REBUILD

MY WORLD

by

Cheryl Norman

DEDICATION:

In memory of

my Pleasure Ridge Park High School classmate

Sherry Carey,

whose brutal 1992 murder

in Long Beach, California

remains unsolved.

ACKNOWLEDGEMENTS:

My apologies to Columbia and Hamilton Counties (Florida) for rearranging their boundaries to construct the fictional Foster County.

I'm indebted to my critique partner, author Dee S. Knight (Anne Krist), for her hours spent helping me polish the manuscript. To the Ladies of the Suwannee Retreat 2009—Judith Leigh Peters, Nancy Quatrano, and Kathleen McMahon—thanks for brainstorming the story with me. I also thank my good friend Glendora "Dorie" Peterson for her expertise in eldercare.

As always, thanks to my two fabulous unpaid publicists, Jo Frye and Rachel Stone; and thanks to my patient and supportive husband, who never complains about the hours I spend sequestered in my office writing. You're wonderful and I love you.

COPYRIGHT & LICENSE NOTES

Love your enemies, do good to those who hate you,
bless those who curse you,
pray for those who mistreat you. ~Luke 6:27 (NIV)

Rebuild My World
Table of Contents

Chapter One
Drake Springs, Florida

The driveway alarm's loud buzzing shattered the quiet evening. Taylor Drake, her heart jumping against her ribs, almost dropped her glass of iced tea. Her hands shaking, she set her drink on the kitchen counter and took a deep breath. The recent addition of a motion sensor had been her brother's idea to alert the family when a vehicle turned in the gate. Because the entrance was a quarter mile from the house, Wil intended the buzzer as an alert of visitors or trespassers. Instead, the contraption nearly stopped Taylor's heart.

Who would be coming at dinnertime? Normal people her age had social engagements on a Saturday evening, but Taylor no longer counted herself among the normal. Alone with her wheelchair-bound father, she couldn't afford to let down her guard, even in her family home. She closed her hand around her pistol, its weight heavy in the pocket of her faded denim apron.

"Are you going to see who that is?" Her father's weak voice drifted from his room across the hall.

"I'm on it, Dad." She tiptoed up the hallway toward the front window.

Sophie, the golden retriever that seldom left her father's side, followed. The dog tensed as if sensing Taylor's uneasiness. These days, uneasiness plagued Taylor's every breath. Gone was the adventurous, confident woman who shot photos in Iraq or Kashmir. Fear kept her a prisoner inside the house where she grew up.

Her fingers still clutching the handgun, Taylor peeked through the slit where the drapes met. The fading sunlight offered little light to the yard and driveway, darkened by the shade of oak trees dripping Spanish moss and the thick growth of Sago palms. A white sedan with green Foster County Sheriff's Office logos on the door approached the house at a slow speed. Bouncing with the uneven surface of the pine needle driveway, it

1

flashed the yard with its driving lights.

What was the law doing at Drake Oaks? Whoever the driver was, he now sat in the parked cruiser as if debating his next move. She waited until he emerged to catch a better look. The motion-sensor security light came on, spotlighting the man. Dressed in a tan FCSO uniform, he wore a hat that obscured his face.

For a brief moment, interest replaced her anxiety. This guy had a lean, muscled physique. He turned his head to look up at the house, revealing an attractive face. He looked to be in his late thirties. Nice.

Why was she ogling? He probably had a wife and three kids waiting for him at home. Giving a snort of disgust, she stepped back from the glass and moved to the door. Her absent brother, the county sheriff, must have ordered a deputy to drive by and check on them. Wil had been reluctant to leave in the first place, though Taylor and Dad had plenty of help with Hazel Porter, the day nurse. A year ago, the overprotective brother routine would have bugged her.

A year ago, Taylor would be living in California, and Roz would be alive. Thoughts of her roommate brought a fresh wave of grief. Gritting her teeth, she shoved aside memories of Roz while squeezing the handle of the .380 caliber Cobra. She'd learned to use the weapon, vowing never again to be helpless to defend herself.

Who am I kidding?

Fear paralyzed Taylor's every waking moment. Sleep brought nightmares more than respite. She fingered the scar at her throat. The physical wound had healed in a matter of weeks, but not the emotional scars. If only she could shake her mental weakness. Taking another deep breath, she fought against the tight knot in her chest and reached for the deadbolt lock with a trembling hand.

Adam Gillespie dragged himself from the Ford and stared up at the house with dread. The last place he wanted to be was Drake Oaks, the home of his father's worst enemy. *Drake* Oaks, *Drake* Springs, *Drake* College—the Drake name mocked him at every turn. But duty called.

2

Adam had promised to check on Sheriff Wilson Drake's self-absorbed sister. He couldn't afford to screw up now, especially with the election in four weeks. He opposed Wil's bid for reelection.

A thin layer of dust coated the hybrid Ford Escape parked at the side of the house. Judging from the California plates, the vehicle belonged to Miss Drake. Adam climbed the wooden steps, crossed the veranda, and then rang the doorbell. From inside, a dog woofed.

A woman edged open the door and peeked from behind the security chain. "Yes?"

Her face vaguely resembled photos of Taylor Drake, but the timid, raspy voice was at odds with the vibrant, prize-winning photojournalist he'd seen on the cover of *Parade* magazine. Her auburn hair was close-cut, except for a few long strands on top that drooped over her forehead.

"It's Chief Deputy Gillespie, ma'am."

"*Adam* Gillespie, right?" At his nod, she unchained the door and opened it partway. "But I thought you were the police chief. When did you change jobs?"

"I guess you were—" He stopped short of saying "globetrotting." No need to be insensitive. "You weren't around when Foster County residents voted to consolidate governments."

She seemed to connect the dots then grimaced. "So you lost your job."

He batted away a mosquito that buzzed at his face. "Yes, ma'am. The city of Drake Springs no longer has a separate P.D."

"I hadn't heard."

More likely she wasn't interested. Adam barely knew Taylor, but he knew her type. And he knew her power-hungry family. "I assumed your brother told you."

"No, he didn't. Or maybe he did. Sorry, I guess I forgot." Keeping one hand in the pocket of her apron, she pulled the door open the rest of the way. "Please, come in."

Holding his hat, Adam stepped inside the two-story foyer. Taylor closed the door behind him, then replaced the chain. A good habit if one

3

lived in L.A., but overkill for Foster County.

"Wil flew to L.A. then drove me back in my car. He talked a lot during the trip, but I guess I wasn't very good company." She motioned him into the living room. "Have a seat."

If she expected him to ask why she couldn't make it home on her own, she'd be disappointed. She wasn't about to suck him into her self-pity scene. He followed her into an elegantly furnished room that showed no signs of use. Several antique pieces, along with large framed paintings—most likely originals—reminded him of a museum exhibit, not someone's home. Adam's circle of friends didn't hire professional decorators, though, so what did he know?

He perched on the edge of an upholstered chair nearest the door. He wouldn't stay a moment longer than necessary. Taylor sat on one of the two matching sofas, the golden retriever sitting guard at her feet. Wearing an apron that resembled an old pair of bib overalls, Taylor looked out of place in the stiff, formal room.

"So Wil and his wife caught their flight this morning?"

"Yes." She cocked her head, a stray lock of reddish hair falling in front of one eye, although she didn't seem to notice. "He worried about leaving so soon after I got here, but it's time—past time—he and Fia had a honeymoon."

"Yes, ma'am." Odd timing, though, considering the man was running for reelection.

"He took time off to bring me back." She spoke as if she had a permanent frog in her throat, which drew his attention to the scar. Her injuries must have damaged her vocal cords. "I guess he told you what happened."

Yeah, he'd heard. Some scumbag had slashed her throat. Miraculously, she'd survived the attack and escaped. "That must have been rough—"

"It was, but we don't need to rehash it." Her expression closed, but her voice vibrated. "It's behind me now."

The cop in him said otherwise. He was here to keep an eye on her

4

safety, though, not provide therapy. "I promised the sheriff I would check on you while he's out of town, so is everything okay here?"

"Fine." She met his gaze with a wide, unconvincing smile, although it might have been a ploy for attention. Suddenly, she straightened and hit her forehead with her palm. "Where are my manners? Would you like a glass of tea?"

"No, thanks. I can't stay." He pulled out a business card from his shirt pocket then handed it to her. "If you need anything while your brother is away, give me a call. Even if you just need to talk, call. I can be out here in five minutes."

Even if you just need to talk. Why the hell had he said that? He didn't want to play therapist, and certainly not with any of the Drake family.

With a trembling hand, she accepted the card. "That's nice to know, but I've paid a shrink a chunk of change to hear my troubles. I'm okay. Really."

Yeah, right. Behind her bravado lurked a vulnerable and shaky woman. Who would've thought? Vulnerable and *scared*. Something in her eyes tugged at his gut. His gaze dropped first to the angry red scar at her throat, then lowered to her apron pocket. Was she armed? Not that he would blame her, but a weapon in untrained hands could pose a greater danger.

"I'll be around evenings while the sheriff is away." He stood to leave. "If there's nothing I can do for you tonight, I'll be on my way."

"Look, as long as my big brother is making you patrol Drake Oaks, why not join me for dinner? Hazel left plenty of stew, and I was just about to have a bowl. Poor Dad. He wouldn't want to be dependent on my cooking, although I did manage to make cornbread from Jiffy Mix."

Poor Dad? The man had suffered a stroke a few years back that left him confined to a wheelchair, but Adam could muster little sympathy for the son of a bitch who had ruined his father's business.

"I need to go, but thanks."

"I didn't think. Your wife must be waiting dinner for you—"

"No wife." Had he imagined it, or was that a flicker of interest in her

5

big ol' green eyes? Just what he needed, the kid sister of his enemy flirting with him.

"If it's because of Dad, he's already eaten. Since the stroke, he prefers to eat alone. But I don't. Won't you stay?"

"I'll take a rain check."

"I'll hold you to it. Arrive hungry tomorrow. Frankly, I'd like the company."

"Miss Drake, let's not—"

"Taylor."

"Taylor, let's not kid ourselves. The Gillespies aren't welcome in this house and—"

"Are you still nursing that stupid feud? I thought we were past that, at least our generation."

"Hardly." Did she believe the Drakes' offenses ended with the last generation? Wil's shabby treatment of Adam's sister still rankled.

"You know, I was in diapers when the trouble between our families began. I refuse to be a part of this nonsense."

"Do you even know why our families are enemies?"

She shook her head. "Not really. Wasn't it something to do with Dad opposing the rezoning of your father's property?"

"That was the start of it. I guess you were too young to remember."

"Then leave me out of it. Life's too short to sweat the small stuff."

Small stuff? "Some old grudges can't be resolved."

"But you work for Wil. Don't old grudges get in the way?"

"We're professionals." Yet hadn't his mother said the same? Adam changed the subject. "Look, if it's company you want, what about your old friends from Foster County High? Couldn't you meet them in town for—"

"I can't." She grimaced. "I'd rather no one know I'm here."

Adam moved to the door, Taylor and the dog following. "That's what the sheriff said. Are you worried that you're still in danger?"

Her shrug, a gesture probably meant to show lack of concern, didn't hide the tension that kept her body rigid. "They haven't caught the guy, but . . . well, I just don't venture outside the house these days."

Curious. No wonder Sheriff Drake had asked Adam to check on his sister. Whether or not Taylor was a spoiled attention-seeker, she seemed terrified. But she wasn't going to be Adam's problem. He would pay his nightly visits for the next week. Then when Wil returned, Adam would shed his babysitting detail.

Taylor exhaled a long breath. "Do you know much about agoraphobia?"

"Not really. Is it like claustrophobia?"

She shook her head. "It's almost the opposite. I fear being alone yet I fear being in a crowd. It's nuts."

"It's normal." He leaned against the doorjamb in resignation. Though eager to escape, he wasn't willing to be rude. "You were a victim of a brutal assault."

"As anxious as I was to leave L.A., I couldn't board a crowded plane. I couldn't leave the clinic on my own—it was my safe place. Now, this house is my safe place. I'm in control as long as I stay here."

He'd seen crime victims suffer worse and come out with their sanity intact, but he'd indulge Taylor with a little sympathy. "What about treatment? You said you had psychotherapy—"

"Right. I had sessions, and I still take anti-anxiety medication. I have an emergency supply of antidepressants for panic attacks. I pray a lot." She gave her head a shake. "I'm sorry. I've taken up enough of your time."

Yes, she had. "Until tomorrow, then." He unlocked the door then stepped onto the porch. "Lock up."

A shiver seemed to seize her body. "I always do."

He stared pointedly at her apron. "I hope you've taken a firearms safety course for that handgun in your pocket."

She stared at him, her mouth frozen in an O. Did she take him for a total idiot? He should've expected her to underestimate him. Her family had little use for the Gillespies, and the youngest Drake—despite her words to the contrary—was no exception.

"In my profession, I know what to look for." He nodded toward her pocket. "May I see it?"

"Sorry, no." A smirk—not quite a smile—eased the tightness in her face. "My weapons instructor says never to surrender my firearm. If I lose my gun, I'm defenseless."

He nodded. "Wil, I presume."

"Not Wil. He set me up with Deputy Peterson. She helped me apply for my permit, too."

Wil claimed *thorough* was Jamie Peterson's middle name. After working a recent cyber-crime case with her, Adam agreed. "I guess that answers my concerns. Jamie's certainly qualified."

"Well, I won't keep you."

"See you tomorrow. Or call if you need me." He turned toward the steps, holding on to his disgust for the entire rotten family. He headed to his cruiser then paused at the door. Something tugged at him, curiosity most likely, but he had to look back one more time.

She stood in the doorway, her thin body casting a thinner shadow across the threshold. "Thank you, Adam."

She called him *Adam*. Why that mattered, he couldn't imagine. But the soft whisper of her permanently hoarse voice and the simple expression of gratitude punched a hole in his resentment. It also scared the hell out of him. He didn't know how to deal with the Drakes without the hatred. Maybe Taylor was worth saving. She'd been gone from Foster County for more than a decade.

But the rest of her family could jump in the Suwannee River. Adam's hatred burned hot as ever, and with good reason. He started the engine and fled Drake Oaks.

Taylor watched the gorgeous chief deputy drive away then closed and locked the door. A smile would improve his face, not that she was likely to see one. For all his handsomeness, Adam seemed downright grumpy. No wonder he had lost to Wil in the last sheriff's race. Small-town people warmed to Wil's relaxed charm easier than Adam's intense seriousness. Or so she'd heard. She hadn't been around to vote for either man.

She'd bet Adam made a good cop, though. His intense hazel eyes constantly moved, his gaze registering everything. Like her concealed weapon. Probably little got past the chief deputy.

Returning to the kitchen, she paused at the door of her father's room, a converted den now equipped with a special bed and plasma screen TV. Wil had ripped out the carpet and re-finished the cedar plank flooring to accommodate the electric wheelchair. Behind two potted plants hid a potty chair that spared Dad middle of the night trips to the bathroom, although he seldom used it. A contraption of metal and leather straps, which was used to lift him in and out of his chair, loomed beside the bed.

"That was Chief Deputy Gillespie. Just checking on us to see if we needed anything."

He gave a single-syllable grunt in response before returning his attention to *Wheel of Fortune*.

"He says he'll check on us each night while Wil's gone."

Her father glared back at her. "That's like asking the fox to guard the henhouse."

"You're not sucking me into this old feud of yours, Dad. Besides, Adam seems like a nice man."

"I don't want him in this house, hear me?"

"Sorry, but it's too late. I've invited him to have dinner with me tomorrow night."

"That's not appropriate."

"Not appropriate? Is he secretly married?" She hadn't seen a ring, and he said he had no wife.

Another grunted response. "What was Wilson thinking?"

"Give Wil some credit. He knows his staff."

Or did he? She'd been away from Foster County a long time. Did she really know anything about her brother's judgment, or about his work as the county sheriff? But Wil loved his family. He'd proven that after Dad's stroke, when he'd left his career in the Jacksonville Sheriff's Office to move back to Drake Oaks. He'd spent too much of his own time following up with the officers about her attack in Long Beach and hounding the

9

doctors about her care and recovery, not to mention dropping everything in the middle of his reelection campaign to come get her. If Taylor could trust any man, she could trust Wil.

As for trusting Adam, she had to wait and see. His aloofness and her neuroses aside, she wanted to trust him. She wanted to see him again, to get to know him better. She was attracted to him, for all the good it would do. She was a Drake, and he hated her guts.

Most of all, she wanted to feel safe again. Yet every night when she closed her eyes, she relived the attacker's knife, slicing the tender flesh at her throat. The slick, spurting blood that soaked her blouse. And the terror of stumbling through the kitchen to escape, tripping over the mutilated body of her friend Roz.

At seven-forty-five, Adam parked the cruiser in the driveway of his twin sister's rented house on Park Street then headed for the front door. Dinners at Amy's were chaotic, especially with her two rowdy boys, but the food was good. Her husband Ben Sawyer was a decent guy, and he seemed goofy-in-love with Amy, even after almost twenty years of marriage. Judging from Amy's devotion, she felt the same.

She stood in the doorway wearing her chin-length hair pulled back in a stubby ponytail. She scowled at him. "Get in here before the food gets cold."

Adam grinned. "Good evening to you, too."

She tugged him inside the small entry that divided the dining area and living room. "Taco casserole tastes better warm."

"Woman, it's piping hot." Ben waved him over to the dining table. "Have a seat and we'll ask the blessing."

"She knows how much I love her taco casserole." Adam pulled out the empty chair across from his nephews, Ray and Travis, and held it for Amy. "In fact, my sister's cooking is far better than mine."

Amy took her seat then motioned Adam to the end chair opposite Ben. "That's because you learned to cook from our mother, whereas I had excellent training in the kitchen of Mama Sawyer."

Eleven-year-old Ray frowned at Adam. "But Granny Gee doesn't cook."

"That's right. Ergo, Uncle Adam doesn't cook."

"True, our mother's talents didn't include gastronomy." Amy turned to her sons. "Gastronomy means food preparation."

"Now use it in a sentence." Adam suppressed a grin when Ray screwed up his face as if contemplating an example. "Just teasing your mom, guys."

Amy snorted. "Before you give me too much credit for my *gastronomy*, remember this dish is just glorified nachos."

"Nothing wrong with that," Ben said. "Ray, would you ask the blessing, please?"

Adam bowed his head and listened to his nephew's prayer, then joined in with the collective *Amen*.

"So what had you running late tonight, little brother?"

Adam grinned at his nephews. "You may be three minutes older, but I'm definitely not your 'little' brother." Travis giggled, and Ray rolled his eyes at the worn joke. "I was out at the Drakes'. I promised the sheriff I'd keep an eye on things while he's out of town."

Amy met his gaze. "As in that younger sister of his?"

"Why would you think she's there?" He held out his plate for Amy to serve him a heaping portion of the casserole.

"I run a newspaper. I know things. So how is Taylor?"

"Shaky. I guess that's to be expected." He took a drink of sugary iced tea. "She doesn't want anyone to know she's here."

Amy dished out servings of the casserole for Ray and Travis. "I won't blab. After such an ordeal, I'd want to be left alone for a while, too."

"What happened to her?" Ray asked.

Amy gave a slight shake of her head. "Someone attacked her and hurt her, but not here. It was in California."

"She's the picture lady, right?" Travis asked. "The one you said the paper could use."

Amy chuckled. "That was wishful thinking, honey."

11

Taylor wouldn't stoop to taking pictures for any small town newspaper—especially one owned by a Gillespie. After Phyllis Gillespie started treatments for ovarian cancer, she had turned the newspaper over to her daughter. "It's not like you need Pulitzer-prize-winning photos of the garden club meeting."

"We have news." Ben grabbed the pitcher of iced tea and refilled his glass. "Enough for a weekly paper, anyway."

"And Drake Springs dot com." Amy beamed. "Instead of a weekly rag, the *Drake Springs Democrat* is now a daily Webzine."

"I'm impressed. I'll bet Mom's proud of that."

Amy nodded. "Which reminds me, I'm taking her to Jacksonville Wednesday to the Mayo Clinic."

"Let me know how that goes." Adam said no more on the subject, not wanting to worry his nephews about their grandmother. But her treatments had left her sicker and questioning their effectiveness, hence the follow-up testing on Wednesday.

The Tex-Mex dish was delicious, but Adam resisted a second helping. Amy had all she could do to cook enough for two growing boys and a hardworking husband. After hurricane-force winds destroyed their home, Amy and her family had started over, almost from square one. They needed more space. The two-bedroom ranch they rented was no roomier than Adam's.

Amy cleared the dishes and brought out dessert, a single layer orange cake with chocolate frosting. She sliced the small cake into eight servings. He'd seen his sister divide a box of cake mix and cut the recipe in half. She stretched her grocery dollars without complaint, and her family didn't seem to mind.

"I'd better skip dessert." Adam patted his abdomen. "Since turning forty, I've had to watch my calories."

Ben snorted. "I wouldn't sign up for Nutrasystem just yet."

"Leanness runs in our family," Amy said. A brief sadness clouded her eyes. "Remember how Megan drank milkshakes with raw eggs to gain weight?"

"Yeah." Adam couldn't think of their older sister without grief, along with a huge dose of hatred for Wil Drake. "You're no tub of lard, yourself."

Ben forked a bite of the cake, pausing with it in midair, and gave his wife a warm smile. "She's perfect in my book."

Ray made a gagging gesture, and Adam winked at him. "Yeah, I think I'm going to be sick, too."

"You're just jealous." Amy ignored his earlier protest and handed him a serving of cake. "Someday you'll be crazy in love, too, as soon as you meet the right woman."

"Are you gonna get married?" Travis asked Adam.

Ben came to his rescue. "Not anytime soon, sport. Your uncle's like me. He's choosy."

"But a lot slower," Amy added. "You'll be a senior citizen by the time you find yourself a special girl if you don't stop working so hard."

"I need to win this election, now more than ever."

"Hey, we'll vote for you. But some folks see marriage as stability. Your opponent's married now, remember?"

"As if I can find a wife and marry in four weeks." Adam steered the conversation away from his love life. "Have you had any word on when you can get your new modular home set up?"

"When the bridge is finished." Amy referred to the bridge that provided the only access to their property across the Suwannee River.

Ben nodded. "It took longer to sort out the funding, between the county, state, and FEMA folks, than it did to rebuild the sucker."

"Dad always said that bridge needed replacing. Too bad he didn't live to see it," Amy said.

Adam gritted his teeth. Just another battle Jed Gillespie had lost to Harold Drake. "It wouldn't be replaced now if it hadn't been washed out in the hurricane. And that was two years ago."

Ben shrugged. "We count our blessings. Nobody got hurt, and we have a great deal with this house.

"Amen to that," Amy said.

"Can we please be excused?" Ray asked.

Adam appreciated his sister's no-TV-during-supper rule. In the small house, watching TV from the dining table would be easy. But Amy insisted on dedicated family time at dinner, a departure from their own upbringing. Their mother frequently worked late at the newspaper office, and their father drank his dinner at the Alibi Bar. Adam's usual supper had been macaroni and cheese that Megan nuked, or one of Amy's bologna sandwiches.

Ben excused the boys, who then scooted from the table and scampered toward the television in the living room. Ray grabbed the remote then joined Travis on the sofa. Sounds of a dog food commercial blared from the TV.

"They're good boys," Adam said. "They have good parents."

Amy picked up the empty cake plates. "Thanks. I think it's because we waited to start our family until we were mature enough to enjoy and appreciate them."

"Me? Mature? First time you accused me of that." Ben scooped up the remaining glasses and forks from the table. "I'll get these, honey. You visit with Adam."

"He's doing this for your benefit. Ben only helps out when there's an audience."

"Hey, it never hurts to suck up to the in-laws." Ben grinned. "Is it working?"

Adam nodded. "Oh, yeah. I'm impressed."

The friendly teasing and relaxed atmosphere drew Adam to the Sawyer house many evenings for supper, especially now that they lived just blocks from him. It bugged him that his sister and brother-in-law had such a struggle to make ends meet. Adam sometimes slipped a couple of twenties to Amy to help with the groceries, especially right before Ben's payday. After all, Adam did his share of eating there.

Tonight, though, Amy pushed the money back at him. "You don't have to do that. I have a full-time job thanks to Mom's retirement."

"Do you know any more about her appointment at the Mayo?"

14

She shook her head. "No, but it has me worried plenty."

"I'm glad you're driving her to Jacksonville, but at least let me give you gas money."

"Not necessary. Mom wants to pay for fuel. Stop worrying about our finances, okay? We're getting by and we both have jobs. We're blessed."

It was about time she and Ben caught a financial break. For too many years, the Gillespies—and now the Sawyers—had struggled, thanks in part to Harold Drake. How could Amy not resent the Drakes? Yet she often lectured Adam about forgiveness, quoting him scripture and speaking psychobabble about negativism. How could she be so charitable when hatred simmered deep in his gut?

"Do me a favor, little brother. Watch out for Taylor."

"Why do you say that?"

"The cops never caught the dude who slit her throat. Danger may have followed her here."

"That's the newspaper editor in you looking for a story."

"Oh, yeah? Why do you think Wil asked you to keep close watch on her?"

"If he seriously thought Taylor was in danger, he wouldn't have left town for a week."

Or could Amy be right? What if the killer had unfinished business?

Chapter Two

Taylor peered over the security chain at Adam. He stood on the porch and removed his sunglasses, which he tucked in the pocket of his dress shirt, the one with the sheriff's department insignia on the collar points. He met her gaze with serious hazel eyes—seriously gorgeous hazel eyes.

"Please tell me you're hungry. I have a homemade pizza in the oven."

His eyebrows lifted. "Homemade?"

"I have to keep busy." She opened the door. She'd left her handgun in the kitchen cabinet drawer and her dowdy apron hanging on its hook on the utility room door. Would he notice the care she had taken with her appearance? "Come on back to the kitchen."

He hesitated in the foyer. "I really hadn't planned to stay long—"

"I know. But I have something I need to discuss with you, and it's dinner time, so why not share a pizza with me? Call it a working dinner, if you must."

His frown deepened. "Is something wrong?"

"Not how you mean, but there is a matter I need your help with." She reached around him to lock the deadbolt and caught a whiff of woodsy cologne. Though still in his dress uniform, he had the fragrance of a man freshly showered. "It's just us two. Dad is eating leftover stew in his room."

"Except for an occasional slice at Vinnie's, my pizzas are the frozen kind." He followed her down the hall to the kitchen. "Don't let the TV ads fool you about frozen tasting like delivery."

She caught the ghost of a smile in his eyes. His mouth refused to budge, however. She'd have to work on that. "Before you're too impressed, I confess my pizza crust comes from the grocery store's dairy counter. But everything else is homemade."

He drew in a deep breath. "The aroma has me sold."

"Great!" Too much pleasure filled her, but she'd had little to celebrate in recent months. "It needs about ten more minutes, so let me get you something to drink."

She poured him a glass of iced tea. He sat opposite her at the breakfast room table, where she had her mother's letters stacked in the opened jewelry box. She pushed them in front of him.

"What's this?"

"It's what I want to talk to you about. Last night, I found these letters while cleaning out my grandmother's closet. My mother wrote them. In the last one, the letter she wrote Dad the day she died, she mentions your mother—"

"My mother?" He shoved the jewelry box toward Taylor. "I don't want to hear any more."

"Look, obviously you know more about this history than I do. No one will tell me anything. The subject of my mother is taboo in this house, and I want to know about her. Whether or not she suffered from alcoholism or anything else, she gave birth to me. I need to know what happened—"

"Why? You're the one who said we need to end this feud."

"For one thing, I have her genes. I need to know what I should worry about in terms of addiction or . . . or mental illness. It's a legitimate concern, Adam."

His mouth tightened, and his jaw tensed. "Why me?"

"I need someone who can be objective and discreet." She met his gaze, trying to read him. "Wil thinks you're a thorough and ethical lawman, or he wouldn't have you as his chief deputy. He certainly wouldn't leave you in charge if he didn't trust you."

"Oh, yeah? We're opponents in the election for county sheriff. What better way to monitor me than to have me working for him? If I sabotage his career, I sabotage my own. Pretty clever."

"You're opposing him again?" She'd missed that important piece of information. Could that be the basis of her father's remark? *That's not appropriate.* "I'm sorry. I didn't realize… If this puts you in an awkward position—"

"It doesn't put me in an awkward position as far as the election goes. But you have no idea what you're asking of me."

18

"And I have no one else I can ask. I've heard bits and pieces. But Gram raised me, and she wouldn't allow any talk of my mother. She must have hated her."

"With good reason, I would think."

Taylor lifted the top envelope from the opened box. "Just read this last letter and tell me what you think it means. Please?"

Adam stared at her for a full minute. She wouldn't blink. Wouldn't back down. He had to understand how much she needed his help. Finally, he held out his hand for the letter.

What began as busy work, cleaning her grandmother's suite for Wil and Fia when they moved from their tiny cabin on the river, became a treasure hunt. Who knew her Gram had hidden away the letters? She'd committed her mother's words to memory:

Dearest Harold,

I will always regret the hurt and shame I brought our family. I admit my own weakness, and humbly ask for your forgiveness. Don't write off our marriage. Give me the chance to rebuild trust. Surely, you hold some affection for me. I beg you to consider the children, too.

I am meeting Phyllis tonight to apologize for my role in this dishonorable affair. I don't know if she can forgive me, but can't you? Life is too short to waste. After I leave Phyllis, I will stop by the house. Please don't turn me away this time.

With all my heart,
Connie

While Adam read, Taylor got up to check the pizza even though she knew it needed to bake five more minutes. She set out plates, a pizza cutter, and a spatula. Then she turned to face him.

He folded the letter. "Did you ask your father about this?"

Taylor shook her head. "I found these hidden in the back of Gram— my grandmother's closet. I'm not sure he read it or even saw it."

"If you're asking me to question my mom about that night, the answer is no. You Drakes have caused my family enough pain." He returned the letter to the top of the stack then slammed the jewelry box closed.

"We're talking about thirty years ago. Your mother moved on. Surely she could answer a few—"

"No."

"Look, I'm in the dark. Give me at least the short version of why you hate my family. Did our parents have an affair years ago—"

"That came later, after Harold opposed rezoning the property Dad had sunk all his money into for a water park on the Suwannee. It ruined him financially, and he started to drink. He hooked up with Connie—your mother. All of Drake Springs knew about their affair."

"I've heard rumors. What else?"

"Maybe you should ask your brother."

"Wil or Sam?"

"Wil," he said through clenched teeth. "Ask him about how he left town after he knocked up my sister Megan. When she died in a car wreck, he didn't so much as attend her funeral."

"What?" Taylor's head swam, and a roar filled her ears. Wil had gotten Megan Gillespie pregnant then abandoned her? The callous man Adam described couldn't be her brother. "I didn't realize he dated Megan. I thought he dated Amy."

"You'll have to ask Wil for that story. As for what became of your mother and whether or not she and Mom spoke, you're on your own."

Adam's rigid posture and set mouth showed his resoluteness. He wouldn't bend, and Taylor wouldn't push. She'd get no sympathy from him if she tried to explain her father's fragile health. Adam's claims about Wil couldn't be right, though. There had to be an explanation, but it could wait until he and Fia returned from their cruise.

"I respect your decision." Adam's bitterness stunned her. So much anger. She picked up the jewelry box and placed it on top the refrigerator, out of her father's sight in case he rode in later in his electric wheelchair. "I'll get the pizza."

Wrapping her hands in two dishtowels, she removed the rectangular cookie sheet from the oven. The cheese bubbled. The mushrooms curled at the edges, and the slices of pepper and onion had caramelized. The diced ham, the only pizza-type meat she'd found in the refrigerator, added the final touch. Perfect.

"Smells good." Adam's voice had lost its earlier tightness. "Need any help?"

"Iced tea is in the fridge." She wheeled the pizza cutter through the crust and toppings. "You can refill our glasses."

Adam topped off their iced teas while Taylor slid two squares of pizza on each plate. Could she stuff down two pieces? She couldn't predict when the tightness in her gut would return. The doctor called it spastic colon, which often led to bouts of diarrhea. *Please not tonight, Lord.*

She returned to her chair and waited for Adam to taste the pizza. He took a bite and nodded. "This is good."

They ate in silence. He made quick work of finishing off his two pieces, and Taylor stood, reaching for his plate. "Seconds?"

"Please. You're a good cook."

"Not really." She slid two more squares of pizza onto the plate then set it in front of him. "I have a couple of things I do well, and that's it. Very small repertoire."

He ate another piece of the pizza, then paused to drink. "You don't expect me to believe you didn't know I was running against your brother for sheriff, do you?"

"I honestly didn't know you were his opponent. It speaks poorly of me as a sister, doesn't it? Neurotics are very self-centered. I'm ashamed to say I focus totally on myself these days."

"How's that working for you?" His tone didn't hold an ounce of sympathy.

"It's not. Agoraphobia is a temporary setback, not a condition I have to accept. Through therapy and lots of prayer, I'm getting my life back."

He stared at his empty plate. "I was hungrier than I thought."

"More?" She started to get up, but Adam stood and reached for her empty plate.

"I'll get it. How about you?"

"No, thanks. I'm stuffed. You take all you want."

"It's good. Some of the best I've eaten." He returned to the table with two more slices and dug in.

Her cheeks warmed at his praise, and she averted her gaze. Like the typical fair-complexioned redhead, she always blushed at the first hint of a compliment, broadcasting to the world her self-consciousness. "I ate two slices. I guess I am making progress."

"You could use a few pounds."

She stopped short of saying "thanks" because he hadn't sounded complimentary. Her weight loss hadn't bothered her at first, since she usually carried about five pounds too many. But the sunken face that greeted her in the mirror these days was undeniably gaunt.

He finished off the pizza then gave her a sheepish grin—brief, but a grin nonetheless. "I should be embarrassed, but I don't regret a bite."

"Thank you." After their earlier tension, she and Adam had settled into a pleasant meal together. She wouldn't spoil the mood by mentioning her request again. There was always tomorrow.

Adam scooted from the table. "Thanks for dinner."

"I guess you have to go now." How pathetic she sounded. "Oops. Was I whining?"

He could have smiled, or at least softened his serious expression. But not Adam. "You're the one who said neurotics are self-centered. Whining is just a form of self-pity."

She nearly gasped but recovered. "You won't cut me any slack, will you?"

"Is that what you want?" His gaze turned more intense, if possible. "Is sympathy going to help you get better?"

"What do you know about—"

"After church today, I booted up the computer in the office and did a Web search on agoraphobia. I read a bit about the treatment. You've already gone the route of therapy and drugs, right?"

She rose from the table and glared. Was he playing devil's advocate, or had he no compassion? "What's your point?"

"Isn't it time to step outside of your safety zone and take a chance?"

"You're talking desensitization."

He held her gaze. "I guess you could call it that."

She placed her fists on her hips. "What would *you* call it?"

"Practicing." His face softened, just a fraction, and a tiny bit of warmth slid into his eyes. "Practice doing the things that you're avoiding."

Practice, desensitization, it all boiled down to stepping outside her safe place. She couldn't do that. More than anything, she wanted to. She just couldn't.

"Reading up on agoraphobia in one afternoon doesn't make you an expert."

He shrugged. "I don't claim to be."

"Why did you, anyway?"

Any trace of warmth in his eyes vanished. "I prepare for all my assignments."

"Right." Taylor pushed aside the disappointment. She was just an assignment, forced on him by his boss. She'd worked all afternoon to impress him. From styling her hair to making pizza, she made it her goal to coax a smile from his humorless face. What had she expected? He hated her family. He probably hated her.

"Try something with me. An experiment." Adam reached for one of her hands and tugged her toward the hall.

She followed him, in no hurry for him to let go. She shunned any physical touch with men these days, but his grip was firm yet pleasant. Or maybe she was desperate for human contact. Yeah, she was pathetic. "What kind of an experiment?"

"Walk me to the car."

"Oh, please, no." She stopped, jerking her hand from his grasp. If Adam witnessed one of her anxiety attacks, she'd be mortified. Humiliated. "I'm not ready for that."

"Why not?"

Damn him and that inscrutable look. Was he punishing her for her earlier request? Did he take pleasure in frightening her? "I can't."

His gaze turned into a glare. A dare. "You mean you won't."

"You're a jerk."

"Yes. Now, walk me to my cruiser and you'll be rid of me."

"You won't leave until I do?" Her teasing tone couldn't mask the panic in her voice.

"The sooner we walk, the sooner I'm gone." He held out his hand. "Come on."

A sudden knot squeezed her stomach, and she regretted every bite of pizza. Sour bile filled her throat. Clamminess engulfed her. The walls of the foyer seemed to tilt. She squeezed her eyes shut. "Don't make me do this."

"Hey, calm down." He gave both her arms a vigorous rub. "Don't pass out on me. Take a deep breath, okay?"

What about her relaxation techniques? She could do this. She wasn't outside. She was here in her safe place. Opening her eyes, she focused on Adam's face, the barest hint of concern in his hazel eyes. She held her breath then exhaled slowly, mentally counting to ten. *Dear God, help me through this.*

"That's better." He continued to rub her arms. "You lost some color for a minute, but it's coming back."

"I hate to panic."

He gripped her shoulders and met her gaze. "Listen to me. You walk me to the cruiser tonight. Then you build on that success, a step at a time, until you regain your confidence."

"You make it sound easy."

"If it was easy, they'd call it Sudoku." He said it without a trace of a smile.

"You made a joke."

"No, champ. Just making a point. This isn't easy for you, but you have to do it. You'll hate me tonight but you'll thank me tomorrow." Still no grin. He wasn't kidding.

"Hurry. Let's do it now and get it over with." This time, she grabbed him by the wrist and tugged him toward the door, pausing to unlock the deadbolt. "Am I allowed to run?"

"Whatever it takes."

She pulled him outside to the porch then stopped. "Just give me a sec, okay?"

"Say when."

"First, I just want to say, I appreciate the thought. I mean, you're trying to help, and you don't have to. Wil asked you to drive by and check on us, not render first aid—"

"You're stalling."

"I am. I guess I'm nervous."

"That's to be expected."

"Let's go." She took a deep breath, as if she were diving under water. In a way, the simile fit. If a panic attack hit her, she wouldn't be able to breathe. She'd drown in mortification.

Adam placed his hand at her elbow and kept pace with her as they hopped down the porch steps and into the driveway. She let out the breath she'd been holding. Then she inhaled another, silently counted to ten, exhaled. No panic. No hyperventilating. No debilitating cramps in her belly.

He opened the driver's door. "You did it, champ."

"Why do you call me that?"

"Because you know and I know that you're a winner. You just have to get your game back."

She smiled, a genuine rush of relief and pride filling her. She wasn't having an anxiety attack, and she was at least sixty feet from the porch. "I still have to return."

"I'll sit here and watch until you're inside, okay?"

"Okay." She drew a steadying breath. "Oh, boy."

"You'll make it." He nodded, then slid behind the wheel. "We'll do it again tomorrow."

"Um, yeah, I guess . . . ." *One step at a time, Taylor. One step at a time.*

"Except tomorrow I'll park farther from the house." With that, Adam shut the door, blocking any protest from her.

Fighting the urge to run, Taylor strode back to the steps then up onto the porch. She turned and waved, forcing a smile. A herd of grasshoppers did calisthenics inside her chest. At least she hadn't hyperventilated. She stepped inside, closed the door, then locked and chained it. Leaning against the doorjamb, she took deep breaths and clutched her chest, her heart beating a frantic tattoo against her fists.

Did her pulse race from anxiety or from Adam Gillespie? He sure had her attention, whether he wanted it or not. Regardless of what he said about her being an assignment, he'd researched her illness and tried to help her. His bedside manner sucked. Or had it? Would she have risen to his challenge if he'd been cajoling and solicitous?

Maybe Adam was just what the doctor ordered.

When Adam drove out the driveway and onto County Road 471, he debated closing and locking the gate at the entrance to Drake Oaks. He had found it propped open both visits. The chain wrapped around the fence post looked as if it hadn't been touched in months. He'd ask Taylor tomorrow.

Taylor. He hated the Drakes, so why couldn't he get his mind off her? Bony and thin, she still was a looker. She had emotional problems, but she showed strength, too. Her steady gaze drew him to look deep into her eyes, mindful of the deep green of a Heineken beer bottle—and just as intoxicating as the brew it contained.

His thoughts returned to Taylor. Her camera skills were legendary. Her homemade pizza awesome. Who would have guessed she had talent in the kitchen? What other talents did she possess? Bedroom talents—

Whoa!

His too-long celibacy had caught up with him. When he thought of *talents* and *Taylor*, his mind wandered from cooking and photography down a very different path, and his body followed. The fragrance of her silky hair lingered with him, and he couldn't shake the vision of her face.

26

Sure, he'd seen the glamorous photos of her in magazines. None of the cover shots did justice to her soft, natural beauty.

He sure as hell didn't want her occupying his thoughts. Since when did he go for red-haired women, anyway? He leaned toward brunettes, with dark eyes and athletic builds, not that he'd had luck lately finding any. The last woman he'd taken an interest in dumped him for a county firefighter. Much as he missed sex, he just didn't miss the effort it took to build a relationship. It never seemed worth the trouble.

He reached the city limits, then took a left on Court Street. Past the FCSO office, he turned up Park Street and headed toward his house. He bought the small ranch as a starter home, at least that's what his realtor called it. Two bedrooms, one bath, and an attached garage made a perfect bachelor's pad. Seven years later, he saw no reason to trade up.

He slowed to pull into his driveway when his cell phone trilled its double ring. He grabbed it. "Gillespie here."

"Adam. I—oh, God, I don't know what to do." Hysteria shook Taylor's voice and drove it up an octave. "Can you help me?"

He shoved the gearshift into reverse. "On my way. Talk to me. What's happened?"

"He's found me. He . . . he's been here!"

"Who's been there?"

"I don't know who he is."

Panic shook her voice, and she made no sense. He had to keep her talking. "I'm almost to the highway. Just calm down and tell me exactly what's happened."

"My cell phone. It said I had a message from Roz. It was her number."

"Okay, who is Roz?"

"She . . . she was my roommate, the one he killed."

"Someone has her phone and used it to call you." He could handle that. The wireless provider probably hadn't deactivated the account. Such matters often were overlooked after a death. Or some crook had cloned the phone. "But that doesn't mean it's the killer or that he's tracked you down.

So what was the message?"

"No message. Picture." She sounded on the verge of hyperventilating. "Just a picture."

A sick prank. Adam gritted his teeth and mashed the accelerator. In her fragile emotional condition, Taylor couldn't handle mind games. She barely handled everyday life. "Slow, deep breaths. I'll be there in five minutes, tops."

She exhaled into the phone. "Be careful. The . . . the picture—"

"What kind of picture?"

"You and me beside your car. Adam, he took it less than half an hour ago!"

Chapter Three

Taylor stood in darkness, peeking through the slit in the draperies. Her eyes strained for any sign of headlights. Her body did a full tremble, and her stomach roiled. Not since her brutal attack had fear gripped her with such force. Her fingers slid around the cold metal handle of the Cobra. Her hands shook too much to risk taking off the safety. She'd probably shoot a lamp or the window.

Twin high beams swept through the dense foliage of oaks and pines, then stopped. Bracing herself for the driveway alarm, she barely flinched when it buzzed. The headlights broke free of the trees and led the vehicle toward the front of the house. Adam bolted from the cruiser, barely pausing to slam the door. Taking the porch steps two at a time, he ran to the porch. Relief swept through her at the sight of him racing to her rescue—a silly thought, though she felt every bit the damsel in distress—and she slid back the deadbolt.

Opening the door, she made no attempt to hide her weapon from Adam. "Thank you for coming back."

He nodded. "May I see your cell phone?"

"Yes. It's in the living room." She led him to the sofa and gestured toward the end table.

"This it?" He reached for her cell phone at the same time she bent to turn on the table lamp.

Their hands collided, and she jerked her hand back as if he'd been a wasp and stung her. She managed to turn on the light with her quivering hand but couldn't ignore the tightening of his jaw. She'd asked for his help then offended him. "I'm sorry. I'm just rattled."

He reached for the hand clutching the Cobra .380, enveloping both in his larger hand. "You're shaking with nerves. Better let me have that."

She sat in the middle of the couch, keeping her distance without being rude. "Like I said, it's not you. It's . . . I feel violated and angry and frightened."

"All normal reactions." His hand hovered over hers, waiting for permission to touch her. "I'd never hurt you."

She reached for his hand then and tentatively placed her palm against his. He didn't move or react, allowing her to touch him at her pace. "I thought I was making progress—"

"You are making progress, Taylor. Let me help."

"Thanks." She gave his hand a quick squeeze. That hadn't hurt. In fact, it felt damned good. It wouldn't do for her to sit and hold hands with the hunky chief deputy, though. Breaking the contact, she nodded toward the cell phone. "It's the last incoming call. Press the telephone icon."

"Taylor? Who's here?" Her father's raspy voice called out from the next room.

"I'll be right back." Leaving Adam to examine the photo, she headed toward Dad's room.

He sat in his electric wheelchair, his good hand on the toggle switch. With a soft whir, the wheelchair jerked back and forth. The rocking was a nervous habit, usually a sign of agitation. He met her gaze with a scowl. "Who's here?"

She hesitated. Dad didn't need to be upset about a Gillespie in the house, but she wouldn't lie. "I'm talking to Adam."

"Humph. I told you—"

"He's my visitor, not yours. You don't have to see him."

Her father's scowl deepened. "I'm ready to get in bed."

"I'll help." She fluffed his pillows so he'd have a clear view of the TV then helped him out of the wheelchair to the side of the bed. Her father had lost weight, but he still weighed enough that moving him was a challenge, even with the hydraulic lifter. How did Hazel manage him every day?

The effort took its toll on him, too. Between breaths, he gestured toward the wheelchair. "Hand me the remote."

By the time Taylor had him settled, she was winded and perspiring. "Need anything else?"

"I'll let you know."

How it must cost him to ask for help when he'd once been an independent and successful businessman, and county commissioner, too. No wonder he was grumpy. She gave him a smile. "Love you, Dad."

Returning to the living room, she marveled at how she'd stopped trembling while helping Dad. Maybe she needed more physical activity. Or maybe she needed to focus on others instead of her own problems.

She rejoined Adam on the sofa. "Sorry about that. Dad needed help getting into bed."

"I imagine he'd be upset to know I'm in his house again."

"I told him you're here." At his look of surprise, she shrugged. "I'm not going to lie. As I said, you two aren't sucking me into this silly feud."

"It's not just a silly feud, but let's focus."

She pointed to her cell phone. "So did you see the picture?"

With a deepening frown, he punched up the photo again and stared at the tiny screen. "It's dark and grainy, but it's us. Judging from the angle of the shot, he or she would've been inside the gate, on your property."

"I realize that. That's why I panicked and called you."

"Officer Newcomb's on his way over now. I called him while you were with your father. He'll search the grounds, although I'm sure our photographer is long gone."

"Brady Newcomb? We went to school together. He's Jamie Peterson's partner now, right?"

"They ride together sometimes. But this is a small county, and we don't have the luxury of scheduling partners on all shifts."

"Even after consolidation?"

"*Especially* after consolidation. We patrol the entire county with fewer officers. That was part of the deal."

"Some deal. I don't believe I would've voted for it, but I wasn't here." Last November seemed a lifetime ago.

"Do you plan to return to California?"

She made no attempt to suppress the shudder that wracked her body. "No way will I go back there to live. I'm not sure I'll go back at all. Right now I can't think about so much as leaving this house."

"The sheriff is worried about you. Does he know about this message on your cell phone?"

"I didn't call him and neither should you. Please. He deserves this vacation."

Adam shook his head. "He won't like it. He'd want to know."

She twisted her hands together in her lap. Her quivering worsened, and the pizza in her stomach revolted. "When it happened . . . my attack . . . . Wil rushed to California to be with me."

"You think you're interfering again with his vacation time?"

"It's more than that, Adam. I don't think he had an hour's sleep the whole time. He was either camped out at the hospital with me or hovering over the police detectives working the case. I'm sure they put up with him as a professional courtesy because it sure wasn't his crime to investigate."

"I know what it's like to lose a sister, and he almost lost you. I'm sure he was no more of a nuisance than I would've been."

"I wish I could remember Megan."

He shook his head again. "It was a long time ago. You would've been a child."

"Tell me about her."

For the first time, Adam smiled. It was a fond memory type of smile, a pleasant grin that relaxed his usual intensity. "We three were latchkey kids with the working mother, which suited Megan."

"At least you had a mother. I can't even remember mine."

"Megan was fun, and Amy and I loved her. But she went too far, and sometimes scared us. Her self-destructive behavior got her killed, though we'll never know for certain what caused her to wreck."

"What happened?"

"Single car accident on the Interstate." His jaw tightened. "Highway Patrol said she was going ninety and lost control."

"Did they do an autopsy?"

"Sure they did. She wasn't legally intoxicated, but she'd had a drink or two. I suspect she was buzzed." His lips thinned, and he ground his teeth. "She was also three months pregnant."

"What a tragedy. You lost a sister and a niece or nephew."

"You lost a niece or nephew, too."

"How do you know Wil was the father?"

"She confided in Amy the day she found out. Megan seemed to think Amy would hate her—"

"Hate her? Why?"

"Amy and Wil dated a long time before he went out with Megan."

"Was she upset with Megan?"

"By then Amy and Ben Sawyer were involved. She was over your brother. But she was concerned about Megan."

Was Megan over Wil, too? Or did she have the chance to tell him-"

"Of course she told him, but he didn't care."

"You know this for a fact?"

"If you don't believe me, ask him. I've always wondered why he abandoned her. I'd honestly like to know his answer."

"I will ask him."

"I was eighteen at the time, and so angry. I wanted to grab Megan by the shoulders and shake some sense into her. I wanted to demand an explanation. Why was she drinking in her condition . . . and driving?"

"Anger is one of the stages of grief."

"It's irrational. Just like your fear."

Fear wrapped her in its cloak on an hourly basis. "I know I'll never feel safe again. My roommate's murderer may not have killed me, but he killed something inside of me, something I can't recover."

"Don't let him win."

Yeah, right. "I always thought of myself as a fighter, an achiever. Now I'm not sure of anything. I have an emotional weakness." Would it claim her as it had her mother?

"Don't start that again."

His lack of sympathy made her smile. "You're right. Thanks for giving me the KITA."

"We all need the occasional kick in the ass. Remember, the creep who shot this photo wants you scared. It gives him control, but only if you let it."

"You sound like my counselor." The driveway alarm buzzed. Though she should've expected the noise, it still rattled her. "I . . . I guess that's Brady Newcomb."

Adam stood. "I'll meet him. You lock the door behind me and stay inside."

"Like I'm going to run out to the mailbox." She spoke facetiously, but he didn't laugh.

He lifted his hand as if to touch her face then hesitated. "We'll work on that."

He gave her one of his rare smiles then opened the door, leaving her with a flutter in her chest that had nothing to do with indigestion or nerves.

Adam stepped onto the porch and waited until he heard the deadbolt slide home. Noisy crickets and frogs filled the warm evening. Two security lamps, one at the gate and one in front of the barn behind the house, created more shadows than light. Brady's vehicle had triggered the motion sensor light on the porch. The humid air formed halos around each bulb.

He met Brady in the driveway and showed him the e-mailed message on Taylor's cell phone. "I figure our suspect hid beside the barn and used a zoom."

Brady followed his gaze. "I'll check it out. You might want to let Jamie have a go with that cell phone."

"Smart thinking. If anybody can trace an e-mail source, it's Jamie."

"I didn't realize Taylor was in town."

"She's keeping a low profile. I assume you know what happened to her."

"Yeah. Wil had to fly out to the west coast to see about her. He didn't mention bringing her back."

"At the time, I guess he figured the fewer he told, the better. But this is stalking and you're law enforcement. I trust you to keep her location secret."

"You bet. Me and Taylor were classmates since middle school. I'd enjoy getting my hands on the sorry son of a bitch who hurt her."

"We don't know he's the same one stalking her now, but he sure wants to convince her he is."

Brady opened the hatch on the Jeep and retrieved his spotlight. "If he was way out here, he needed transportation. I'll check for tire tracks."

"Or he could've slipped in by boat."

"If I don't find tracks, I'll comb the path to the boat ramp."

"I'll get Taylor to turn on the outside lights. When I got here, she was sitting in the dark, terrified."

"She's had a rough time." Brady slammed the hatch then faced the house. "How is she now?"

"Still shaky." But at least now she wasn't waving a loaded pistol with her trembling hand.

"Stay inside with her. I can handle a little CSI." Brady spun on his heel and headed toward the barn.

A *little* CSI? Adam started to remind him the Drake Oaks estate covered eighty acres, much of it pine forest, but he let it go. The younger officer had given him a chilly reception as the new chief deputy. At least tonight he'd seen none of Brady's frostiness. Given time, Adam hoped to win the respect of all the FCSO employees. After all, next year he planned to be their new boss.

He stepped onto the porch and called out, "Taylor, it's Adam."

She unbolted the door and opened it. Harold's golden retriever stood beside her. "Find anything?"

"Brady's doing a search of the grounds. But your prowler is long gone by now."

"Come in before the entire bug population does."

He stepped inside and waited while she relocked the door. Taylor took security to a new level. "Could you turn on all your outside lights? It'll help Brady."

"Sure will." She reached past him to flip the switch by the door. "Have a seat while I turn on the back porch lights."

35

He returned to the sofa and waited, staring at the cell phone he clutched. His mother would have a hissy fit if she knew how he had made himself at home—sitting in the fancy living room, eating pizza in the Drake breakfast room—not that he would tell her. A minute later, Taylor returned. This time she sat on the matching sofa opposite him, the dog making a circle then settling at her feet.

"Does your dog think I'm a threat? I thought she usually stayed with Harold."

"Sophie spends most of the time with him. I think she's more curious than protective. We rarely have visitors at night." She nudged the dog. "Go say hi to Adam."

"How long have you had her?" Sophie approached him, tail wagging. He held out his free hand for her to sniff. That went well, so he reached behind her ear and scratched. She leaned into his hand and closed her eyes.

"I think Wil got her about five or six years ago when she was a puppy. He was still in Jacksonville working as a homicide detective. She belonged to a murder victim, and no one would take her. Wil didn't have the heart to send her to the pound."

"I can see why." He switched to scratching Sophie's other ear. "She's beautiful."

"And now she stays with Dad almost all the time. We call her his therapy dog because she really lifted his spirits after the stroke."

He chuckled. "I think she'd let me scratch her ears all night."

"You now have a friend for life." She pointed to her cell phone, which he still clutched in his other hand. "Now, can you explain how someone could use my cell signal to locate me?"

"No, but I believe Jamie Peterson can. I'd like to borrow this and see what she can do. She's the techie on our force."

Taylor nodded. "Sure, if it'll help."

"If we're to get to the bottom of this, I'll need to ask you a few questions about the attack. Are you up to that?"

She sighed, her damaged windpipe rasping. "Where do you want to start?"

"You said Wil dogged the detectives. Did he bring back any reports about the crime scene?"

"He read the reports and saw crime scene photos, but he didn't bring anything home."

He couldn't fault Wil for that decision. Taylor had enough to battle without running across crime scene photos. "What items did the intruder steal?"

"Electronics, I presume. He took every piece of my camera equipment, plus both my laptop and desktop computers. Even my media cards and flash drives. Roz had a netbook, and he took that, too." She shuddered. "Nothing worth killing for."

"Anything else stolen?"

"I think that was it. He might have stolen more but when he discovered I'd escaped, he probably panicked."

"How did you escape?"

"After he . . . cut my throat and threw me to the floor, I pressed against the wound hoping to slow the bleeding. I lay still so he'd think I was dead." She squeezed her eyes shut and paled. "When he left the room, I managed to flee. In the kitchen, I stumbled over Roz—"

"You don't need to go on. I'm sorry to upset you."

Taylor met his gaze. "Anyway, I had a lot of expensive equipment, thousands of dollars' worth. He took my camera bag, which had everything in it from my cameras and special lenses to my tripod and film."

"Film? Isn't everything digital now?"

"Digital is convenient, especially for covering a story. But I won my awards with traditional photography, using thirty-five millimeter film and my single lens reflex. Nothing will replace the rolls of exposed film from my nature shoot in the desert."

"Talking about this isn't easy for you, but we need to figure this out."

"What's to figure out? The killer took Roz's phone, and now he's followed me to Florida. The question is, why? I never saw his face. I can't identify him."

"What about your cell phone?"

"I'd left it plugged in my car charger, so it wasn't in the apartment. But my number was in Roz's. That much I can understand. How did he track me here?"

"That's not my area of expertise. I know it can be done." He pulled out his notepad and jotted a list of the stolen items. "What about photographs? Had you taken any pictures prior to the break-in that anyone would want?"

She frowned. "The desert shoot was artistic. I shot that earlier in the week. I did my own developing in the bathroom, usually when Roz was gone. It was the only room with no windows, and it had a sink."

"Any other shoots someone would have known about?"

"Oh." She rubbed the scar at her throat. "I had a routine assignment for the local paper covering the Teamsters picketing the docks. I shot about thirty digitals, which I never delivered and won't get paid for. I'd forgotten about those until now."

"When was this?"

"The morning of the attack. That's right. I remember uploading the memory card to my computer to make sure I'd gotten enough good shots. I'd planned to e-mail the best ones to the editor that evening. Never happened."

"I wonder if something connects your photo shoot to the theft of your files and equipment. Too bad we can't look through those photos."

"Oh, but we can."

"How? I thought you lost all your files and—"

"After a digital shoot I back up everything to an online alternate storage account. Uploading the photos took so long, I didn't have time to preview and select photos to e-mail. I was late for another appointment."

"I suggest you log on and print out those pictures so we can examine them. I'll send Jamie by tomorrow with her laptop and photo printer, if that's all right with you."

"Sure, if you think it will help."

He shrugged. "It's a long shot, but we need to try. If you accidentally photographed something you shouldn't have . . . . "

Taylor shuddered. "I get where you're going with this. I could be in danger if somebody wanted to destroy my picture files. I seriously doubt a bunch of picketing longshoremen object to being photographed, though. They welcome publicity."

"Humor me. I'm paid to be thorough in my investigation, and you're on my watch now." Adam's cell phone rang, and he raised a finger to Taylor. "It's Brady. Let's see what he found."

"Boss, I think you better see this for yourself," Brady said. "I'm beside the barn."

Boss? Brady must be troubled if he called Adam "Boss." He normally reserved that for Wil.

Adam stood, startling the dog. "Be right there."

Sophie rushed to Taylor's side when she bolted from the couch. "What is it? What did he find?"

"Don't know yet. I'll check back with you before I leave."

She and the dog followed him to the door. "I'll lock up behind you."

What had Brady found?

Chapter Four

Taylor bolted the door lock and replaced the security chain just as the telephone rang. She rushed to the kitchen to answer it.

"Taylor, it's Sam. Hope it's not too late to call."

"Dad's in bed, but he may still—"

"I'm calling you, actually. How are you?"

She strained to hear her brother's words over a low hum on the phone line. "Not so good. But if I tell you why, you have to promise not to call Wil."

"I promise. Just tell me how I can help." As the dean of Drake College, Sam seemed too busy to call or visit. Why the sudden attention?

"Oh, Sam, that's sweet, but you're busy with the college. You don't have to—"

"I can listen. Tell me everything."

Starting with Wil's request that Adam drive by each night to check on her, she told Sam everything, including the fact that Adam and Officer Newcomb were outside now checking for her stalker.

"This certainly impedes one's recovery from agoraphobia. Will you continue to work the desensitization approach?"

"Adam says he'll help me, but it's baby steps. I've made it no farther than the driveway."

"How's our father reacting to this latest development?"

"He doesn't know about the photo e-mail. He thinks Adam and I are socializing."

"I can't see him reconciled to having a Gillespie as a guest at Drake Oaks."

"He's not, but I refuse to be drawn into that old feud."

Sam snorted. "An admirable goal, dear sister, but unattainable. As long as we Drakes live and breathe, we'll be adversaries of the Gillespies."

"Why, exactly, is that? I know it involves our mother, but nobody ever talks about it. None of you will tell me a thing."

41

"That's our grandmother's legacy. She ruled the house and trained us that speaking of her deceased daughter-in-law was a breach of etiquette. We never questioned her because we were forbidden to question her."

"About anything. Gram's dead and gone now, so I want to know about our mother. Tell you what. Come by some night and I'll show you her letters. Interesting reading."

"Letters? You have letters written by Mother"—his voice caught—"to us?" She could hear him swallow in spite of the humming connection. Stiff, controlled Sam . . . emotional?

"To Dad." She explained how she'd stumbled upon the jewelry box while cleaning Gram's room. "I didn't say anything to Dad yet. He's . . . he's so weak, Sam. I think four years of confinement to a wheelchair have taken their toll."

"I thought the physical therapist said he'd made progress." Sam had regained control of his voice. Or had she imagined his emotional lapse?

"She said his speech, especially, is much clearer. And his paralysis isn't as widespread as it was, which could mean some nerves are rerouting themselves—"

"Neuroregeneration. I've read about that. Father isn't nearly as helpless as most stroke victims in his condition. He's a fighter."

"That's just it. The fight is exhausting him. He sleeps most of the time. Wil put a safety belt on his wheelchair so he doesn't fall out of it while dozing."

"I have a couple of hours free tomorrow. I'll pay Father a visit. Then you and I can read those letters."

"Come for lunch."

"Meanwhile, report your telephone to repair service. Your transmission is weak."

"Oh, okay. I thought it was on your end."

"My connection worked perfectly until I called you."

She had bigger fish to fry than a hum on the line, but she'd humor her perfectionist brother. "See you tomorrow." She hung up the phone and her dad called to her. She entered his room. "You need something, Dad?"

"Sophie." Sophie ran over to the bed then stood with her front paws on the mattress. Her tail wagging, she nuzzled his paralyzed hand. He reached over with the other hand and petted her. "Good girl."

"Sophie, stay." Taylor leaned over and kissed her father on the forehead. "Want me to turn off the TV?"

"I can do it." He cut his gaze toward the remote control lying within his reach. Because of the stroke, he sometimes slurred his words and she had to listen carefully to understand him.

"Good night." When she pulled the door closed, she heard footsteps on the front porch.

Adam called to her as he had earlier. She turned the deadbolt and unlocked the door then slid back the security chain. The nighttime insects swarmed the porch light, eager for a chance to move indoors. Opening the door, she waved Adam inside. "What did you find?"

He seemed to understand the race with the bugs and quickly entered the house but he made no move to sit and chat. Tension lined his face. "You didn't have a prowler tonight, at least not exactly. We found a surveillance camera installed on the barn, aimed at the driveway in front. Brady found no fresh footprints or tire tracks, so we don't know how long it's been there. Someone is monitoring your family, and they're doing so remotely."

"How? I thought surveillance cameras had video tapes or cards inside."

"Usually. But this is more sophisticated. As I told you, technology isn't my area of expertise. I'm not sure this is within Jamie's, either. We may need to call in the state."

"I know a little about it. Wildlife photographers sometimes use surveillance setups in shoots where human presence would scare away the subjects. I don't know how they retrieve the data remotely, but I could find out."

"Good. I'll send Jamie in the morning and you two can put your heads together. Meanwhile I'll see what I can learn from the forensics staff at FDLE."

"Just leave Wil out of the loop, okay?"

"For now." He turned to leave then hesitated. "I'll stop by again tomorrow evening, but it may be late. I'm having dinner with my mother."

"No problemo. I'm up late."

"One more thing. Do you have a lock for that gate?"

She shrugged. "Are you suggesting we get one?"

"Think about it. Better yet, why not an electric gate with a coded keypad? It may not keep out trespassers, but it'll bring them to your attention."

"That's what the driveway alarm is for."

Adam shook his head. "The motion sensor catches traffic after it enters the driveway."

She pictured the wooded entrance off the county road, along with the long stretch of pine trees between the driveway and the barn, all a blind spot from the first floor of the house. "I see what you mean."

"If you need someone reputable to install the equipment, talk to Jamie in the morning. She's better acquainted with the contractors."

After Adam left and Taylor locked the door, she went upstairs to log on to her e-mail account using Fia's netbook. The time had come to open Jim Russo's e-mails. Like it or not, she needed to acknowledge his messages. She should've responded sooner. He'd been a good friend and she'd ignored him. Now he was the one photographer who had the capability to help her.

The Monday afternoon flood of emergency calls and reviewing reports receded, so Adam grabbed a cup of stale coffee and a bag of peanuts from the vending machine. Working two jobs challenged him. While acting Sheriff, he had Wil's responsibilities and his own, too. When he took over as sheriff, who could he move into the chief deputy position? He needed someone experienced and reliable.

Deputy Geraldo Blanco wandered in, examined the coffee carafe, and scowled. "Let me brew a fresh pot."

"I'll drink to that." He tossed the stale coffee into the sink. "I wanted to have a word with you, anyway."

"Uh oh." Geraldo tucked the premeasured packet of coffee into the filter basket. "What'd I do now?"

He chuckled. "Nothing I know about. It's your brother Buzz."

"Brady told me about Saturday night. I had a chat with little brother yesterday. I don't think he'll sneak around Cari Mercer's windows again."

"That's good to know."

Geraldo poured the filtered water into the reservoir then turned on the brewer. "Cari got herself a weekend job waiting tables at the Hurricane Lantern, and Buzz feels neglected."

"Did you remind Buzz she needs the money to afford college?"

"You know kids. He's not thinking about college or earning money. He's thinking about one thing and one thing only."

Well, let's hope Cari's smart enough for the both of 'em." He rinsed his stained coffee mug at the sink. "I remember seventeen. It's a wonder I lived to graduate from high school. College never occurred to me. I headed for the Army."

"High school seems a lifetime ago, doesn't it?" Geraldo snapped his fingers. "I almost forgot. Jamie Peterson wants you to call her. She thinks she has a lead on that cell phone. I guess that means something to you."

"Sure does. I'll be right back." He finished off the peanuts while hurrying to his office, pausing for a quick sip at the water fountain. Instead of calling Jamie, he found her headed toward his office. "I was just going to call you."

"I wanted to bring you these." She handed him a tan clasp envelope. "Copies of the photos from Taylor Drake's last photo assignment."

"Thanks. Come in and have a seat." He slid the envelope under his desk blotter, away from prying eyes. He'd examine them later. "How did it go this morning with the Drake woman?"

Jamie sat across from his desk. "Great. When I first met her for her firearms safety training, she was nothing like I expected. After I spent some time working with her, I found myself forgetting the weird voice thing. I'm sure she's self-conscious of that."

"I know what you mean. She's lucky to have no more injuries than she did, considering."

"Jumpy, though. Edgy. But who wouldn't be? She's smart and cooperative, and a real nice person. I hope I can help the lady."

"I hope so, too." At what point had he stopped thinking of Taylor as an enemy? "So what about the surveillance camera?"

"I got the model number, but left it for now."

"Good thinking. Whoever is spying may not realize we've found it."

"I was careful to avoid the lens. We think a guy posing as a building inspector installed it about a month ago. Hazel Porter didn't think to question his phony credentials so she gave him access to the barn. The camera is accessed remotely by cell phone for retrieving the images. I intend to get the records and figure out who's dialing in. I'll know more then."

"So there wasn't a trespasser last night, in the physical sense, and the photo and e-mail could have come from anywhere?"

Jamie nodded. "Anywhere with cellular service."

"That should ease Taylor's misgivings about a prowler being on her property last night."

"It's going to take a heap more to ease that poor woman's misgivings. That is one nervous wreck."

"Anything else I should know?"

Jamie consulted her notes. "Taylor's colleague out in California is named Jim Russo—does mostly wildlife photography and is familiar with remote surveillance equipment. She's contacted him for information on his remote camera setups, but I'm checking him out. Seems to me he makes a good suspect."

"Did she mention anything about their friendship? Have they dated? Competed? Anything that motivates him to stalk her?"

"In a way, they're competitors, although they sometimes work together. Taylor says he's only a friend, although she concedes they dated once. He wanted a relationship; she didn't."

"Jamie, you learned all that from Taylor? Good job. Definitely check this dude out."

"Thanks." Jamie stood. "I'm on it."

Adam returned to the break room for his freshly brewed coffee. He'd just taken his first sip when his cell phone trilled. Caller ID showed *Mom*. "Hello, Mom."

"Are we still meeting for dinner?"

"Unless you'd rather I pick you up."

"No, no. Save us a booth. I should be there by six."

He didn't need to ask where. Aside from a few franchised fast-food eateries, Drake Springs had only one restaurant open in the evenings—the Hurricane Lantern on 471. The Alibi Bar had a limited menu, but his family never stepped foot in that joint. Bad memories. The Alibi had been Dad's home-away-from-home too many years.

After his mother disconnected, he took his coffee into the dispatch office for a status report. Rebecca Gibbons was on duty. A Bluetooth headset was stuck behind her ear amid a mass of brown curls. Not much older than Adam, she kept her youthful appearance using cosmetics she sold on the side.

She looked up from her console and smiled. "Mighty quiet today."

"It's Monday. Kids are back in class."

"Whatever the reason, I'm not complainin'."

"I'm going to make a pass through town before I stop for dinner. If you need me, call my cell."

"Will do."

He finished his mug of coffee, stopped by his office to lock up, then halted at his desk. A corner of the tan envelope peeked out from beneath his month-at-a-glance desk blotter. Before he left, he scanned the photographs Jamie had given him, the ones from Taylor's last photo shoot. Four sheets of photo quality paper with a series of thumbprint images revealed nothing unusual. Just shots of a crowd of people gathered at the docks, some carrying picket signs, some standing to the side. At first glance, he saw nothing but spectators and picketers.

He'd take the photos with him and look at them again with Taylor.

Perhaps she'd have more of an eye for something out of place. He ignored the zing of anticipation that punched him in the chest. Just because she was a babe didn't mean he should look forward to sitting beside her on the sofa, their heads together examining the photos, so close he could feel the heat from her skin and the tickle of her breath. Even if she hadn't been the daughter of Harold Drake, she was fragile and unstable. He wouldn't take advantage of her emotional vulnerability, and that was that.

Taylor jumped at the sound of the gate alarm. She'd been a bundle of nerves since everyone had left for the day. After serving her father a hamburger and fries she managed to pull together from the freezer stock, she'd logged on to see if Jim Russo had answered her e-mail. An automatic vacation reply that he was out of the office and would read her message as soon as possible had been the only response.

With nothing to occupy her mind and no one to talk to after *Wheel of Fortune* claimed her dad's attention, she'd been as jittery as a chicken on a hotplate. Now Adam was here, and she couldn't deny the rush of pleasure that swept over her. Or had she confused pleasure with relief? She did feel safer with him in the house. His being illegally handsome didn't mean she felt an attraction to him, right?

Wrong. He attracted her too much, and it had nothing to do with the silly feud between their families marking him as forbidden fruit. He exuded confidence, just shy of arrogance. Furthermore, he didn't coddle her. His attitude toward her emotional disorder inspired her to overcome her self-centeredness. It shamed her how she needed to learn focusing outside of herself. No wonder he saw her as a spoiled rich bitch. Until recently she'd had an easy life.

Now Sophie had skittered up the hall to stand at Taylor's side by the door. "It's okay, girl. Go back to Dad."

The dog obeyed and backtracked. Taylor followed and peeked inside the room. Her father lay asleep in his bed with some reality show blaring from the TV. She pulled the door closed and tiptoed back to the front of the house.

As soon as she saw Adam climb out of the car, she unlocked the door. He dragged up the steps with a weariness she'd not seen in him. "Come inside."

Without a word, he stepped into the foyer and removed his hat. Following her into the living room, he sank into the sofa, laying his hat and a tan envelope beside him.

"You look exhausted, Adam. Let me get you something to drink."

"I wouldn't turn down a cup of decaf if you have any. Instant's fine."

"Hey, coffee sounds good. Let me brew us a pot." She paused at the door. "Want to sit in the kitchen and talk, or would you be more comfortable here?"

He stood abruptly, as if he'd rather be anywhere but abandoned in the formal living room. "Kitchen's fine."

She led him to the kitchen breakfast nook. "Have a seat and I'll start the pot."

"I talked briefly with Jamie." He held up the envelope. "I thought we'd look through these photos together."

"Sure." She pulled the coffee maker toward her. "Did she tell you about the Bluetooth setup on the surveillance camera?"

"Yeah." At the end of the table he pulled out a chair, on which he placed his hat and the envelope, then sat in a side chair facing her. "She said you agreed to go about your daily routine as normal and pretend you didn't see it. How's that working for you?"

Normal? Yeah, right. She reached for the canister of decaffeinated coffee. "Fred Fischer arrived after lunch, and I had to explain what was going on. He worked all afternoon and left around six, but the bulk of the repairs are inside the barn."

"Fred's retired law enforcement. He understands."

"There hasn't been much for the camera to record. I've stayed indoors." She opened the refrigerator for the pitcher of filtered water. "Did Jamie tell you Dad's nurse quit? At least until we catch the stalker."

"What will you do? Can you handle your father by yourself?"

"Hazel called a retired nurse in Live Oak named Judy Wood, but she can't start until Wednesday. I figure I can manage one day." She swallowed, shoving her unease to the back of her mind.

"You don't sound convinced of that."

She pushed the button on the coffee maker. "I'm trying to convince myself. The truth is I'm not good with Dad, not like Wil. He inherited the nurturer gene in our family."

"*Nurturer* gene? I thought women were naturals at taking care of people. Someday when you have children, it'll kick in."

Turning to face him, she gave him an eye-roll. "Oh, please! I can barely take care of myself. I can't see me with a baby."

"Don't you want children someday?" He suddenly broke eye contact, as if uncomfortable with the question.

"Not really. What about you?"

He shrugged. "It's easier being Uncle Adam to my nephews."

"I wouldn't mind being Aunt Taylor someday, if Wil and Fia will cooperate. Sam's a confirmed bachelor, I fear."

"Can Sam help you out tomorrow with your dad?"

"I wouldn't ask. Sam is as deficient as I am when it comes to care giving. But Dad can do quite a bit for himself. If you don't rush him, he can dress himself. He can feed himself, too, as long as nothing needs cutting up. He just has trouble with balance since he's mostly paralyzed on one side."

"I'll run a quick background check on this Judy Wood."

She grabbed two coffee mugs from the cupboard. "I appreciate it. Normally I'm not so paranoid."

"Checking on employees is just good business." He pulled a pen and a small spiral notebook from his shirt pocket. "Judy Wood, you say?"

"Right. No *S*. But Hazel knows her."

"Even so, it pays to be cautious." He scribbled in his notebook. "I also need to know your roommate's full name in case we come up with anything on her cell phone."

"I made the rent check out to Rosalind Williams." Picking up the tan envelope, she sat down across from him. "May I?"

"They're your pictures. Be my guest." He stuffed pen and notebook into his pocket. "Look carefully at each one and see if anything seems out of place. Or anyone."

While the coffee maker gurgled and hissed in the background, she unclasped the envelope and pulled out the four sheets. She'd already seen the pictures when she'd downloaded them for Jamie, but now she took a closer look. Each sheet contained nine different frames except for the last, the contact sheet that contained all twenty-seven images. She frowned at the poor composition of several of the shots, and one picture was overexposed. Two others needed to be cropped to remove a couple of people unrelated to the picket line.

"Some of these need to be purged—"

"Don't delete anything. Call it a hunch, but I think something about your photo shoot could lead us to your attacker."

"I thought it was a random burglary-turned-murder."

"Probably, but I believe in leaving no stone unturned."

That's why Adam was in law enforcement and she wasn't. No way she could collect and examine all possible clues to solve a crime. Clutter annoyed her. She needed simplicity and order in her life. She traveled light—*used* to travel light. It wasn't as if she'd be going anywhere now.

"You're frowning," Adam said. "Did you find something?"

"Not yet. I was just thinking about how so much has changed."

"What do you mean?"

"I lived in Long Beach with Roz because I wasn't home enough to justify paying rent on an empty apartment. I owned a couple pieces of furniture and not a lot of clothing. My camera equipment was the exception. I loved my cameras and took them wherever I traveled. I couldn't wait to get to the next assignment, whether it was in Alaska or Paraguay. Now I've lost my cameras, and I don't even want to walk out the front door."

"You want to. You're just afraid."

"Terrified. But I'll survive." She slid the photo sheets back in the envelope.

"Perhaps what you need is a new camera, something to get you back to doing what you love."

Funny that she hadn't thought of that. She loved all kinds of photography. "You're right. I could order one online and have it shipped here."

"There you go."

"Meanwhile, let me grab the netbook so we can look at the photos enlarged. Be right back."

On her way to the stairs, she paused to check on her father. He still dozed, but Sophie had jumped onto the bed and lay at his side. Easing the door closed, she hurried up the steps. Minutes later, she returned to the breakfast nook clutching Fia's netbook. "I downloaded the pictures to a folder so we can look at them with the zoom feature." Enlargements would have worked better, but the ten-inch netbook screen would do.

"Good idea." The weariness in his voice had returned.

"You need coffee." She grabbed the carafe and filled their mugs. "Cream or sugar?"

Adam sipped from his steaming mug. "Black's fine."

She doctored her own coffee with half-and-half and a sweetener. "Are you all right? You seem . . . distracted."

He straightened in his seat and seemed to remember his posture. "I'm fine. It's just been a long day."

She didn't buy it, but what business was it of hers? Perhaps dinner with his mother had taxed his patience. Rumor had it Phyllis Gillespie was a control freak, although Taylor couldn't be sure how much old grudges tainted that gossip. "It's going to be a long week with Wil gone. You have his duties as well as your own."

He gave her a look so filled with gratitude she nearly gasped at the strangeness of it. What had she said? "You're the only person who seems to realize that."

"No, I'm not, Adam. Wil said as much when he left. He felt he was leaving you with the lion's share of the work while he goofed off for a week."

"That's how vacation time works."

"That's what *I* told him, but you know Wil." She took another drink of the coffee then turned her attention to the netbook. "Let's take a quick look at the pictures so you can go home and decompress."

"Decompress. That's one way of putting it." No smile accompanied his words, so she let the comment pass.

One by one, they studied each of the photos, zooming in when necessary. But the tiny ten-inch screen didn't show much of a photo at a time. Sitting opposite each other with the small computer on the table between them, she and Adam craned their necks until their heads nearly touched. The faint scent of citrus from his cologne drew her, but she resisted resting her head against his. What a ridiculous notion. He'd probably bolt for the door and never return.

"What about this one?" Adam tapped the photo she thought needed cropping. "Those two guys don't belong there."

"Right. I would've cropped them out—"

"They also don't belong together. Look at how differently they're dressed."

She zoomed in on the two men. The one with his back to the camera had his head turned, giving the profile with a large hook nose, kind of like that of a Halloween witch's mask. He wore baggy, low-rider shorts and a black muscle shirt. Tattoos covered his arms, neck, and legs, and his hair hadn't seen a barber's scissors in months. The older man wore a business suit. His clean-shaven face seemed to stare directly into the camera, although she'd been a good distance away and had made the shot with her telephoto zoom.

"Could be a parolee and his parole officer. Something about the suit makes me think cop."

"I don't think so. Check closer. Cops can't afford four-hundred dollar suits."

She zoomed in on the shoes. "Calfskin, I think. Ka-ching. There's another four-hundred."

"Lawyer, maybe. Anyone else look out of place?"

She browsed through the twenty-seven photos again, studying the longshoremen and their supporters in the crowd. One unkempt teenage girl appeared in one of the last photos. "She looks like a runaway."

Adam leaned back and sighed, unable to mask his fatigue. "Who can tell anymore with the way kids dress?"

"More coffee?" She shut down the Net book. "Or shall we call it a night?"

"Unless you need me for anything, I'll head home." He picked up his hat and stood. "Thanks for the coffee."

A mixture of relief and disappointment swept through her. He hadn't mentioned a repeat of her desensitization exercise. Was she that starved for attention? Or just lonely? Considering the surveillance camera, it was probably just as well she stay inside. "I'll walk you to the door."

"Walk me to my car." So he hadn't forgotten. He paused in the hallway and tapped her nose with his finger. "Show the son-of-a-bitch you aren't afraid."

She'd love to show her peeping Tom he hadn't spooked her, but he had. Could she walk to Adam's car without a panic attack . . . a panic attack photographed and viewed by strangers?

"Don't think about it. Just do it. Take a deep breath, open the door, and walk with me. I'll even hold your hand."

She almost smiled. "What an incentive."

"All right, I *won't* hold your hand." He seemed to mistake her teasing for sarcasm. Any trace of tenderness in his voice vanished. "Either way, get your butt going."

Focus outside yourself. Consider Adam's feelings.

With renewed determination, she reached for his hand. "You *will* hold my hand. It'll be a wonderful diversion."

His shell-shocked gaze nearly made her laugh. Had the man no idea how attractive he was? Any woman in her right mind would drag him upstairs to bed and jump his bones right now. Unfortunately, she hadn't been a woman in her right mind for some time.

Inhaling a breath for courage, she unlocked the door. "Let's go."

He put on his hat as she led him onto the porch. "Now remember to put on a show."

Put on a show. She could do this. Instead of fear, she clung to anger. How dare this bastard terrorize her? How dare he invade her privacy? With head held high, she marched down the porch steps toward the police cruiser. Not one moment of panic intruded.

Standing beside Adam at the driver's door, she smiled at him. "Thank you."

A hint of a smile flirted with his lips as his hand gripped the car door. "You'll get through this, champ. You're tougher than you think."

"I . . . I don't feel tough, but thanks for saying that."

Some trace of admiration warmed his eyes, and his voice softened. "I mean it, Taylor. You're smart and resilient. Don't let the bad guys win, okay?"

"Okay." Her smile grew. Adam was one of the *good* guys— absolutely. "Let's give the surveillance camera a real show."

He cocked his head and gave her a quizzical look. "What do you mean?"

She grabbed him by the shoulders and tiptoed to reach him, touching her mouth to his. At first he didn't react, just stared at her in astonishment. Then his eyes closed, and his lips moved with hers, barely open yet bold and warm. He tasted like black coffee and bedroom sex. Their tongues touched. His breath hitched. So he wasn't immune to her!

Resisting the urge to wrap her arms around his neck and really have her way with him, she withdrew. The poor guy's stunned expression made her smile. "Good night."

She strolled up the steps, crossed the porch, then checked his reflection in the living room window. He hadn't moved. At the front door, she turned and waved, but he either didn't see or ignored her. He climbed into the car and left. She'd closed the door and locked up when it hit her— she hadn't panicked. Furthermore, she'd kissed him. And it had felt damned good. After three months of fearing even the slightest contact with a man, she had progressed to kissing one.

With Adam's taste still on her lips, she touched them with her fingertips. Pride warred with perplexity. She'd been unprepared for the sheer jolt of pleasure from that kiss, and the joy that lingered long after he'd gone.

Chapter Five

If Adam had been rude to Taylor, he couldn't help it. Her comment that he seemed distracted nailed it. Why else had he stood there like a damn department store mannequin when she'd kissed him? He had no idea what triggered such affectionate behavior nor why it had shocked the hell out of him. Worse, he couldn't stop the buzz of arousal still tingling throughout his body. But even Taylor's sweet, luscious taste couldn't keep his mind off his mother and their conversation at dinner. Her prognosis had worsened, and her upcoming visit to the Mayo Clinic was a last resort.

As soon as he got home, he grabbed his phone and punched in his sister's number. She seemed to expect his call.

"Mom came over tonight after she left you at the restaurant." She paused to blow her nose. "I was afraid something like this would happen."

"It's as if she's given up."

"She's lived too long with the poison."

"Poison? You mean the cancer?"

"You'll scoff at my theory—you always do—but her bitterness and anger have festered for so long, ever since Daddy betrayed her—"

"Bullshit. Opinions and emotions don't give you cancer." He'd heard too many of Amy's forgiveness-is-good-for-the-soul speeches, and he was in no mood for one now. "She has every right to feel bitter."

"But negative feelings weaken the immune system. Look at Harold Drake. Do you think a healthy sixty year old man should have had such a stroke? He's as full of resentment as Mom. I'm telling you, Adam, for your own health, let go of this grudge."

How could she suggest he forgive and forget? Harold Drake had ruined their father's business, Connie Drake had destroyed their parents' marriage, and Wil Drake had deserted their sister Megan without a backward glance. "Can you honestly say you have?"

"A long time ago . . . and I'm happier for it. But I worry because you and Mom haven't."

He clenched the edge of the counter until his knuckles whitened. "That family doesn't deserve forgiveness."

"None of us *deserve* forgiveness. You're missing the point."

"Yeah, yeah." Next she would quote Bible scriptures unless he got her back on track. Now wasn't the time to debate religion or the longstanding feud between the Gillespies and the Drakes. "Did she tell you about the surgery scheduled for Wednesday?"

"Yes. I think it's like exploratory. I'll stay with her as long as it takes. No way she'll go through that alone."

"Good." A rush of affection overwhelmed him, along with a dose of relief. Thanks to his tenderhearted sister, Mom wouldn't be alone when learning her prognosis. He could overlook Amy's cockamamie theories on metaphysics or her Pollyanna philosophy. "Thank you. I offered to take her, but she wouldn't hear of it. Is there anything I can do to help, like pick up the boys after school?"

"Mama Sawyer's taking care of Ray and Travis. You concentrate on winning this election. That's what will make Mom feel better fast."

"Nothing like a little pressure."

"Pressure? You're the one determined to defeat Wil Drake."

Drake may have beaten him four years ago but he had a less than stellar record. "I may not like the bastard, but I'm opposing him because I want the sheriff's job. I have more experience—"

"Okay, okay, I get that. But—"

"He has two unsolved homicides that are now in the cold case file—"

"In all fairness, those two murders are solved. The killer may never go to trial because the DA didn't have enough evidence, but that's not Wil's fault." She sounded like a reporter for the *Drake Springs Democrat*, not his twin sister.

"Whose side are you on, anyway?"

"Yours, of course. Your comment about pressure concerns me, though. I love Mom, but I've seen her push you to run for office. Just be sure it's what *you* want."

"Don't worry. I may pretend to be a mama's boy because it's the course of least resistance. But I make my own decisions."

He ended the call yet remained at the breakfast counter, staring at nothing. The similarities between his sister and Taylor Drake amused him. Both women naively believed the trouble between their families could be settled with prayer, a group hug, and a stanza of Kumbaya. He excused Taylor because of her age. She'd been two . . . three years old, tops, and didn't remember the trouble her family had served up to the Gillespies. But Amy dated Wil in high school and had suffered from his perfidy. She knew better. Could she so easily forgive Wil and forget Megan?

He slid off the stool in search of a beer. Though not much of a drinker, he needed a nice cold one tonight. Unlike his father Jed, Adam understood that alcohol solved nothing. One lone Samuel Adams lay on the top shelf of his refrigerator.

He could drink a dozen bottles and not erase the taste of Taylor on his lips, though. And God help him, if he had the opportunity, he'd kiss her again.

Taylor checked the deadbolt locks on each door. After double-checking the windows, she retrieved her pistol to take with her upstairs to her bedroom. While having the electric gate installed, she'd check into having a security system added to the house. Although Dad had a medical monitoring device with its special telephone, he could afford to add a burglar alarm.

She grabbed the cordless telephone from the upstairs hall and carried it to her room. After her facial, she brushed her teeth. She returned to her room just as the telephone chirped. "Hello."

"Hi, darlin'. How's it going?"

"Oh, Wil. Must you micromanage? Everything's under control. Fred Fischer started renovations on the barn today, and I've been cleaning house."

"Did you save anything for the cleaning service to do?"

Cleaning service? "Refresh my memory. When do they come?"

"Every other Wednesday. It's a service out of Lake City called Home

Maid Bonnie. I thought I told you. They change bed linens and do the heavy cleaning, like bathrooms and vacuuming."

She had no memory of a cleaning service, but she'd fake it. No need to worry Wil. "I just moved some stuff to storage. There will be plenty for Home Maid Bonnie to do. Are you lovebirds having a good time and relaxing?"

"When Fia's not seasick. I worried about traveling in the Caribbean during hurricane season, but the weather's been calm. Still, she's had a time with nausea."

"Hm. Does the nausea come and go?"

"She usually feels better later in the day."

"Have you considered that your bride may have morning sickness?"

"I didn't, but…that would be wonderful. We do want a family."

"It'd be nice to become an aunt." Now wasn't the time to ask him about Megan. Surely Adam had been mistaken about Wil's behavior.

"Don't say anything to anyone else yet."

"I wouldn't dare. That'll be your news to share."

"Thanks." The connection crackled. "I may be losing the signal."

"Before you hang up, do you have any objection to my moving into Dad's old suite upstairs? It'd give me more room and a private bath, a bigger one where I might do some developing."

"That's a terrific idea. Does this mean you're staying?"

"Yeah, I'd say so. My plans right now are . . . indefinite at best."

So is Adam patrolling?"

"Every night. Dad grumbles but he seems resigned to having him around. I keep them in separate rooms."

"Wise move." Wil chuckled. "So everything is all right?"

"Sure. Sam came by today and had lunch with Dad."

"Excuse me. I think I'm losing the connection. I thought you said *Sam* came—"

"I did. Dad enjoyed his company, I could tell."

"Hm." For once, her chatty older brother seemed speechless.

"Sam seemed different today, Wil. You think he's in love or

60

something?"

"Who with? He isn't even dating anyone that I know of."

"Something else is going on, then. He even called last night to see how I was doing. He's definitely more thoughtful. You'll see for yourself soon enough."

"We'll be home Sunday afternoon. We have to drive all the way from Port Canaveral."

He'd told her this countless times, but she let it slide. "Relax and enjoy the cruise, and stop worrying about things here. I have everything under control."

She was a lousy liar, but she did her best to convince him. He said goodbye and ended the call. He'd be calling again, though. No doubt.

She laid the phone on her nightstand and reached for the netbook to surf the Internet for cameras. Adam's suggestion that she get back to photography made sense. He was good medicine for her in many ways. Memories of their one kiss triggered a goofy smile. Yeah, good medicine.

A sudden flash of light swept the room. Lightning? She snapped off the lamp and crept to her window to peer out between the mini blinds. The bedroom's only window overlooked the pine forest and offered a partial view of the barn. Clouds gathered in the sky and hid the almost full moon. Tree limbs swayed and dipped with a strong breeze. Thunder rumbled in the distance.

She started to return to the netbook to check the weather forecast when a creature's silhouette flitted across the barn's roof. Her breath caught in her throat. Had she imagined the shadow? Had it been animal or human? Eyes straining to watch, she saw nothing but the painted metal roof reflecting the outdoor security lamp. A brilliant flash of lightning startled her and she closed her eyes to refocus.

She stared again at the empty roof. Probably her imagination or the shadows of wind-blown tree branches. But what if the creep who had watched her through the surveillance camera had come back to remove it? If he suspected they'd discovered the device, he'd want to take the evidence. Why hadn't Jamie removed it this afternoon while she had the chance?

Then a figure came into view, just in her line of sight, furtively crawling across the barn roof. She hadn't imagined it. Another flash of lightning revealed a blond man of medium height clutching something—the camera?—in one hand while scrabbling toward the roof's trap door.

A strong mixture of anger and fear choked her, but she gave both emotions a ruthless shove. How dare he spy on her and her family? She needed to stop the trespasser. No time to waste calling the cops. What could she do? She picked up her pistol but she needed a rifle at this range, not that she wanted to kill anyone. Still, a gunshot might startle him, buying her time until help arrived.

She unlocked the safety, shoved open the window, then held the Cobra with both hands. Her body shook and her heartbeat thundered in her ears. Aiming in the direction of the barn's roof, she squeezed the trigger and fired.

After dialing 9-1-1, Taylor then had the unpleasant task of telling her father. Sophie howled and paced until Taylor finally calmed her. Oddly, Dad seemed more curious than upset.

His dull eyes flashed with excitement. "You might want to put the gun away."

"Uh, right." She left his room and placed her pistol in the kitchen drawer just as the driveway alarm buzzed. The sudden noise drove the bumblebees in her stomach into a frenzy. She crept to the front window and peered between the drapes. Two deputies, having arrived in separate vehicles, got out of their cars and ran to the front door.

With shaking hands, she removed the security chain, unlocked the deadbolts, then opened the door, coming face to face with Deputies Devon Winston and Brady Newcomb. Before either officer had a chance to speak, she gave a rapid-fire account of what had happened.

"He's in the back lying on the ground by the barn. I don't know whether I shot him or he fell, but I'm sure he needs medical attention." She wheezed the words in one breath then gulped air into her lungs while her heart played bass drum against her breastbone.

"Calm down, Miss Drake. EMS is en route." Deputy Newcomb gestured toward her door. "Lock up while we take a look."

The way the deputy stared at her, he may have meant EMS was en route for *her*, not her injured trespasser. Immediately, the ambulance lights cut through the trees as EMS triggered the driveway buzzer. The deputies returned to their vehicles and Taylor locked up. She watched from the utility room window, straining to catch sight of the stalker, but he was blocked from her view. Had she shot him? Would he recover?

The driveway alarm sounded a third time, rattling her as it usually did. Now who? She rushed to the front window. The familiar FCSO sedan rolled to a stop in front of the house. Adam Gillespie parked, shut off the bar of strobe lights on the cruiser's roof, then got out and headed toward the porch steps. He didn't bother masking the weariness in his face. Poor guy had barely had time to get home and relax before having to return.

She wasted no time working the chain and locks to open the door. "I deliberately didn't call you. You need your rest."

"I'm the acting sheriff, Taylor. My deputies know to notify me."

"They're around back with the paramedics." She told him about firing a shot at the trespasser on the barn roof.

"You should've called 9-1-1 first and—"

"And let him get away? I don't think so. I am so tired of being afraid. I need to know who's spying on me and why."

"Well, now's your chance." He reached for her hand. "Come on."

She recoiled. "What do you mean?"

"You're coming with me. You need to take a look at the offender and see if you can identify him."

Her brain saw the wisdom in his words, but her body refused to move. The bees in her chest morphed into angry hornets. "I . . . I can't."

He gave a none-too-gentle tug on her arm. "You have no choice. This is a crime scene now and you're involved."

Gone was the patient, gentle man she'd kissed. Who was she kidding? Adam was rarely patient and gentle. He hadn't coddled her, and he wasn't going to now.

"Okay, okay." A stiff breeze kept the flying insects at bay and warned of an imminent thunderstorm. Lightning streaked the distant sky. But the storm outside paled compared to the one in her chest. She took a deep breath and prayed for courage. "Let's get this over with."

He gripped her elbow and led her onto the porch. "We don't know the extent of the victim's injuries—"

"I'm okay. Just . . . just catch me if I pass out."

"You won't." He kept a grip on her elbow and they stepped into the driveway. "You're made of stronger stuff than you credit yourself for."

"Or not. What if I take after my mother?" Her greatest fear. "She was emotionally needy."

"You said you don't remember her." He stopped at the car and popped the trunk. "I need to grab a flashlight."

She stared at the Ford logo and the *Crown Victoria* insignia, focusing on the details of the vehicle. But she couldn't stop the memory of the last time she'd stood by his cruiser, earlier in the evening when she'd boldly kissed him. Her lips still tingled and her breath quickened, not that she could expect a repeat performance. He was on duty. He'd returned because she'd shot a prowler—nothing more.

He slammed the trunk, clicked on the flashlight, then reached for her arm. "Let's go."

"You can do this, Taylor," she whispered.

"Yes, Taylor, you can. Tell me why you say your mother was emotionally needy."

"That's what Gram said. Nobody talks to me about my mother, and nobody wants to. It's why I asked you to help me retrace her steps the night she died."

He tightened his grip on her arm. "It's not police business."

"I understand. But all I know is she hit a tree while driving drunk."

"And you think your agoraphobia makes you a candidate for self-destructive behavior? I don't see it that way. But if you choose to, that's up to you."

64

"Oh, so I can *choose* to be mentally unstable?"

We all have choices— Oh, no, now I sound like my sister." His ensuing chuckle held no humor.

She forced her legs to move and her mind to ignore sudden stomach cramps. "How's that?"

"She believes our attitudes draw things to us, so we need to stay positive."

"That's part of being a Christian." She saw through Adam's attempts to distract her with chit chat, but she never lost sight of her surroundings. She'd already exceeded previous forays from the house. So far, so good . . . if she didn't double over from the pain in her gut. She concentrated on deep breathing to ease the tightness in her chest.

"This your ride?" Adam glanced at her Ford Escape as they hiked past it.

"Yes. It gets terrific gas mileage for a four-wheel drive." Or it did last time she drove.

"Why would you need a four-wheel drive in L.A.?"

"I don't. But photography can take me off road. One of my last projects was in the desert. I sure didn't want to get stuck in sand."

A flash of lightning preceded a distant roll of thunder. "A storm is coming."

"Keep talking to me, even about the weather." *One foot in front of the other, Taylor.*

"That's the idea."

She'd suspected as much. "I probably should sell it."

"Your SUV?" They rounded the house and headed toward the barn, where the emergency vehicles illuminated the yard with numerous spotlights and emergency lanterns. The faint sound of thunder rumbled again in the distance. "Why?"

She couldn't stop the shiver of dread that shook her body. "I haven't driven since . . . since I left the clinic. I tried once. Got behind the wheel, started the engine, then . . . I don't remember anything."

"Panic attack?" He seemed focused on the scene beside the barn.

"Wil said he almost had to use the Jaws of Life to pry me out of there." She glanced at the light coming from the windows in her father's room. "Dad hates being left out of things."

"I can help you with him and bring him out here."

She stopped suddenly and stared at him. "You'd do that? You two hate each other."

"True." He urged her toward the EMS van, where figures in white and black uniforms stooped beside a gurney, and they resumed their trek. "But I'm a professional."

"Thank you, but it won't be necessary. I'll just have to fill him in after I finish out here."

They finally reached the EMTs, one a fair complexioned female Taylor recognized but couldn't name, and one young Latino man she didn't know. They rolled the gurney toward the back of the van. Their patient appeared conscious.

"Wait a sec." Adam held up his hand, and the EMTs stopped. "What are his injuries?"

The male EMT answered. "Appears to have a broken leg and dislocated shoulder. Maybe a fractured wrist. He'll live."

Thank God! Relief swept through her, easing the tight bands of guilt squeezing her insides.

"No gunshot wound?"

"The lady didn't shoot him, if that's your question."

Adam stared at the injured man. "Miss Drake, do you recognize this man?"

He tugged her closer to the gurney, and she gazed into the scowling face of a man she knew well. Confusion warred with rage. Heat flooded her body, and she clenched her hands. "Jim? What are you doing here? Why were you spying on me?"

"You know this joker?" Adam asked.

"This is a colleague of mine, Jim Russo."

Jim snorted, then grimaced, as if in pain. "Yeah, *colleague.* That's all I am to you. But you sure as hell don't mind sucking face with this guy."

He'd scared the hell out of her and then whined as if he was the victim? How dare he put her on the defense? He had the audacity to embarrass her and Adam in front of the deputies and EMTs? Outraged, she shook her fist toward him.

"Whose face I suck is my business. Now answer my questions. What were you doing on my barn? Why are you spying on my family?"

"Why did you try to shoot me? I was only trying to watch over you, to keep you safe."

"That's hardly what I'd call—"

"Not now." Adam tugged her back from the gurney and spoke to Jim. "After you receive medical attention, you'll answer more questions, pal, starting with how you ended up with a murder victim's cell phone."

Ignoring Adam, Jim glared at her. "I don't know what you're talking about—"

"You used Roz's cell phone to e-mail me the photo." She tried to shake free of Adam's grip but he tightened his fingers around her arm. She glared at Jim. "You . . . you sick whacko."

Jim closed his eyes and dropped his head against the padded stretcher. "Think what you want."

Adam turned to Deputy Winston. "Did you read him his rights?"

"First thing."

"Take him to the medical center and keep a guard on him. Soon as he's released, bring him back to the jail."

Jim's eyes opened. "For trespassing? Like hell. I want an attorney."

"Wait a minute." Taylor turned to Adam. "I might've killed him. At least let me talk to him before they take him away."

Adam nodded and released his grip on her arm. "Make it quick."

She stood over the man she'd called friend, someone who shared her passion for photography. "I didn't intend to hurt you, Jim. You're the last person I expected to be prowling around my family's home."

Jim gazed at her with pain-filled eyes. "You shut me out, babe. You wouldn't answer my e-mails or phone calls. I thought I meant more to you than that."

She started to ask again about the e-mailed photo, but a quick glance at Adam's frowning glare kept her on safe legal ground. "I shut everybody out, not just you. I . . . I needed to be alone to recover."

He cut his gaze to Adam. "Yes, I see how alone you are."

"Take him." Adam nodded to the EMT then gently pulled Taylor out of the way, turning her toward the house. "You okay?"

She exhaled a deep breath, shaking her head in disgust. "Sure."

With his palm splayed at her back, he led her toward the house. "Let's go back inside."

Inside?

Realization hit her full force, along with a tiny dose of pride. She'd been away from her safe place . . . without passing out. "I didn't panic."

He held the flashlight to illuminate their path along the sandy driveway. "Told you so."

"You are so smug." She injected a smile into her tone to soften the words. A flicker of pure joy lit her heart. Though she'd been frightened out of her wits then forced outside her comfort zone, she'd coped. She'd almost forgotten to be afraid. Surprise and anger at Jim's behavior had overshadowed her insecurities. But she knew enough about agoraphobia to be cautiously optimistic. Relapses often followed successes. "To think I trusted him."

"Old boyfriend?"

She shook her head. "We went out to dinner once, but that was the extent of our dating. I worked with him on some projects, competed with him sometimes, professionally."

"Is he the wildlife photographer you mentioned to Jamie?" They approached the house and he directed the flashlight's beam toward the back door as if checking for hidden intruders.

"Yes." She snorted. "I planned to pick his brain about remote surveillance camera technology." She couldn't bring herself to laugh at the irony. Jim's hurt, accusing face stayed with her. "He says he's in love with me."

"And you discouraged him?"

"I thought I had. I explained to him that I cared for him as a friend but couldn't feel romantic about him. I never dreamed he'd go to such lengths. He must really be in love—"

"That's not love, Taylor. That's obsession."

"You're right, of course. Still, I'd feel horrible if I'd hit him with my shot and killed him."

"From that distance? No way."

"It's difficult to think of him as dangerous, though." They drew near the corner of the back porch, at the end of the wheelchair ramp Wil had built for Dad.

"I've seen my share of battered women who underestimated the danger posed by the men in their lives."

"I'm sure you have." She touched his arm to slow his pace. "I'm sorry I put you in a compromising position *vis-à-vis* your deputies."

"What do you mean?"

"Jim's remark about 'sucking face.'" Heat crawled up her neck even now, but she wouldn't shy away from the subject. "I regret the deputies and paramedics having to hear him say that. Such gossip will be spread throughout the county by daybreak."

"I'm not that important a—"

She stopped walking and groaned. "You're running for sheriff. The last thing you need is gossip about your personal—"

"Don't tell me you didn't think of that."

"I didn't!" Was he accusing her of political sabotage? His stride seemed to lengthen and she hurried to catch up. They rounded the corner and approached the cruiser, bathed in the light from the front security lamp. "You're . . . you're infuriating."

He stopped so suddenly she nearly slammed into his back. Turning off the flashlight, he turned to face her. "Is that why you kissed me?"

She searched her brain for a clever retort, but his heated gaze seemed to empty her mind. She broke eye contact to look at his mouth. Big mistake. His almost-smile held a touch of self-satisfaction. She stared at even white teeth peeking from behind his full lips, lips she longed to taste again.

His arm snaked around her waist and pulled her against him. He lowered his head, barely grazing her lips with his. *Oh, yes.* She tiptoed to meet him halfway—hell, more than halfway—and plastered her mouth against his. Not that he seemed to object. Groaning, he nudged her lips apart with a touch of his tongue to deepen the kiss.

She sank into his arms and closed her eyes. He relaxed his embrace and pulled back, resting his forehead against hers. "I shouldn't have done that."

She opened her eyes and stared at his strong chin, his moist lips. She wanted to kiss him again . . . and again. She cleared her throat. "Why not?"

"You're vulnerable—"

"Is this where I get the noble speech about how you don't want to take advantage of a victim of crime and emotional illness? 'Cause it won't fly. I'm outside the house, after shooting at a trespasser. And I'm not having an anxiety attack. So don't think of me as a vic—why are you laughing?"

He tugged her closer and kissed her forehead, then laughed again. "You don't have to beg me to kiss you again, sweetheart. I'm only too happy to oblige."

"Why . . . you . . . of all—"

He silenced her sputtering with his seriously hot mouth. She moaned, surrendering to the powerful longing that shook her down to her toes— longing to have a man in her life. Not just any man, but Adam. Lights flashed behind her eyelids. Thunder vibrated the heavens. The flashing lights brightened and turned colors and—

Adam abruptly ended the kiss and stepped away, a sheepish grin softening his features. The bright kaleidoscope of lights was in reality the emergency flashers on the ambulance idling past them. The female paramedic smiled and gave Taylor a thumbs-up when they rolled past the cruiser. Oh, boy. More grist for the rumor mill.

"Uh oh. I've been caught sucking face with the sheriff's sister." His voice held amusement, and not a shred of dismay.

More heat flushed her skin. "I . . . I need to go inside."

"Sure." He walked her up the steps and to the front door. "Thank you."

"For what?"

His grin turned from sheepish to wry, and then to mischief. Or had she imagined the devilment in his eyes? "I believe you just gave me your endorsement, Miss Drake. Folks will be wondering for sure now. Will Taylor Drake vote for her brother or her—"

She rounded on him. "My *what*?"

He didn't answer. Had he orchestrated the whole scene? Surely he knew the ambulance would be pulling around the house. How like the arrogant jerk to set her up.

"I can't vote for either of you. I'm still a California resident." She bit back adding *I wouldn't vote for you even if I could*. The twitch of his lips belied his amusement with her, as if she'd stuck out her tongue at him in a childish quarrel.

Childish quarrel or not, if she were a violent woman, she would've slapped the smug grin from his mouth.

Not true. What she really wanted to do was throw herself in his arms and *kiss* his mouth.

He spun toward the steps and left her standing inside her door. She'd missed her window of opportunity to make a fool of herself.

Correction: to make a fool of herself *again*.

Chapter Six

Adam stopped at the gate to allow a vehicle to turn and enter. Samuel Drake's Saturn edged past him in the narrow driveway. No doubt someone had gotten word to Sam about the shooting. Adam let out a weary sigh. Exhausted by the long day, he could do without an encounter with that particular family member. The dean was a prick of the first order, an intellectual snob.

Adam had no use for any Drake family member, so why had he kissed Taylor? Kissed, hell. Who was he kidding? He'd had his tongue down her throat and his body pressed into hers so close she couldn't have missed the boner tenting his trousers. Why did he lose all reason around that woman? Fatigue and stress. Had to be. No other excuses came to mind for his ridiculous attraction toward her.

Adam drove back to town, headed for his empty house. How nice to be greeted by a friendly, faithful dog like Sophie after a long day. Maybe he should visit the pound and adopt one. Funny how he'd not thought of his home as empty until tonight. An unexpected yearning filled him, staggering him with the outrageous idea that he needed a wife. And the only face he could put to that fantasy was Taylor's, with her short red hair and luminous green eyes.

His parting remark had left her with hurt and confusion in those eyes, but damn! He couldn't have her kissing him again. His goals didn't include a fling with anyone, especially her. He had an election to win, and his mother to help nurse back to health. Amy couldn't take care of Mom alone, not with the responsibilities of her family and the newspaper.

Amy had too much on her plate, yet she never complained. She seemed content and filled with joy from her hectic schedule. Was that from building a family with the guy she loved? No matter the setbacks she and Ben endured, they had a happy home. In comparison, Adam's life was sadly lacking. No wonder he often felt surly and alone. But with his busy schedule, how could he find time to do justice to a wife and family?

The first splat of a huge raindrop hit his windshield . . . then a second and a third, picking up speed until he had to switch on the wipers. Why couldn't the storm have held off another day? Though the area needed rain, it would hamper the collection of evidence at Taylor's. Fortunately, Devon and Brady had gotten a jump on processing the scene before he'd arrived. Good men, both, and he planned to develop them with further training when he became sheriff.

Once he took over as sheriff, the real work would begin. Much as he hated the Drake family, he would offer the chief deputy position to Wil. Whether or not he accepted didn't matter. Adam grinned.

He looked forward to turning the tables on Wil.

Zelda Brooks, the sheriff's office secretary who as of last year was eligible for a pension but had postponed her retirement, handed Adam a message slip as soon as he arrived at the station. Her inky black curls had been freshly touched up to hide her silver roots. She made no secret that the makeup she ordered regularly from Dispatcher Rebecca Gibbons accounted for her glamour.

"Your hair looks nice."

"Thanks for noticing." She pointed a red polished nail at the message slip. "Better call your sister right away. She seems all agog about something."

"And I thought I was getting here early." He'd been on the job and on his cell since he'd pulled into the parking lot, talking to the physician in charge of Jim Russo's medical treatment.

"Amy's earlier." Zelda winked. "I'll get your coffee. I already washed your mug."

"Now, Zelda, I told you that isn't part of your job."

She frowned at him. "Don't spoil my fun. I'll see if I can rustle up a muffin for you, too. I know you don't take time for breakfast."

"You're pampering me."

She breezed toward the back and he continued toward his office, hiding a smile. *Don't spoil my fun.* Nobody was ready for Zelda to retire.

Around the sheriff's office, she *was* the fun. She often boasted that at her age, she couldn't be intimidated, manipulated, or humiliated. However, it was her incredible efficiency rather than her age that earned her the run of the place.

She had written the office telephone number for the *Drake Springs Democrat* on the message slip. Adam punched in the number, half expecting his mother to answer. How could he forget? Mom had retired. And her cancer seemed to be worse. His empty stomach felt as if he'd eaten a cup of metal screws. He swallowed the unpleasant taste of dread.

Amy answered on the first ring. "Don't hold out on me, Adam. I've already got the police reports from yesterday."

"Good morning to you, too."

She sighed into the phone. "Look, I know you said Taylor Drake wants to keep a low profile, but she shot somebody. All bets are off—"

"Shot *at* somebody. The prowler sustained injuries when he fell—"

"Great. Fill me in over lunch. You can pick us up something on the way. I'll take a plain burger and fries from Hardee's. I have Cokes here."

"You've sure become bossy now that you're managing the paper."

"I mean it. This is a story. Work with me."

"See you at lunch."

As he hung up, Zelda darted in carrying both his coffee and a muffin wrapped in a paper towel. "Breakfast is served."

He picked up the muffin, and the aroma of bananas and spices chased away his nausea. "This looks homemade. Did you—"

"Of course not. I don't bake. But Rebecca Gibbons does. You're lucky I looked out for you before the vultures arrive."

"If you weren't married already, I'd propose."

For a moment she seemed flummoxed. "Now, that's the kind of thing I expect to hear Wil say, not you."

To hide a grin, he took a huge bite of the muffin and took his time savoring it. He'd managed to take Zelda by surprise. Maybe if he loosened up, he'd do better at the polls. Yet he campaigned as the candidate who took the sheriff's job seriously, the implication being Wil was laidback to a fault.

"I'm just not used to you teasing me, Adam."

"Who said I was teasing?" he deadpanned then laughed.

"So you *do* have a sense of humor." She broke into a wide smile.

"I have to work at it."

"Don't worry. Your secret's safe with me." She crossed her arms and leaned against the doorjamb. "You have your mother's disposition. Even back in high school, she was intense and serious. We couldn't get her to lighten up."

At the mention of his mother, his appetite vanished. How could he joke with Zelda or enjoy a banana nut muffin while his mom was fighting for her life? Irrational guilt settled over him, and filled him with gloom.

Zelda frowned. "Did I say something wrong?"

"No. I didn't get much sleep." That much was true. "I'd forgotten you and Mom were classmates."

"Oh my, yes. I ran around with Phyllis and Connie."

"I was old enough to remember the scandal, Zelda. I knew my dad and Wil's mother had an affair. Who in this little town didn't know?"

She shrugged, still not meeting his gaze. "Your mother took it real hard. So did Wil's father, but . . . ."

His curiosity piqued, he fought the temptation to question Zelda further about Connie Drake. He refused to investigate her death, no matter how many times Taylor kissed him. He needed to work on current crimes, not ancient history.

She shook her head. "What a shame people hang on to their grudges so long."

"Yeah." Zelda's none-too-subtle hint reminded him of his earlier conversation with Amy. This whole forgiveness thing eluded him. What about justice and fairness? But he wouldn't debate philosophy with yet another idealistic female.

"Phyllis and I can't seem to find time to get together, though."

"Give Mom a call, today if you can." If ever his mother could use a friend, it was now.

Her frown suggested she, too, worried about his mother's prognosis. "I'll do that."

He nodded then motioned her back to her desk. "I need you to find Jamie Peterson for me."

A few minutes later, Jamie entered his office lugging her laptop. "I heard about last night."

"The camera device—or what's left of it—is locked up in evidence. I doubt it works after being crushed beneath our suspect."

She dropped her laptop case and wrinkled her brow in confusion. "We got the guy. What difference does it make now?"

"Don't you ever get a gut feeling?"

She nodded. "So what's yours tell you?"

"That we're missing a piece of the puzzle." He indicated the chair across from his desk. "Have a seat. The offender is one James Russo from Torrance, California. Although he was caught in the act and admitted spying, he seemed confused about the photo e-mailed from the murder victim's cell phone. He claimed to know nothing about it."

"Are you buying it?"

"Let's just say, I want to connect all the dots. We need to prove he e-mailed the photo. If not, who did, and why?"

"Was he in possession of the cell phone?" Jamie asked.

He shook his head. "Not at the time we apprehended him. Devon and Brady did a search of the grounds before the rain hit."

"I'm working on the wireless phone records. What do you know about the investigation into the murder of Taylor's roommate? Need me to talk to the LAPD?"

"Yeah. Contact the lead detective on the Rosalind Williams homicide."

"Want me to interrogate Russo?"

"The doctor on duty last night medicated him and told Devon not to expect him to be fully conscious before this afternoon. *I* want to be there first to question him."

Jamie grinned. "Figured you would. Don't be surprised if he lawyers up, though."

"He already has, though we haven't heard from his attorney yet."

"Anything else?"

He pulled his notepad from his shirt pocket. "I need a background check on a Live Oak woman named"—he flipped open the notebook and read— "Judy Wood. She's a retired eldercare nurse."

"The woman Hazel Porter recommended to Taylor. But won't Hazel be back on the job now that we have the stalker in custody?"

"Probably, but I promised we'd check the woman out."

"Won't take but a minute." Jamie hesitated. "For what it's worth, this Russo guy could be telling the truth. I'll know more when I have call records, but that e-mail could've come from anywhere with a wireless signal."

"How would a third party manage the e-mail without Russo providing the photo file or giving him the Bluetooth number to access?"

"Don't know yet." She reached for her laptop case. "As Wil would say, let's examine the evidence, not waste time on theories."

"Wil's right."

Jamie left his office, and he swiveled toward his computer to check e-mail messages. One caught his attention, an e-mail from his boss, but it was a short note thanking Adam for checking on Taylor during his absence. Wonder how Wil would feel if he knew about those fiery kisses? It was certainly far less than Wil deserved after what he'd done to *his* sister Megan. He now had the opportunity to use Taylor to exact retribution, but he refused to stoop to Wil's level.

In truth, he wouldn't use Taylor, regardless of how much he hated her family. He couldn't shake the notion that she was untainted. She'd spent much of her life away from Foster County, and she'd been a toddler when the trouble began. Who was he kidding? It was far more than that. He liked Taylor.

Her protests to the contrary, she was spunky and brave. Her intelligent humor and guilelessness, in spite of the horrific trauma she'd suffered, drew him. Whereas he'd dreaded his patrol duty that first night, now he looked forward to visiting Drake Oaks and talking with her. Kissing her, nevertheless, had been reckless and indiscreet. He couldn't allow himself an encore, regardless of the temptation.

Zelda returned with a stack of police reports for his review, and he pushed the lovely Taylor from his mind. By the time he'd worked through the e-mails, reports, and telephone calls, it was noon. Like it or not, his sister was waiting for him. He paused by Zelda's desk, but she had already left for lunch. He circled the sheriff's office, cutting through the dispatch room, where he paused at Rebecca's console.

He leaned over the cubicle partition. "Thanks for baking us muffins. Mine was delicious."

"You're welcome. Going to lunch?"

"Yes." He stepped back from the cubicle. "I'm expecting a call from Foster County Medical Center. You can reach me on my cell or at the newspaper office."

He did a quick drive-through at the Hardee's then proceeded to face the inquisition with his sister.

Taylor's gaze followed Fred Fischer and his helper as they unloaded materials from Fred's pickup. The sun shone directly overhead, the sky a cornflower blue with an occasional wisp of white cloud. Rain from the previous night's thundershower had cleansed and cooled the air, bringing with it the first nip of autumn. She'd turned off the air conditioning and opened all the upstairs windows.

Everything appeared normal from her bedroom window, the one from which she'd fired a shot at Jim Russo, her onetime friend who'd been skulking across the rooftop of the barn. Where had she found the moxie to confront a prowler? For that matter, how had she managed to leave her safe place without an anxiety attack?

Adam.

Since his first visit, he'd challenged her to live again, to choose courage over cowardice, to test her self-imposed limits. Warmth rushed through her when she relived kissing him. Funny how her earlier anger had dissolved. Instead of being irritated, she longed for another chance to lock lips with the hunk. Or as Jim had so indelicately phrased it, *suck face*.

She liked Jim, though not romantically. At the very least, their friendship would suffer the strain of his crossing the line into stalking. Or he might serve a jail sentence. She'd miss him, but who said she'd return to work? Last night's victory did not mean she'd cured herself of agoraphobia.

Fred disappeared from view, and she turned from the open window. The driveway alarm jolted her, but only for a second. She expected Miller's IGA Market to deliver the order she'd called in that morning. Dashing down the stairs, she headed for the front door, reached for the deadbolt, then froze. Since when did she throw caution to the wind? She stepped into the dining room to peek through the windows. The same white van that had hauled last week's grocery order sat parked in front of the house.

The sight of the familiar figure of Ed Miller calmed her. He lifted two sacks from the vehicle. He'd owned the town's only supermarket for as long as she could remember. He had to be at least seventy, maybe older, and had lost most of his hair. What remained had turned snow white.

She opened the door and met him on the porch steps. "Good afternoon."

"I'll take these inside for you."

"Let me help." She relieved him of one of the brown paper sacks and followed him inside. "I thought you retired."

He hoisted the sack onto the kitchen counter. "I left both young'uns running the store. I like getting out once in a while."

"Is this everything?"

"Nope. One more bag."

She followed him back outside, stopping at the steps. She took one tentative step then a second. No anxiety attack. Taking a deep breath, she met Ed at the bottom step. He held a sack in one arm and a clipboard under the other.

She reached for the groceries. "I'll carry these."

"Thanks. How's your dad?"

"Why don't you say hi to him and see for yourself? He'd like that."

"Think I will." He followed her into the foyer and handed her the order form. "I won't stay too long if you think it'll tire him."

"On the contrary. Your visit will perk him up."

She led him to her father's room. The door stood open, and Sophie leapt to her feet to welcome Ed. Dad sat in his wheelchair beside the bed. He picked up his remote and muted the television. "Hey, Ed."

"Howdy, Harold." Ed strode into the room and claimed the only chair.

Juggling both clipboard and sack of groceries, she pulled the door closed to give them privacy. Back in the kitchen, she checked each item off the order form. She signed the bottom, authorizing the charge, leaving the clipboard on the table for Ed to pick up. Then she lined up all the ingredients for her chili recipe and went to work.

In the middle of dicing onions, the telephone rang. Placing the chef's knife on the counter, she wiped her hands on her apron and swooped up the receiver on the second ring. "Hello."

"Miss Drake? It's Chief Deputy Gillespie." At the sound of Adam's velvety southern drawl, her pulse stuttered.

"Why the formality, Adam?"

"I'm here at the office of the *Drake Springs Democrat*." His tone turned clipped and professional. "I realize you prefer to keep a low profile, but last night's events put you in the news. Would you be willing to do a telephone interview with the editor for the next issue?"

So he had an audience. No wonder he seemed all business. Yet this was her opportunity to question Phyllis about the night her mother died. Maybe she'd agree to a bit of reciprocity. "Your mother wants to interview me?"

"My sister, Amy Sawyer, is the editor now. Will you speak with her?"

Disappointment filled her. Soon everyone who remembered her mother would be dead or senile. Unless . . . "On one condition."

"Which is?"

"You'll investigate my mother's death."

She held her breath during his lengthy silence. Finally, he exhaled loudly into the phone. "I'll find out whatever I can."

"Does that include talking to your mother—"

"I can't do that. But I promise to help you in any other way. Do we have a deal?" The weariness in his tone raised her suspicions. Why wouldn't he talk to his mother?

"Deal. Put Amy on the line now, but you and I need to talk."

"I'll be by later."

As Adam left the newspaper office, his cell phone rang. He flipped it open. "Gillespie."

Caller ID said Geraldo Blanco. "Still pulling guard duty outside the suspect's room. He's able to talk now."

"Will he be released today?"

"Probably. Doc Evans said he was lucky. Clean breaks in both the wrist and leg. He'll have trouble getting around for a few weeks, though." Geraldo snorted. "He may not have far to walk if he's in jail."

"We'll talk when I get there. I'm leaving now."

"It's Room 211."

Adam shifted into gear and nosed the cruiser onto Third, working his way over to First Street. The new hospital took up the square block past Desoto, behind Miller's IGA, and the road had been widened to accommodate a separate turning lane. The services offered by Foster County Medical Center were limited to basic treatment, but at least now local residents didn't have to travel to the next county to get emergency medical attention.

Despite the county commissioners' efforts to curb expansion, Foster County's population had exploded. Like it or not, people had discovered Florida's best kept secret, and the small town of Drake Springs suffered growing pains. The newer residents had pushed the referendum to have consolidation put on the ballot. Much as he hated to admit it, merging the duplicate services made sense, even if it had cost him his job. But he missed the status of his police chief position.

He turned right on Desoto and took the rear entrance into the FCMC parking lot. After parking in one of the spaces reserved for the sheriff's office, he strode into the emergency room entrance. The smell of new paint overrode the normal antiseptic odors of a hospital. Fixtures, walls, and floors still wore that new-building gleam. He turned past the ER and followed the hall toward the elevator bank. Rather than wait for an elevator, Adam took the stairs and emerged from a door next to the nurses' station. One nurse plowed into him as she ran toward one of the rooms.

A man he recognized as Doctor Evans jogged past him, his stethoscope dangling from the pocket of his white coat. Responding to some emergency, no one seemed to notice Adam. He followed the commotion in search of Room 211 and froze. The nurse and doctor, along with two other hospital employees, crowded inside the room and blocked his view of the patient.

What happened? Did it involve Russo? Adam clenched his hands into fists at his side, tightly controlling the urge to charge into the room and interrupt the medical personnel. Apprehension filled him then mushroomed into alarm.

Geraldo Blanco stood at the door, his complexion paling in contrast to his dark hair and mustache. When he caught sight of Adam, he grimaced and dropped his head.

"What's going on, Geraldo?"

"I screwed up."

From inside the room, urgent whispers grew louder. Then the doctor returned to the hall, approaching Adam. "We lost him."

"What?" Disbelief and shock drove his voice up an octave. "What do you mean?"

"Cardiac arrest, though the autopsy will determine the exact cause of death—"

"Death? You're telling me Russo's *dead*?" He resisted the urge to grab the doctor by the lapels.

"Murdered." Geraldo drew a ragged breath. "On my watch."

Chapter Seven

Adam struggled to absorb that someone had killed the suspect.

"We suspect an injection into the IV port. Our nurses know not to leave a syringe . . . ."

No!

He tuned out the doctor's calm monotone. This couldn't be happening. Who would want to kill Taylor's stalker unless . . . ? Would the powerful Harold Drake be behind the homicide? Though stuck in a wheelchair, he still had influence. Not only would killing Russo exact revenge for stalking Taylor, it would cast doubt on Adam's ability to handle the responsibilities of sheriff. Harold had to know Russo's death would hurt Adam's chances at the polls.

Jamie's words echoed from that morning. *Let's examine the evidence, not waste time on theories.* He would stick to solid police work. First he needed to secure the scene. He took a deep breath and focused.

"I need everyone out, please. This is a crime scene." He waved the nurse and aides from the room. "Stay close. We'll need to question each of you. We need to preserve any evidence." He turned to Geraldo. "What did you mean about screwing up? Did you leave your post?"

Geraldo shook his head. "No, but I let in a woman without verifying her credentials."

"When was this?"

"Just minutes after I phoned you. She said she was from the lab, here to draw blood. She looked like a lab tech. She carried a tray with tubes and such, and wore a uniform."

"What else do you remember about her appearance?"

"She was young and sturdy, with almost no neck. You know the type, so husky you'd expect her to have a beard?"

"So it could have been a man disguised as a woman?"

Geraldo rubbed his chin. "I doubt it. For one thing, no whiskers—"

"Did she wear makeup?"

"Well . . . yes, but it didn't cover that hairy mole on her chin."

Adam grabbed his cell phone. It was probably too late, but he ordered a lockdown of the hospital parking lot. "Don't let anyone leave. We suspect she or he wore a disguise."

He slipped his tattered notebook from his shirt pocket, along with his pen. "Let's cover the description. A masculine-looking woman with makeup and a mole on her chin . . . what else do you remember about her?"

"Am I free to leave?" asked Doctor Evans. "I haven't had anything to eat all day."

"Sorry, no. I need statements from everyone who had contact with this patient. But we can have food brought in—"

"That won't be necessary. I'll just grab a sandwich at the canteen."

Adam nodded. "That'll work. Just stay close."

Geraldo waited until the doctor disappeared into the elevator. "I'm sorry I didn't—"

"Not now, Geraldo. Let's do our jobs. I'm designating you first officer on the scene. Contact FDLE. We'll need their crime scene technicians over here. I'm calling in Devon to help."

Geraldo snapped to attention and pulled out his cell phone. "I'm closing the door to make the room off limits until the techs arrive."

"Better block it off, too." Unlike television shows and movies, real-life crime techs had one shot only at collecting admissible evidence, so protecting the scene from contamination was imperative. He called Devon Winston, who answered on the third ring. "Hey, I realize you worked a late shift last night, but we have a homicide. Can you meet me at the medical center, Room 211?"

"Give me five minutes. Who's the vic?"

"The guy you arrested last night, James Russo."

Devon wasted no time with further questions. "On my way."

Adam spun around and collided with Geraldo. "It may be another hour before the FDLE team will be here, but they're en route."

"That gives us time to conduct interviews and start the reports. I'll need your chronology up to the time I arrived."

"I know the routine." Geraldo fingered his mustache. Not even the slightest hint of an accent laced his southern drawl. He looked every bit the Latino but spoke pure Dixie. "How come those cops on TV never have to write reports?"

"I hear ya."

"What about Miss Drake? Wasn't this guy a friend of hers? She'll need to be notified."

His gut told him Taylor was no suspect. "I'll give Jamie that job." He'd also have her snoop around about Harold Drake's recent visitors or phone calls.

"My secret ingredient." Taylor stirred the contents of three cans of beer into the ground meat. After the meat cooked, she added the rest of the ingredients for chili, filling the kitchen with the aromas of hops, cumin, and sautéed onions.

Dad slept and Sophie lay on the rug in front of his entertainment center, so Taylor spoke only to herself. The stainless steel pot held enough chili to feed a dozen people. She planned to freeze half of it. Some would go on hotdogs for her dad. Next to fried shrimp, chili dogs were his favorite food. When the driveway alarm buzzed, the beer can she rinsed for recycling slipped from her fingers and clanged into the sink. Fred Fischer still worked in the barn, so someone else had triggered the sensor. Her racing heart dizzied her. She abandoned the aluminum cans, turned off the water, then wiped her hands on a paper towel.

When she finally reached the front window, Jamie Peterson was climbing the porch steps. Jamie bore a strong resemblance to Roz, and grief squeezed Taylor's heart. She pushed aside the memory of her dead roommate, and unlocked the door.

"Hello, Jamie. What a pleasant surprise."

Jamie hesitated at the door. "I'm afraid it's not so pleasant."

She motioned Jamie inside. "Don't keep me in suspense. What's wrong?"

"I need to talk to you—"

"Is this related to last night?" She replaced the security chain and dead bolted the door.

"I'd say so."

"Follow me to the kitchen. I need to lower the heat under a pot of chili."

"It smells delicious." Jamie followed her to the end of the hall and into the kitchen.

She set the temperature to simmer, then she turned to face Jamie. "Won't you have a seat?"

"No, but you may want to. I have bad news, honey."

"Tell me." Her head swam. She wiped her clammy hands against her denim apron. "Is it Wil? Sam? What's—"

"They're fine. It's James Russo, your colleague. I'm sorry, Taylor, but . . . he's dead."

"Oh no. No!" Guilt replaced anxiety. Her reckless actions had caused Jim's death. "But I don't understand. The EMT said he'd live, that he'd only broken—"

"Someone murdered him. You had nothing to do with this. The hospital was going to release . . . ."

Jamie's voice receded into an echo chamber, her words distorted and muffled. Jim . . . *murdered*? Was someone else involved in stalking her? Nothing made sense. Jim had an accomplice at the other end of the camera's transmission. An accomplice willing to kill. Who would kill *her*.

Oh, God!

She fingered the long scar at her throat and fought the nausea. Everything in her field of vision turned snowy. Then the kitchen walls spun around her. Dizziness consumed her. Bile burned her throat. She lost her balance and plummeted toward the floor. Escaping into blessed unconsciousness, she never knew when she made impact.

Adam braked the Crown Vic in front of the Drake mansion between the county EMS van and a white Yukon that looked exactly like his sister's. He squinted at the woman behind the wheel; it *was* Amy. What was she doing here? For that matter, why was fire and rescue?

Amy turned off the engine and opened the door of the SUV. "What's going on?"

His temper already on short fuse from too little sleep, he glowered at her. "Have you become an ambulance chaser now that you're the editor?"

She stepped out of the Yukon, her camera in hand, and faced him. "Chill, little brother. Taylor invited me. She thought we could do the interview better in person, and this way I could photograph the scene."

"She did?" He took off his hat and finger-combed his hair. "Look, she's been through a lot lately. She's emotionally fragile. I want you to respect her privacy—"

"Are you falling for her?" He must have hesitated a bit too long because her frown deepened. "Oh, Adam, you mustn't get involved with her. What are you thinking? She's a Drake, for—"

"Whoa. I'm not 'falling for her.' This is about my boss—the man I'm running against for sheriff—asking me to look out for his sister during his absence. I can't afford to screw this up."

"That's right. Don't screw it up and don't screw around with her." She slammed the Yukon's door as if to drive home her point.

"Nothing could be further from my mind. You're imagining—"

"I am not imagining it. Why are you here now?"

He didn't have an answer for that one. After he and Devon finished interviewing the hospital staff and potential witnesses, he left Devon to wait for the FDLE techs. In truth, he'd wanted to see for himself that Taylor was all right. Russo's murder must have been a shock for her. Had Jamie had to call the EMTs for Taylor or, possibly, for her father?

Amy huffed. "You act entirely too . . . too proprietarily where Taylor is concerned. I picked up on it earlier today."

Proprietarily? His twin sister knew him too well, but he couldn't admit it. "What you picked up on was fatigue. I've slept maybe three hours, tops, in the last two days. With Mom getting worse, and now a homicide to investigate, I have a lot on my mind."

"Okay, I'll drop it for now. Let's find out why the—" she grabbed his arm "—did you say *homicide*?"

"I figured you'd be on top of that story, *Brenda Starr*. Did you forget to turn on your police scanner?"

"Don't torment me. Spill. Who was murdered?"

"I did not use the word *murdered*. It's a homicide, and that's all we know until the medical examiner performs the autopsy."

"Don't split hairs. I know not all homicides are murders, but you suspect intent to do harm, right?"

"Off the record, yeah. We're looking for a suspect we think deliberately caused his death."

"So it's a *him*."

"James Russo, the guy we arrested here last night." He glanced at the ambulance. "I'd better see what's up. I sent Jamie here to break the news to Taylor—"

"See? The way you say her name, Taylor . . . it's full of affection. You *like* her. Admit it."

He spun and headed toward the porch, Amy at his heels. "Not the way you think. She's not like the rest of the family."

"Just keep your perspective. It would devastate Mom if you—"

"That's rich coming from you, queen of forgiveness." He hesitated at the door.

She lowered her voice. "You can *marry* the woman for all I care, but it's Mom you need to think about now."

"Get a grip. No Gillespie will be marrying anyone in this family." Yet last night he'd fantasized that very scenario.

"What's wrong?" Amy's voice jarred him. "Aren't you going to ring the doorbell?"

Adam pulled his emotions together and pushed the doorbell button. "I can't stop worrying about Mom and her surgery tomorrow. No matter what else has happened, I keep thinking about her."

"I know. I'm the same way. It's this dark cloud hovering over me, reminding me that we may lose her."

He wanted to scream, to shake his sister by the shoulders for saying such a thing. But he couldn't deny the decline in his mother's health.

Jamie answered the door. "Come on in. The paramedics are with Taylor."

His heartbeat faltered. "What happened to Taylor?"

"She passed out. But I think she's all right now."

Amy stepped inside the foyer and swiveled her head, taking in the opulence. As far as he knew, this was her first time inside the inner sanctum. He bet she was itching to snap photos, but she showed unusual restraint for a reporter.

Jamie shut the door behind them. "I told her Russo was dead, an apparent homicide, and she hyperventilated. I told her it wasn't her fault, but I don't think I got through to her."

"Does her father know?" he asked.

Jamie gasped. "I forgot about him. He's probably in need of attention. I'll ask one of the EMTs to help me with him." She rushed to the rear of the house.

"I thought Harold Drake had a nurse," Amy whispered.

"Hazel Porter. But she bailed when the stalker showed up."

"There's a smart lady. I wouldn't want to be around an emotionally unstable woman and her loaded gun—"

"I said she was emotionally fragile. That doesn't mean she's unstable."

"There you go again. You really don't get it, do you? You are *so* into her."

"Stop it," he whispered. "I don't have time for your nonsense. Just let me do my job."

She moved toward the kitchen. "Fine. Let me do mine."

He bit back a retort. Amy was right. He couldn't afford an emotional entanglement with Taylor, and he wouldn't run interference for her. He stepped back to allow Jamie and one of the paramedics to pass.

The aroma of chili filled the kitchen. Taylor sat on the floor staring into space, her back propped against the leg of a dinette chair. EMT Karen

Fox squatted beside her, talking in low tones. Adam stooped at Taylor's other side and took her hand.

"May I talk to her a sec?"

Karen stood. "You can try." Then she met his gaze and mouthed "Good luck."

Amy watched from just inside the doorway, yet he focused on Taylor. He'd witnessed anxiety attacks before, but not with someone who mattered. Like it or not, he cared about her. The sight of her in a zombie trance set off emotions he couldn't afford to examine. The tightness in his chest and the difficulty he had swallowing around a lump in his throat drove him to bring her back from wherever she'd retreated.

"Hey, look at me." He took her chin between his forefinger and thumb, nudging her to face him. "Are you giving up, or are you going to fight this? Say something, Taylor. Talk to me."

Her eyes unfocused, she stared at him and seemed to frown. Then she blinked a few times. That was a good sign, right? Maybe he was getting through to her. But then she faded into another world.

"Dammit, Taylor, snap out of it." He gave her shoulders a gentle shake. "Talk to me."

She frowned, her face screwed in concentration. Then she closed her eyes. *No! Don't leave me!* He shook her again and she shuddered. What the hell? Big fat tears rolled from her eyes, and her lower lip trembled. She started to cry then and quietly sobbed. His heart squeezed for her suffering, but he much preferred tears to the zombie routine.

"I . . . I . . . killed Jim."

"No, not you. Someone else killed him."

Ignoring Amy's stare, he gathered Taylor into his arms and patted her back, letting her cry. She said nothing for a long time. Was she grieving her dead friend? Or were those tears of relief?

Karen handed him a paper cup of water and a pill. "Officer Peterson found these tranquilizers upstairs in her medicine cabinet. See if you can get her to take one."

Taylor wiped her eyes and hiccupped. She looked pale and drawn, but at least her eyes now seemed focused. "I save . . . save those for . . . emergencies."

"I think this qualifies." He handed her the water. Then he slid the tiny tablet between her lips. The slightest touch of her tongue against his fingertip, though innocent, triggered all kinds of erotic—inappropriately erotic—thoughts. He glanced at Amy, who gave a slight shake of her head. Judging from the disapproving glare, she read the guilt written across his face. He couldn't worry about her now.

Taylor drained the water. "This is humiliating."

"Don't worry about it." He stood and stretched the kinks from his legs. "You'll be all right now."

The bleakness in her eyes when she looked up told him she was anything but all right. He had a homicide to solve, though, so he left her in the hands of the trained professionals. He took Amy by the elbow and guided her into the foyer.

"You are so not sending me away, Adam. She invited me—"

"I just wanted to talk to you in private a minute . . . about Mom's surgery tomorrow."

"Oh. Okay." She let him lead her to the front door.

"I'll be working around the clock trying to figure out who killed Russo, but call me as soon as you talk to the surgeon tomorrow, hear?"

"Yes, of course." She nodded toward the kitchen. "So are you going to call Wil?"

He nodded. "He'd want to know about the homicide."

She followed him out onto the porch. "Can't it wait a day? If you solved the crime in his absence, it'd make good press. Win some votes."

"And if I don't solve it? His supporters could argue—"

"You're right. I wasn't thinking."

He gave her a quick hug. "You get your story and then forget about everything but Mom's surgery. That takes priority now."

She nodded. "Sorry I rode you about Taylor. I see what you mean. She's a mess."

"Yeah." He headed toward his cruiser, his mind torn between his homicide case and his mother, and his heart aching for Taylor.

Days earlier, he'd thought her a spoiled heiress and celebrity. But that wasn't the woman he'd gotten to know . . . and kiss. His sister had nailed it. He *was* falling for Taylor.

Nothing he could do about it, either.

The chill pill took effect. Breathing came easier for Taylor, and she emerged from her crippling attack. With the EMT's help, she moved from the floor to a chair at the dinette.

Karen Fox smiled. "Your color is back. Feel better?"

"I do. But I need to see about my dad."

"Officer Peterson and my partner helped him to the bathroom and to his wheelchair. Your dad's fine. Are you going to be all right?"

Would she ever be? "This happens sometimes. It's embarrassing."

"Miss Drake, after what you've been through, it's perfectly normal. I've dealt with post-trauma symptoms, and yours will diminish. Trust me."

"Thank you . . . for everything."

After the paramedics left, the woman she assumed was Amy Sawyer walked to the kitchen doorway and smiled. "You look like you're feeling better."

"I am."

She moved into the room and shook Taylor's hand. "I'm Amy Sawyer, but I guess you figured that out."

"Yeah. And I'm the basket case named Taylor."

"Still up to an interview, or would you rather I leave?"

"No, stay." Amy had already seen her at her worst. What was the point in delaying the interview? With her hazel-colored eyes and thick brown hair, Amy resembled her twin brother. Dressed in a plain tan blouse and brown slacks, she wore a wide camera strap around her neck— attached to an impressive Sony Alpha DSLR. "That's a nice digicam. May I see it?"

"Of course." Amy pulled the strap over her neck, then handed her the camera. "Although I'm sure you're used to fancier equipment."

"This is super. Single lens reflex, just what I like. Gives you better depth of field."

"The selling point for me was the image stabilizer, since my photography skills suck."

"If it wouldn't insult you, I could give you a few pointers."

Amy seemed taken aback. "Insult me? Don't be silly. I'm open to any guidance you can give me."

"Ooh, interchangeable lenses. I like that. You don't have to lug around a lot of different cameras."

"I plan to buy a telephoto zoom, but can't decide exactly which is best."

"I can help you with that, too." She cradled the camera, and her heart ached for all her lost equipment—

No. Not the equipment. What she sorely missed was the weight of the camera in her hand, ready for a shot, and the view through the lens, framing and composing the picture. Why hadn't she followed up on Adam's suggestion to buy a new one?

Jamie stopped by the kitchen door. "You want me to stay?"

"No, I'll be all right. These spells come and go."

"Remember what I told you." Jamie gave her a meaningful stare.

"Yes, I will." No matter what spin Jamie or Adam put on it, though, Jim died because Taylor had shot at him. If he hadn't fallen from the barn, he wouldn't have needed medical attention. Being laid up in a hospital bed left him vulnerable for the killer.

"I mean it, Taylor. I can see those 'what if's' running through your head."

"Busted." She gave Jamie a wry smile. "And thanks for seeing about Dad."

"Keep your doors locked." Jamie winced. "Why am I telling *you* that?"

"Yeah, I'm obsessive about security. I'll walk you to the door so I can lock up behind you." She handed the camera back to Amy, then motioned her to follow. "Let's sit in the living room, where it's comfier."

"Suits me." Amy followed her and Jamie into the foyer.

After Taylor secured the door locks, she turned toward the living room, where Amy sat on one of the sofas. "Where are my manners? Would you like something to drink?"

"No, thanks. I don't expect you to entertain me." Amy grimaced. "I'm sorry. I'll bet you need a cold drink. It must hurt your throat to talk."

"It hurts the listener more." Her damaged voice must grate on people's nerves, but at least she was alive. "I'm fine for right now." Moving toward the sofa, she sat beside Amy. "What did you want to ask about last night? Or is it still a news story now that Jim's . . . ."

"First, let me assure you that nothing about your medical episode today will be reported. I respect your privacy."

"I never thought otherwise. I trust you to be fair."

Amy leaned back and crossed her arms over her chest. "How can you trust anyone after all you've been through?"

"I have no reason to be afraid of you—"

"My brother is running against your brother for sheriff. I control the town's only newspaper. You aren't worried about what I might print?"

"Should I be?" She placed her hand on Amy's arm and squeezed it. "Look, as I told Adam, I refuse to be a part of this feud between our families. I believe you're a good person because Adam is. If he wasn't trustworthy or good at his job, Wil never would've hired him and made him second in command. So if Adam asked me to talk with you, it must be all right."

"Wow, you are naïve. But I'm beginning to understand what Adam meant about—" She unfolded her arms then reached into her shoulder bag. "Never mind. Let's do this so I can get out of your hair."

"What Adam meant about what?"

Amy seemed to study her face. "He just said you were different after living away so many years."

"He's right." She fingered the scar at her throat. Her attacker had reduced her from confident achiever to disabled neurotic. "I'm not the same person who left here for college."

Amy pulled a ruled pad from her purse. "How's that?"

"You're going to take notes?" Boy, she *was* naïve. Amy came here for a story, not a friendly chat. She bumped her forehead with the palm of her hand. "Duh. Of course you are."

"Not if you object." Amy dropped pad and pen to her lap and sighed. "You and I are on the same page as far as this feuding goes. I wish we could find a way to make peace between our families. Mom raised us to be Christians yet I don't know if she can ever forgive."

Taylor shook her head. "Same with Dad. But Wil wants peace."

"During the hurricane, Wil loaned his boat to Adam to rescue me and the boys, then later picked up Ben. Fia first-aided Ben, and loaned us her house to live in until we can replace ours."

"So I heard. I remember teasing Wil about his old girlfriend living in his new girlfriend's house."

"Old girlfriend? That was high school. My point is I have no reason to nurse grudges against your family."

"I don't, either. But Adam hates us."

"I blame Mom for that. She can't seem to let go of the anger, even after thirty years. She manages to fuel Adam's resentment toward the Drakes. I'm not sure why he can't see past her bitterness."

"It mostly has to do with Wil and Megan."

Amy frowned. "What?"

"He said Wil got Megan pregnant and then ran out on her."

Amy gasped. "He told you that?"

"I intend to ask Wil about it as soon as he gets home. There has to be some misunderstanding—"

"There is." Amy shook her head. "My brother doesn't know what he's talking about."

"He doesn't?"

"Megan never told Wil she was pregnant. She made me promise not to, either, so he doesn't need to hear it now. What good would it do?" Amy shook her head. "My God. This explains a lot."

A huge weight lifted from her chest. Adam *had* been mistaken! For the first time since her anxiety attack, the tightness in her stomach eased. "But you told Adam."

"No, I never told a soul."

"He said Megan confided in you the day she found out. She worried that you would hate her, since you and Wil had dated first."

"I wrote that in my diary. The only way he'd know that is if he read it. I can't believe he'd invade my privacy like that—"

"Unless he found out another way that she was pregnant. Maybe he felt justified in snooping."

"It must have been in the autopsy report, but I never saw that. And neither he nor Mom ever mentioned it. All these years I thought Megan took that secret to the grave."

"To be fair, Adam hasn't let his feelings interfere with his professionalism."

Amy harrumphed. "Here I am defending your brother, and you're defending mine. I think we are perfect for this peacemaking job."

"I'd sure like that." Could she and Amy be friends? Except for Jamie, she hadn't had a girl-talk fix. She'd lost more than a roommate when Roz died.

"Unfortunately the timing is bad right now. Adam doesn't want to do anything to upset Mom. I guess he told you she's ill."

She frowned. Was illness behind Adam's reluctance to question Phyllis about the car accident? "No, he didn't. I hope it's nothing serious."

Anxiety filled Amy's eyes, and she shook her head. "It is. We'll know more tomorrow after she has more testing, but she's battling cancer."

She reached for Amy's hand and squeezed it. "I hope the results are encouraging."

"Thanks. All prayers are appreciated." Amy smiled then, chasing the worry from her eyes. "So. What about your other brother? Think we can persuade him to make peace between the families?"

"Sam will come around."

Amy picked up her pad and pen. "Let me ask you about last night, then I want pictures of the scene."

"Just don't photograph me. At least not until I've seen a good hairdresser."

"I was wondering about your style. Is that something California-ish?"

Taylor snorted. "No. Blame this bad cut on me. It's a long story."

"I'm guessing that after your attack, you felt vulnerable with long hair."

"Yeah. I took the scissors to it in the hospital. I vow never again to have hair that's long enough to be grabbed." She shivered at the memory.

"It's severe but not bad looking. I promise to take no pictures of you, though."

By the time she told Amy her version of last night's events, she could hardly swallow. "I'm parched from talking. Let's grab a soft drink."

"I'll take you up on that." Amy stood and stretched. "Thank you for inviting me and letting us talk in person."

She stretched, too. "It's been the highlight of my day, actually. I'm a boring recluse."

"You've taken some down time to recover. That's not the same as boring."

"Maybe. Lately I've been a real stick-in-the-mud." She led Amy toward the kitchen. "After we drink a Coke, I'll take you upstairs where we can get some photos. From the window, I can show you the exact view where I first spotted Jim."

Her mood crashed. Clamminess returned, along with the tightness in her gut. How could she forget Jim Russo was dead? No matter what anyone said, she was, at least in part, responsible.

Thanks to her, Jim had been murdered.

Chapter Eight

The FDLE van took up both parking spaces reserved for law enforcement, forcing Adam to drive around the hospital lot in search of a parking spot. The ordered lockdown had slowed the departure of visitors while his deputies checked each vehicle. The mysterious lab tech had escaped apprehension. She—or *he*—could be anywhere now.

He needed to meet with the FDLE staff then check in with his deputies working the case, which was pretty much all of them. Homicides were rare in Foster County, despite its recent population explosion. By the time he finished and returned to the sheriff's office, it was after five.

He'd just sat down at his computer when Jamie stopped at his door. "Got a minute?"

He motioned her to sit. "What's up?"

"First, Judy Wood checks out." She opened her laptop case and handed him a single page printout complete with a headshot photo of a gray haired lady in her seventies. "Also, I talked to Troy Raizor, the Long Beach detective on the Williams homicide, like you asked."

He stuck the single page report on Judy Wood in his middle desk drawer. "Any progress in closing the case?"

"Not yet. The offender knew forensics, although they collected biological evidence. A single strand of hair. I think."

"It could be enough. Even the most careful criminal makes mistakes."

"Troy's still waiting for the DNA profile."

"If they're as backlogged as Florida, it'll be months."

"Too bad real life isn't like television. We could have a profile within an hour."

"Did you get a chance to talk to Harold Drake?"

"Sure did. I have to tell you, I don't think he's had much outside contact. He had one visitor, Ed Miller, who dropped off a grocery order for Taylor around one o'clock. I don't think Drake had Russo whacked, if that's what you're thinking, but I still requested his phone records."

"Just want to cover all the bases." Adam suppressed a weary sigh. It wouldn't do to show fatigue when he had deputies working overtime. "Devon finished the interviews, and the vehicle checks at the FCMC parking lot turned up zilch. The killer got away."

"For now. I also asked the telephone company to check the Drakes' phone line. There's an annoying low hum, and transmission's reduced. Could be tapped."

"Good thinking. Russo could have tapped her phone line. But that brings us back to the same question: Why?"

"I'm meeting the telephone repair supervisor at the terminal box on County Road 471 at six."

Adam glanced at the clock. "It's almost that now. You'd better take off."

Jamie hesitated. "Taylor doesn't want you calling Wil."

"That isn't her decision. He'll need to know about the homicide."

"So you're going to call him?"

"Already did. He must be out of range but he'll get back to me as soon as he can pull his messages."

After Jamie left, he wandered to the locker room to get a vending machine dinner. With a busy night ahead, he knew better than to take time for a real meal. Too bad he couldn't drop back by for a bowl of Taylor's chili. The aroma stayed with him long after he'd left, with a foolish notion of having her cooking for him on a permanent basis. He pictured her in her faded denim apron, preferably without a pistol in her pocket, waving a wooden spoon and greeting him with a kiss . . . .

Whoa! He really needed to have his head examined. Even if Taylor hadn't been the daughter of his family's enemy, she was no stay-at-home mom who'd have supper waiting. She was Taylor Drake, career woman. The vicious attack on her had set her back, but only temporarily. When she regained her confidence and health, she'd hit the road with her camera and her celebrity life and never look back.

Taylor . . . gone?

The notion sucker-punched him in the gut. An emptiness engulfed him. How could his ache for her be so strong? He barely knew her. They'd shared a couple of kisses. Yet facing a day without seeing her filled him with a powerful sadness. She'd captured his heart, and he was hooked.

How had that happened?

Taylor overslept, thanks to the extra dose of medication she'd taken. The driveway alarm jolted her awake with its abrupt buzzing. Squinting, she reoriented her fuzzy brain to her new surroundings in the master suite. Grabbing her khaki shorts, she pulled them on. She rushed to the bathroom, finished dressing, and did a quick pass with the toothbrush.

Before heading downstairs, she slipped into the front bedroom once shared by her brothers to view the driveway below. A white pickup truck with matching camper shell passed the front of the house to circle around back. What in the world? That wasn't Fischer's truck. Returning to her room, she grabbed her .380 caliber Cobra and slipped it into her shorts' pocket.

She rushed down the steps and headed to the back door for a better look. Two young women, dressed alike in white Capri pants and shirts, hopped down from either side of the cab. They convened at the tailgate, where the driver of the truck extracted a mop and an upright vacuum cleaner. Her companion hoisted two caddies filled with various bottles. Cleaning supplies? *Home Maid Bonnie.* The logo on the truck finally penetrated her foggy mind. Right. Wil said the cleaning service came every other Wednesday. She unbolted the lock and opened the door to admit them.

"Morning, ma'am." The one carrying the caddies—*Esther* according to the name stitched on her shirt—held the door for the other woman. "We usually start upstairs, if that's all right."

Maudell was embroidered on her companion's shirt. "Gives Hazel a chance to get Mister Drake up in his wheelchair and feed him breakfast."

Dad! A strong dose of guilt overwhelmed her. How could she be so irresponsible and oversleep? Her father needed help getting out of bed. "Evidently I need to do that since Hazel isn't here today."

While Esther and Maudell lugged their supplies through the kitchen and into the foyer, Taylor rushed to her father's door and tapped. Sophie nosed open the door. "You need to go out, girl."

Her father called from the bed. "Her leash is by the back door."

"I know, Dad. Be right back to help you up."

Her deception tugged at her conscience. She'd led her father to believe she walked Sophie when, in fact, all she did was open the back door and let the dog out to do her business on her own. Dad seemed overprotective of the golden retriever, although Wil had warned her that rattlesnakes and cottonmouths ventured into the yard. She prayed nothing happened to the dog. She just wasn't ready to venture outside alone yet. Or was she?

Maybe the next time, she'd clip on the leash and go with Sophie. What was the worst that could happen? Sophie could be as much help with an anxiety attack as a human . . . perhaps more so.

Just as she let Sophie out the back door, the driveway alarm buzzed again. Racing to the front, Taylor peered out the dining room window. A red Honda Pilot with Suwannee County tags backed in and parked. Probably Judy Wood, the retired eldercare nurse. Good thing the woman was late since Taylor had overslept. The woman got out of the car then stood for a moment examining the exterior of the house. Although Taylor had grown up in the big house, she realized some people thought of it as a mansion. She once had, too, until she'd driven through Beverly Hills. Drake Oaks was a fine estate but nothing like the opulence of the rich and famous.

Judy Wood was a short, stout woman with ridiculously big hair. In fact, she may have been wearing a wig. If so, it was an attractive gray wig, just unnaturally thick for a woman in her seventies. She wore a loose-fitting, colorful set of scrubs. A large vinyl purse hung from her arm.

Sophie raced around to greet her, her tail wagging like crazy. She held out her palm for Sophie to sniff and waited for the dog's acceptance. She laughed when Sophie nearly knocked her over with an enthusiastic dog kiss. If Sophie accepted her, she must be all right.

Taylor unlocked the door and the woman stepped onto the porch. "I'm Judy Wood. Sorry I'm late."

"You're just in time. Dad's in his room waiting to be helped out of bed and to the bathroom."

"Lead the way, young lady."

She took Judy to her father's quarters, Sophie close behind them. Dad lay in bed watching *Good Morning, Jacksonville* but turned to face Taylor with a scowl.

"Dad, this is Judy Wood. She's filling in while Hazel takes a few days off. Judy, meet Harold Drake."

Judy dropped her purse in the corner before approaching the bed. Dad gave an unintelligible response, sort of a cross between a grunt and harrumph. He reached for Sophie and rubbed her behind the ear.

"Let's get you up, Mister Drake." With strong, capable hands, Judy pulled Dad up and helped him into the wheelchair. She didn't bother with the hydraulic lift device.

"I'll make breakfast." She left Judy to wheel Dad into the bathroom, then returned to the kitchen.

The muffled drone of the vacuum cleaner in the background, Maudell and Esther did their thing upstairs while Taylor started cooking Dad's oatmeal. What a relief to have help with him. She didn't have the muscle power to lift him, and it was a struggle the few times she tried to help him in or out of his wheelchair.

Guilt nagged at her. Dad must be depressed and frustrated to have to depend on others. He'd always been strong and independent, and very active. Instead of considering his isolation, Taylor had compounded it. So fearful of leaving the house, she never offered to push his wheelchair onto the veranda or out back onto the deck. She could do that much for Dad, couldn't she?

To keep his mind occupied instead of worrying about his mother's surgery at the Mayo Clinic, Adam focused on the Russo homicide case. At nine, he called a quick meeting with Devon Winston, Geraldo Blanco, and

Brady Newcomb. When Jamie Peterson walked past the conference room, he called her in to join them. She lugged her laptop into the room and claimed a chair by the door.

He closed the door, turning to face the deputies seated around the table. "Where are we on this homicide investigation?"

Devon shook his head. "Russo's killer has vanished."

"What do we know about her so far?"

"Or him," Geraldo muttered. "The more I think about her, the more I wonder if it was a disguised man."

"Good point." Adam paced the room. "Keep an open mind about the suspect's gender."

Devon opened his case binder. "One witness, a patient named"—he scanned his notes—"Carl Montoya, claimed to see her ride off on a small motorcycle. He didn't see well enough to know the make or model. In fact, he said it could have been a moped. But he thought she was a woman because of her short stature and the color of her helmet."

"Color of her helmet?"

"Light purple," Devon said.

"You mean lavender?" Jamie asked.

"Whatever." Devon shrugged. "The thing is, the killer seemed to have had time to put on a helmet and ride away before we discovered the crime."

"Who else saw anything? What about the nurses?"

"No one saw the suspect." Brady shook his head. "As Devon said, she vanished."

"Hospital staff's invisible," Geraldo added. "The nurses are busy and understaffed. If they see people in scrubs carrying medical paraphernalia, they don't look at faces."

Adam claimed the chair at the head of the table. "How much time elapsed from when you saw the suspect enter the room and when the staff responded to Russo's alarm?"

Geraldo shrugged. "Five or six minutes. If she injected him with something, it probably took a few minutes to take effect."

Adam nodded. "Enough time for the killer to rush down the stairs and flee. Probably parked the bike by the fire exit door."

"The room was close to the stairs."

Devon read from his notes. "FDLE found a discarded set of scrubs in the trash can by the second floor storage room."

Geraldo nodded. "That's next to the victim's room."

"Did FDLE take the scrubs to their lab for forensics testing?"

"Yes, but that could take weeks," Devon said. "They also took the hypodermic left at the scene. It could be the murder weapon."

"We'll know more after the autopsy." Adam turned to Jamie. "Keep working on the California connection."

After opening her laptop case, she handed him a two-page printout. "Here's my report from yesterday to add to the file."

"What are you calling the California connection?" Geraldo asked.

"We can't rule out a possible connection between Russo's homicide and the attack last summer on Taylor Drake."

Geraldo frowned. "When she got her throat slashed? Wasn't that a robbery-gone-bad?"

Adam frowned. "That's how it looked, but the case is still open."

Jamie continued. "Here's my question: Was Russo stalking her for personal reasons or spying on her for someone else?"

Devon nodded. "And that someone killed Russo before we could question him."

Jamie looked up from her laptop. "Possibly. The Drake phone line was tapped. The phone company supervisor found clips on the line at the cross-connect box hooked to a vacant cable pair, whatever that means—"

"It means the service is unassigned," Adam said. He'd been down that road before with phone company security. "There's no subscriber to investigate."

"Well, somebody has been listening to every telephone conversation for . . . who knows how long." Jamie hesitated. "There's more, but I'll fill you in later."

"More about the wiretap? Let's have it."

"It's . . . uh . . . ." She hesitated again, and her eyes flickered with discomfiture. This wasn't like Jamie. "The supervisor traced down the vacant pair to a terminal across the river."

"But you said it's unassigned," Devon said.

"It still connects at the terminal box. Somebody rewired it to terminate elsewhere."

"Across the river? So who owns the property?" Adam pressed.

She averted her gaze. "That's the thing. It belongs to Ben and Amy Sawyer. Your sister."

Adam fought for composure. Someone was using his family's land? "Amy isn't living there. Nobody is."

"I realize that," Jamie said. "Until the new bridge is finished, the only way to access that property is by water."

"Wait a minute." Brady held up his hand. "How did the phone company trace this unassigned number to the Sawyer place? In a rowboat?"

"I rode with the supervisor to the terminal. It's located on this side of the river. As he explained it, the hurricane didn't take out phone service. The Sawyers' service is disconnected at the central office until they move back and are ready to reinstall."

"Right. Amy didn't even have to change her number." But where had the offender set up to monitor? "So the wire tapper is camped out at her place listening in on calls with a test set?"

Jamie shook her head. "Not likely. The supervisor said the tap probably hooked up to a transmitter monitored elsewhere. Our suspect had removed his equipment and disappeared by the time we discovered the tap."

"Adam, do you think the person tapped in to the Drake phone line is Russo's killer?" Geraldo asked.

"Let's not spin our wheels with theories. We'll see what the medical examiner's report finds, and let FDLE study the forensics. Meanwhile, basic police work, people. Interview witnesses, track down sightings of motorcyclists wearing lavender helmets, and look for more witnesses."

Jamie closed her laptop case and stood. "I'll keep working with Troy Raizor, the detective in L.A."

"Hold up a sec, Jamie." Adam waited until Devon, Brady, and Geraldo left the room. "I talked to Wil yesterday, and he's worried about Taylor."

"Aren't you? She seems to be the target in all this mess."

"Right. I know we're stretched thin, but I'm going to need to go out there as often as I can. I promised Wil."

"You'd do it, promise or no promise." She gave him a warm smile. "You're good people, a first-rate lawman. Good as Wil . . . but don't you dare tell him I said so."

He gave her his politician's grin. "I hope to convince voters I'm a better lawman than Wil."

"Right. But I'm not worried about the election. Either way, the residents of Foster County will end up with a good sheriff."

Jamie left, and Adam turned off the conference room lights. Jamie's job was secure regardless of who won the election, but who would she vote for? How loyal were Wil's deputies? Adam pushed politics from his mind and headed toward his office, pausing at Zelda's desk. "Any messages?"

"None from Amy, if that's what you're wondering." She handed him three memo slips, her eyes filled with worry. "I visited Phyllis last night."

"I'm glad. Mom needs a friend, especially now."

"She told me what's going on with her. I hope you don't mind that I added her to the prayer list at church."

"Of course, I don't mind."

"I also gave her a Malachy McCourt book to read. I think it will help."

Malachy McCourt. A vague memory of the name floated around in his head. Probably one of the inspirational writers Amy read. "I'm sure Mom appreciates it."

"You'll let me know when you hear from Amy?"

"You bet." He'd promised Taylor he'd investigate her mother's death.

109

Why not start with Zelda? "Do you have a minute? I need to talk to you in private."

She followed him to his office. "Am I being reprimanded? Fired?"

He chuckled. "You know better than that."

"Should I close the door?"

"No need. I just have a couple of questions for you. Taylor wants to know about her mother's death. She needs answers, and her family's not talking."

"Poor little thing." Zelda sat across from his desk. "She was a toddler when Connie died. I doubt she remembers her."

"Bottom line: Was Connie an alcoholic, and did she die as a result of drunk driving?"

"Connie did bend the elbow, but alcoholic? All I saw was a brokenhearted woman who overindulged." Zelda shrugged.

"Brokenhearted over my dad?"

The question seemed to make Zelda squirm. "I'd say he made a fool of her, but break her heart?" She shook her head. "Only Harold Drake could do that. She loved him beyond reason."

"Then why did she sleep around?"

"Your father . . .I'm uncomfortable talking about this with you. He and Connie aren't here to defend themselves, and all I have is rumor."

"I know. But I knew Dad's faults. Mom made demands on him he just couldn't live with, so he drank." Adam shrugged. "Why did you say he made a fool of Connie?"

"Remember how angry he was when the county commissioners denied his request to zone his property to commercial?"

"He had every right to be mad. It destroyed him financially."

"He blamed Harold because Harold argued against developing the area. But Harold had the state environmentalists breathing down his neck. He wasn't alone in thinking your dad's business plan was unsound. Even Suwannee River Water Management showed up to protest."

"He wouldn't compromise or offer Dad alternatives."

"The septic system wasn't adequate. Neither were the roads. The county couldn't afford those improvements, and your father thought taxpayers should foot the bill."

"They could have shared in the expense, but Harold struck down Dad's plan."

"Jed saw it that way, true, but the entire council backed up Harold."

"So Dad's affair with Connie was for revenge, I'm told."

"And it destroyed Harold and Connie's marriage."

He snorted. "Of course it did. Uncompromising Harold Drake couldn't budge and give his wife a second chance. Mom weathered the infidelity, and she and Dad salvaged their marriage."

Zelda frowned. "Phyllis never seemed happy after that. But you know her better than I."

"Mom is intense." Had his mother ever been happy? When was the last time he heard her laugh with joy? For that matter, when had he? No wonder Zelda thought he had his mom's disposition. "How well did you know Dad?"

Zelda sighed. "After he and Phyllis married, we all just drifted apart."

"What about you and Connie? Did you drift apart, too?"

"I threw her a baby shower when she was expecting Wil. But later on, after she had Taylor, we were both involved in our own lives. Harold had little time for the family and expected her to handle the home front."

"I guess that made her lonely and susceptible to Dad's revenge scheme. If only I remembered more about that time, I'd know what questions to ask."

"You were ten or eleven. It's not the sort of thing you needed to be worrying about."

"True. I didn't pay a lot of attention to grownups."

"Wish I could tell you more. Maybe you should read the autopsy report. I'll pull it for you."

"Thanks. I'd appreciate that."

"It's gonna take time, though. That thirty year old stuff's in storage."

"I understand." The telephone buzzed, and he nodded for her to answer it. "We're done here."

Zelda hurried to her desk to grab the phone. He read his message slips and returned calls, pushing thoughts of Taylor and her mother's death from his mind. Yet one thought lingered. Why had Connie arranged to meet his mother before the fatal accident? Only one person alive could answer that nagging question, and she lay in an operating room at the Mayo Clinic in Jacksonville. The last thing she needed was his digging into a painful chapter in her past.

Or was she the only witness? Could he find anyone else who'd been present when they'd met . . . *if* they'd met? Maybe he'd talk to Luke Meiners, who owned the Alibi Bar. That's where Connie purportedly met his dad for drinks. Of course, that's where his dad met everyone for drinks. Odds were that's where Connie planned to meet his mother, too.

Regardless of his promise to Taylor, questioning Luke would have to wait. Adam's open homicide case, election campaign, and ill mother all took precedence over a thirty-year-old automobile accident.

Chapter Nine

Heading toward her father's room, Taylor nearly collided with Maudell and Esther. The two lugged their supplies toward the kitchen. "We usually do Mister Drake's room first, if that's all right," Maudell said.

"Actually, it's perfect. I'll take him outside and give Judy a break." She pushed the door open to Dad's room, and Sophie dashed out. "Come on, girl. We're taking Dad for some fresh air."

She wouldn't dwell on the fact she'd be leaving her safe place. She wouldn't. This was about her father. She could do this for him. When his eyes lit up at her words, her heart squeezed. She *would* do this for him. Before losing her nerve, she breezed into the room and grabbed the back of his wheelchair.

Judy frowned. "He just had his bath. Do you think it wise to take him outdoors?"

Her father grumbled, "I can take myself. The chair's electric."

Taylor read between the lines. *Don't talk about me as if I'm not in the room.* Ignoring Judy, she gave him her best smile. "It's your call, Dad. Want to sit out on the porch with me while your room is cleaned?"

"Yes." He lifted his chin the tiniest bit, and pride filled his eyes.

"Judy, you can take a break. There's iced tea in the refrigerator."

Judy seemed to take the offer grudgingly. "I guess I could use a few minutes." Then she added, "Thanks."

Taylor pulled open the door as far as she could to allow her dad space to navigate his electric wheelchair through the opening. "Front porch or back?"

In answer, he turned his chair toward the front door. She followed, concentrating on breathing. Her heart pounded. Perspiration dampened her palms. *You can do this, Taylor. You will do this. Do it for Dad.*

He bumped into the threshold at the door and stalled. "Hold on." She tugged at the chair to no avail. Finally she grabbed the directional toggle

113

and worked it until she freed the wheels from the threshold strip.

Dad took control of the joystick and whirred his wheelchair to a sunny spot at the edge of the porch. "This suit you?"

She collapsed into one of the wooden rocking chairs and sighed. So far, so good. "It's fine."

"You need your medicine? You look pale."

"I'm okay." She forced a smile. Though she hadn't talked about her attack or her fears with her father, she knew Wil had. "I save the meds for extreme circumstances."

"Like yesterday?" He pursed his lips. "I'm aware of a lot more than you think, Little Strawberry."

Little Strawberry. He hadn't called her that in ages. "I didn't want to worry you—"

"Don't treat me like a child. The stroke damaged my body, not my mind." His voice was low but his tone loud and clear. "If not for Wilson, I'd never know what's going on."

More than once Wil had cautioned her and Sam to keep Dad in the mainstream, not baby him. But she couldn't get past the dichotomy of the once vibrant and powerful man now confined to a wheelchair. "I told you about Jim Russo's murder. I haven't babied you."

"You were almost murdered, for God's sake. You need help to recover. Tell me about your treatment."

"I figured Wil filled you in. I spent time in a clinic and got victim counseling. I saw a psychiatrist and have prescriptions for anxiety. I really am better, Dad."

"Still agoraphobic, though, right?"

"I . . . I never told you that—"

"Precisely. So tell me now. Stop discounting me."

"Oh, Dad, I never meant to. I was being protective." She gave him a rueful grin. "I guess that is a form of discounting you. I'm sorry. It won't happen again."

"So talk to me."

A weight lifted from her chest, and she told him everything.

Everything except her attraction to Adam Gillespie, that is. She talked about her panic attacks, the triggers, the calming exercises she'd tried, even her efforts using desensitization.

"You're a strong person, Taylor. Remember that."

"Am I? I wonder sometimes—"

"I was told I'd wear adult diapers, yet I manage to use the bathroom. It's a challenge, and sometimes I'm discouraged. And sometimes I fail. But I don't give up."

"I know how hard you worked with both the physical therapist and the speech therapist, long after most people would've quit."

"My point is, you take after me. You won't give up."

"What if I don't? What if I'm weak like my mother?" The words tumbled out. She shouldn't have mentioned her mother.

Dad looked stricken, as if she'd insulted him. "Why did you say that?"

She shook her head. "I'm sorry. I know you forbid us to talk about her, but I need to know. Gram said she was weak and addicted to alcohol, pain killers—"

"That was your grandmother's opinion."

"Did you think she was an alcoholic?"

"Nope. But I guess I didn't know your mother as well as I thought."

"What do you mean?"

He turned his gaze toward the stand of trees blocking their view of the county road, and for a long time he stared in silence. Finally, he closed his eyes. "I never thought she'd leave us for that stinkin' Jed Gillespie. I . . . I thought she was happy here."

"She knew it was a mistake. That's why she tried to get you to take her back—"

"You don't know what you're talking about." His voice trembled, and he gripped the wheelchair toggle with his good hand. His eyes flashed. "She didn't call or—"

"You refused to see her."

"At first." He dropped his chin. "I was too angry with her and

115

Gillespie. But she never tried after that."

"Evidently she did. Did you not see the letters? Did Gram hide them from you?"

Suddenly his eyes widened as if he'd finally processed what she'd said. "Where did you find letters?"

She explained about cleaning her grandmother's room and finding the jewelry case hidden in the walk-in closet. "Gram didn't want her to come back, did she?"

Again he took his time in answering. "Your grandmother needed to be here. She'd just lost my father and felt displaced. But I didn't think she'd . . . interfere. Could I"—he swallowed— "could I see the letters?"

"Absolutely. I'll read them to you if you like."

"Yes, please. I still don't focus all that well since the stroke."

She patted his hand. "I'll be right back."

The jewelry box was on the refrigerator where she'd left it the night she'd shared pizza with Adam. Excitement buzzed through her, both for her father's willingness to talk about her mother and for her lack of anxiety. In concentrating on her father's feelings, she'd forgotten to fear the outside. She'd succeeded in expanding her safe place. Maybe later she would hook up Sophie's leash and try walking her.

The maids worked in her father's room and Judy Wood was absent, so she found the kitchen empty. She grabbed the jewelry box and hugged it to her chest. Maybe now she'd get answers. How wrong she'd been not to ask Dad. She certainly didn't want to insult him by handling him with kid gloves.

She hurried back to the front porch, where she settled the box in her lap to remove the letters. "I'll read them in date order, if that's all right."

"How . . . many did she write?"

"I found six in the box. I wonder why Gram kept them if she didn't plan on showing them to you."

He didn't respond to that, so Taylor began to read.

Dearest Harold,

Since you refuse my calls and have barred me from the house, I'm trying to reach you in writing. Charlotte says I'm no longer welcome at Drake Oaks. Is that her directive or yours? She's never liked me much, and has made no secret of it, but she is the grandmother of my children and I will respect her.

Sweetheart, we need to talk. I don't want a divorce. I made a mistake, a bad one, true. But this isn't Victorian times. Surely we can heal this rift if only you'll talk with me. I love you and miss you. I realize that now more than ever.

With all my heart,
Connie

Dad sighed. "Must've been when she figured out Jed Gillespie had just used her to get at me."

"I guess we'll never know now. Want me to keep reading?"

"Yeah."

Dearest Harold,

Charlotte told me you are filing for divorce. Don't write off our marriage. Give me the chance to talk to you face-to-face. Please?

If you insist on following through with divorce, don't expect me to go away quietly. I love my children and will fight for them. It's the twentieth century, and no judge is going to award you custody because of an indiscretion. Don't force this into a battle. Please call me. I'm at the Holiday Inn in Lake City.

Love,
Connie

"You were going to divorce her?"

"I . . . I never said that. Read the next one."

She read through the next four letters, which were more of the same. Connie Drake regretted her brief affair with Jed Gillespie and begged for a second chance. At the end of the last letter, Taylor waited for some response from Dad. He sat for several minutes, staring dry-eyed into the distance.

Fred Fischer's truck rolled through the gate and Fred greeted them with a short honk of the horn. Then the pickup circled the house and headed toward the barn. Taylor waved back, but Dad seemed oblivious to the contractor's arrival.

Finally he cleared his throat. "You must think me hard-hearted—"

"No." She reached for his hand and squeezed it. "I think Gram was hard-hearted for hiding these letters from you. She interfered where she had no right."

Misery filled his eyes. "I refused your mother's phone calls. I did that. But I didn't know about her visits. Or these letters."

"You can't reinvent history. Gram did wrong, but she's gone now, too. There's been enough hurt. I just want to know…to remember my mother. Am I like her?"

His eyes softened. "You look like her. She was blond, like Wilson, but both your brothers favor me. Lucky for you, you inherited Connie's pretty face."

Except for hair color, Sam and Wil looked enough alike to be twins. As Dad said, they both looked like younger versions of him. "But we all have your amazing green eyes."

"Connie's eyes were green, too. I guess you don't remember."

"I remember her soft skin, and the scent of her lotion." An old memory surfaced, of her mother applying hand lotion to her own hands then tenderly rubbing the excess on Taylor's, caressing her tiny hands in the process. "I remember her touch."

"Connie was quiet and kept things to herself. She seemed content, which is why her behavior with Jed Gillespie shocked us all. In that way, you're nothing like her."

Taylor chortled. "No, I'm more in your face—"

"Like your old man." His grin was lopsided. "We Drakes speak our mind."

"You were stronger than Mother—"

118

"That's not what I said. Quiet doesn't mean weak."

"Too bad you two couldn't have worked things out, but I remember how intimidating Gram could be. She had certain rules we all had to follow. I guess she took her role as family matriarch too far."

"I let her. It's my fault—"

"Shh. It's not all your fault. You were left with three children to raise, and the job fell to Gram."

"She had founded the college, but after it was up and running, she didn't have much to do there. Then your grandfather died, and I guess she needed to keep busy."

"She needed something else to run, and our family was the substitute for the college. Oh well . . . ." A deep sadness filled her. What would life have been like if her parents had reconciled? Would Gram have withered away without the family needing her? Would Wil have applied himself more in school and stuck around instead of moving to Jacksonville for so many years?

"She and I agreed to avoid talking about Connie to you kids. I wanted to protect you."

She gave his hand another squeeze. "All that's in the past. I just need to know more about my mother and her medical history. Her mental health."

He scowled. "Connie wasn't mentally disturbed. I'm sorry you thought she was. I guess you heard that from your grandmother."

"What made Gram say she was addicted to pain killers?"

"The autopsy. She had something like barbiturates in her blood. So even if she hadn't had too much to drink, she would've been drunk."

"Barbiturates? So she drank while taking a prescription med—"

"No. That's the thing. Cops checked around. She wasn't on a prescription for anything except birth control pills. Maybe somebody supplied them to her illegally."

"I guess we'll never know." A dark cloud cast a chilly shadow across the porch, and Taylor shivered. "Are you ready to go inside yet?"

"Yes. But let's do this again."

"Come sit on the porch?"

"That, too." He smiled again, a little crookedly, but enough to convey his pleasure.

She'd seen too few of her father's smiles since the stroke robbed him of his active life. "Thanks for talking to me about my mother. I needed that."

"Long overdue, Little Strawberry. Long overdue." He toggled the electric wheelchair control and whirred past her toward the door.

She hurried to the front door and held it open. "Do you need help?"

"I'll make it." Two tries later, he bumped across the threshold and into the foyer.

"I just realized something, Dad. I've been outdoors all this time talking with you and I didn't panic."

He stopped and gazed up at her. "Told you you're like your old man."

"I think you're right."

Though the week had been tumultuous and stressful, Taylor had victories to celebrate. Since returning home to Drake Oaks, she'd made more progress in her battle against agoraphobia than with weeks of therapy. *Thank you, Lord.*

Finally, she was beginning to heal.

At five o'clock, Amy called Adam's cell phone. "Finally," he answered. "How'd it go?"

"Not good." Her weary sigh spoke volumes. "It's been an exhausting day. I'm at the hotel now, but Mom is in a room at the clinic. She'll be released in the morning."

"Tell me what they found."

"Adam, she's eaten up with the cancer. It spread to her pancreas and colon. We're meeting with the doctor in the morning to discuss her options."

The bottom dropped from his stomach and bile burned his throat. He swallowed hard. "Treatment options?"

Amy hesitated. "More like extended care and Hospice."

Anguish tore through him. "That sounds so . . . final."

"Yeah." Amy inhaled a ragged breath. "We talked on the drive over this morning. It's as if she expected to die . . . as if it's inevitable."

"It's not like Mom to give up. She's always been a fighter."

"Some fights can't be won."

"We need to meet as a family tomorrow when you get back and make some decisions. Much as I appreciate your taking her to Jacksonville today, I don't expect you to bear the brunt of this. She's my mom, too."

"Thanks. I won't argue with you. I want the boys to spend as much time with her as . . . ." She broke down then and sobbed. "This is so hard."

"Oh, Amy, I'm sorry I'm not there. Why don't I pick up Ben and drive—"

"No, don't." She sniffled. "I'll be fine, really. The day's stress has caught up with me, that's all."

Torn between the need to be with his family and the demands of filling in as the sheriff, Adam felt the beginning of a headache seize the back of his head. Wil picked a hell of a week to go on a cruise. "I'm just a phone call away if you change your mind."

"Thanks, little brother." Her use of the nickname usually made him smile. Not this time. "Well, I better go. I still need to call Ben. See you tomorrow."

"Take care driving home." He disconnected, then he buried his head in his hands.

"Was that Amy?" Zelda stood in the door, purse in hand, ready to leave. She'd been eavesdropping, no doubt. He nodded. "Bad news I take it?"

"The worst."

"I'm so sorry. Let me know if there's anything we can do."

"Just one thing. Let's keep it private for now." He snorted. "I know how ironic that sounds, considering Mom's a newspaper woman and felt everyone's business was fair game."

Zelda's eyes held no judgment. Only sympathy. "I understand how you feel. I won't say a word."

"Thanks. See you in the morning."

Zelda left, and Jamie appeared in her place. "We have a stolen vehicle report on a Yamaha motorcycle matching the description of the suspect's. The lavender helmet was stolen with it. Belongs to a woman in Jacksonville."

Adam forced his attention back to the homicide investigation. "Does Devon know?"

"Yes, I told him just now." She shrugged and stepped back from the doorway. "I'll get back to my laptop."

"How about going home and getting some rest."

"Not when the other deputies aren't—"

"It's not preferential treatment, Jamie. I need you rested to relieve Devon tomorrow. He's working 'round the clock."

"Gotcha. So who's going to relieve *you*?"

He forced a chuckle. "Doesn't work that way, and you know it. Now get out of here."

"Yes, sir." She offered him a salute and turned to leave.

"I mean it. Get some sleep."

"Oh, one more thing. You can return Taylor Drake's cell phone to her. I've copied her SIM card, so I don't need it." Pulling the cell phone out of her jacket pocket, she laid it on his desk. "But she might."

"Explain the SIM card."

"SIM is an acronym for subscriber identity module. It's the little removable card inside a cell phone that contains the service-subscriber key, along with other user information."

"I'll try to remember that."

She laughed. "I know everybody around here thinks I'm a geek. I can't help it. I like this technology stuff."

"I don't think you're a geek, but I often think you're a genius."

"Thanks." She ducked her head and grimaced. "But techno-nerd better describes me."

"Techno-nerd?" Whatever label she put on herself, he marveled at her expertise. He waved her off. "Home. Now."

After she left, he sat for a long time staring at Taylor's cell phone. He probably should drop it off tonight when he drove out to Drake Oaks to check on her. His heart stuttered just at the thought of seeing Taylor. Yet he longed to be alone to think about his mother. He'd heard Amy's words, but the reality of his mother dying hadn't sunk in. Surely there'd been a mistake. Maybe he'd awaken and find Amy's telephone call a bad dream.

His headache worsened. He swallowed a couple of aspirin and washed them down with the last of his cooling coffee. At a standstill with the Russo homicide investigation, he called it a day. He locked his desk and grabbed his jacket, then stopped by the dispatch desk.

Adjusting her headset, Rebecca Gibbons looked up and smiled. "Evening, Adam."

"You're here late, Rebecca."

"I traded shifts. Nancy has a hot date, and Otis is showing rental property to a client."

Otis Gibbons handled most real estate transactions in Foster County. As for Nancy Fox, Adam had no idea she dated, and he wasn't about to ask. He needed to be working, if not on the homicide then something. Anything to keep his mind occupied.

"You wouldn't happen to know if Luke Meiners still owns the Alibi Bar, would you?"

"He still owns it and still runs it."

He nodded. "That's where I'll be. I need to question him about something, then I'll head out to the sheriff's place. You can reach me on my cell."

The idea of questioning Luke had been the farthest thing from his mind, yet could be the distraction he needed. If he learned anything from Luke to feed Taylor's curiosity, maybe his promise to her would be fulfilled. No way he'd question his mother about the night she was supposed to have met Connie Drake for a drink. In fact, he'd see to it that Mom didn't hear the Drake name at all.

The Alibi Bar was so old it was back in fashion now as retro. Adam remembered Luke Meiners the moment he walked in and saw the man wiping the nicotine-stained Formica countertop. His eyes crinkled with a welcoming smile. "Well, Adam Gillespie, I haven't seen you since—"

"Since the last time you had to help me drag Dad out to the car." Adam stepped up to the bar and shook hands with Luke. "How've you been? You look well."

"Fit as a fiddle. Tracy sees to it. She watches our fat grams and makes me walk with her in the mornings."

Although at least seventy, Luke looked about fifty-five. "Tracy must care about you."

Luke grinned. "She does. Foolish woman thinks I'm worth it. Now tell me what I can serve you. I even have lite beer now."

"Nothing, thanks. I really wanted to ask you a question, and it's going to seem off the wall."

"I tend bar. I'm used to 'off the wall'."

Adam took a deep breath. *Here goes nothing.* "It's about my mother. Did she ever come in here on her own? Without Dad. Or would you remember?"

Luke frowned. "Now, I have an off the wall answer for you. I'll be damned if I don't remember. She came in exactly once, and she was pissed off, let me tell you."

"When was that?"

"Oh, hell, Adam. That's going back twenty-five—no, thirty years, at least. She was out for blood, I remember that much. I wasn't used to seeing Phyllis as a customer, although your dad was a regular. So it stuck in my mind."

"Was she meeting someone?"

"That's the weird part. She was meeting some woman she claimed was sleeping with Jed. I didn't recognize her or know her, but she came in and sat at the booth with Phyllis." He nodded toward the booths lining one wall of the tavern. "Pretty blonde. Sorry. I know it's your daddy I'm talkin' about."

"That's okay. Go on."

"The blonde ordered wine then vamoosed. I'm not sure she even finished her drink. I can't tell you what was said, but I expected a real uproar and nothing happened. Your mom musta held her temper."

"I'd say your memory is sharp if you can recall all that from thirty years ago."

Luke shrugged. "It was out of the ordinary, or I wouldn't. Like I said, Phyllis made no secret of the fact she hated this place. Hated that Jed drank and made this his second home. So for her to show up here as a customer . . . ."

"I see. Would you remember if the blond-haired woman was intoxicated?"

"Near as I could see, she was fine. She strode in here all purposeful-like and headed for Phyllis's booth, like she was on a mission. Then strode right out the door a few minutes later. After seeing how upset your mother was, it was all kind of . . . a letdown."

Adam snorted. "Gee, Luke, you sound disappointed."

"At the time, we all was. Thought we was going to see a real cat fight. But Phyllis proved to have too much class for that."

"Did Mom leave right after that?"

"Now that much I can't say. Seems Jed came in, maybe, and they stayed a bit, but don't take that to the bank." Luke leaned forward on his elbows. "I'm real sorry about your dad. He was never no trouble. Just a happy drunk. I liked the guy and missed the hell outta him when he passed away."

"Yeah." Reliving his father's drinking problems wasn't on Adam's agenda. "I'll let you get back to your customers. Thanks for the information."

Luke motioned to the only two men in the joint, two guys at the bumper pool table. "Yeah, I can hardly keep up with all these customers."

Adam turned to leave. "Take care."

"Wait a sec. Aren't ya gonna tell me what this is about? You got my curiosity going."

"The woman my mother met here died in a car wreck that night. It was an accident, but the family has some questions and I agreed to look into it."

"Holy shit! That was that Drake woman, wasn't it? I didn't know her but I remember now hearing about her and your dad—" Luke shrugged with a rueful smile. "Oops. Sorry."

"No, it's all right, Luke. Tell me what you heard. Frankly, I've wondered myself about the fling that caused so much turmoil."

"Well, I heard it was Jed's idea. He was nuts about that woman, but she wanted to go back to her husband. I think her old man wasn't the forgive-and-forgettin' kind. She was living in some motel in another town, and Jed took up with her there. Tried to get her to run off with him. Least that's what I heard. But you need to know something, son."

"What's that?"

"Most of that rumor I got from your momma."

Adam thanked him and left, but his headache returned. If he reported what he'd just learned, Taylor would have more questions . . . questions for his mother. And there was no way in hell he'd resurrect the pain of that affair with her now.

The growing darkness matched his mood. He needed a long, relaxing hot shower and a cold beer. Some mind-numbing sit-com on TV. Unbidden, a fantasy intruded of him sitting beside Taylor on the sofa, sharing a bowl of popcorn and watching television. What on earth made him think about living with Taylor? Yet, he fantasized about it all the time, ever since they'd sat together in the Drake kitchen and shared her homemade pizza. Considering the hatred between their two families, he'd lost his mind. He and Taylor? *Not going to happen.* Rest would clear his thinking. He needed a few quiet hours alone to recharge his batteries.

Just as he reached his car to head home, his cell phone rang. *Harold Drake.* So much for his relaxing evening at home.

"Adam, it's Taylor. I'm sorry to saddle you with one crisis after another, but"—her scratchy-throated voice rose an octave, as if she was fighting hysteria —"someone's been in my bathroom and tampered with my meds. I . . . I don't know when he could've gotten in."

His heart raced, and his protective instincts kicked in. "Did you take any?"

"No! I didn't touch them."

Good girl. "I'm on my way."

Chapter Ten

Adam rang the bell while holding both an evidence bag and Taylor's cell phone. She met him at the door, flushed-faced and armed with her pistol. Flushed-faced was better than her pale and vacant look of yesterday. At least she didn't appear to be in panic mode.

He handed her the cell phone. "Jamie's finished with this."

"Thanks. I'll plug it in its charger." She locked the door again then stuffed the cell phone into the pocket of her zippered sweatshirt. Her weapon went into the opposite pocket.

"You need a holster if you're going to carry that pistol all the time."

She stopped in the middle of the foyer and faced him. "I hadn't carried it at all until now. I was actually starting to feel safe—"

"Safe? Russo's killer is at large." She paled then, and he could've kicked himself for his abruptness. "Look, I didn't mean to scare you. I've just had a rough day."

She exhaled a long sigh. "I know, and I'm sorry to add to your burdens."

You have no idea, lady. "Goes with the job. Where are the pills?"

"Capsules, actually. Come on. They're upstairs." She turned toward the wide staircase.

He stilled her with a touch on her arm. "The medicine I gave you yesterday was a pill."

"That was a tranquilizer. The capsules are my anti-anxiety meds." She shrugged. "It's complicated. I try not to take either—"

"So you need an anti-anxiety drug tonight?"

"No. But the bottle wasn't where I'd left it. At first, I thought it was Maudell and Esther, the Home Maid Bonnie team."

"Home Maid Bonnie?"

"The cleaning service. But they worked upstairs first, and afterward I'd seen the capsules in their usual place. Then later, the bottle had been moved. Not much, but I knew I hadn't touched it."

He followed her up the stairs and to the end of the hall. She opened one of a pair of double doors leading into a carpeted suite. To the left, another set of double doors led from the empty sitting room toward the screened porch. Taylor turned right, leading him through the huge bedroom that dwarfed the single bed. A small chest of drawers and dresser barely made a dent in the spacious suite. She then led him through a small dressing area that divided twin walk-in closets. The carpet continued into the area in front of a mirrored vanity.

"In the bathroom." She seemed calm, but her voice trembled.

He stepped beside her at the long vanity and faced their mirror images, ignoring the warm rush of seeing them standing together so close. A barely discernible floral fragrance filled his senses, and he swallowed, a knot of pure desire squeezing his gut. He had no business being alone with Taylor, especially in her sleeping quarters.

She pointed to the corner of the counter, to a bottle of prescription medicine, its lid removed. A single capsule lay inside the cap. Snapping on the latex gloves, he took the bottle and sniffed. The smell of bitter almonds replaced her feminine scent.

"I know my medications, Adam. These aren't the original capsules. Someone switched them. I don't know what these are, but I'm not taking one. Can you have it analyzed?"

Taylor wasn't overreacting. He'd read enough to know the odor could mean the presence of cyanide. Thank God she hadn't touched the capsules. "Let me bag this. I'll send it to the lab."

"Do you think Jim's killer did this?"

How could he answer her? He placed both bottle and capsule into the sack, then removed his gloves. "Tell me about everyone who came out here today, and try to account for as much of their activities as you can."

Taylor's earlier anxiety faded. Adam was here. He made her feel safe. After securing the evidence bag, he set it on the marble vanity, then he followed her into the bedroom. She led him to her twin bed to sit, despite the intimate setting; but she didn't have a chair in the room or furniture in the sitting room, and she was too drained to go back downstairs. It seemed another emotional battle followed each small victory. Yet she wasn't discouraged. Not anymore. She'd turned the corner on her agoraphobia, and as her dad said, she was strong. She *would* prevail.

"I'm sorry to seem so paranoid—"

"You aren't paranoid. You've had very real threats."

He sat at the foot of the bed, putting as much distance between them as possible, not that she blamed him. She told him all she could remember, from oversleeping that morning to sitting on the porch with her father without having an anxiety attack. She left out details of their conversation about her mother, although she still wanted answers about the auto accident. Answers about her intruder took precedence now.

"The whole time you were outside, where were the cleaning people?"

"In Dad's room, the downstairs baths, and the kitchen. They cleaned upstairs first."

"And Judy Wood?"

"Well . . . now that I think about it, I didn't see her when I came in the kitchen for a minute. I'm not sure where she went, but I told her to take a break."

"So she, or anyone, could have slipped upstairs unnoticed while you were on the porch with your father?"

"I guess so. I would've seen anyone going in the front door, and Fred Fischer was out back. I'm not sure that he'd notice a stranger going in the back door, though."

"I'll talk to Fred. Meanwhile, keep your doors locked."

She snorted. "Today's the first day I haven't. The maids were going in and out the back, and I was on the veranda with Dad."

"Jamie checked out Judy Wood, but I'll have her verify the two employees with Home Maid Bonnie."

"They seemed to know their way around. They'd been here before, and Dad recognized them. Oh, and Sophie took to Judy right away."

"Sophie took to me right away, too. Except for trained K-9s, dogs aren't reliable, regardless of what you see in the movies."

"Oh. Well, as you say, Judy checked out. And she seemed to know how to care for Dad."

"We know Fred wouldn't tamper with your medications." His troubled frown tugged at her heart. Sadness filled his eyes.

"Have you heard from Amy about your mom's procedure at the Mayo?"

The question seemed to startle him, and he hesitated. "Amy told you?"

"Yes." She longed to squeeze his hand, but he sat just beyond her reach. "Do you know the results yet?"

He slumped forward, burying his face in his hands. "Yeah, and it isn't encouraging."

"I'm so sorry."

He straightened then and glanced at her. "Why? You don't know Mom. She hates your family."

"I know *you* . . . and now I know Amy. You're good people I care about. You're hurting because of your mom's illness, and I can sympathize. Is that so difficult to accept?"

"You really don't buy into this feud, do you?"

She stood, planting her fists on her hipbones. "I told you. Life's too short to hold grudges."

"Life's short for Mom." He swallowed hard. "She's dying."

"The ovarian cancer?"

"It spread. Amy's words were 'she's eaten up with it.'"

"You both must feel so helpless."

"Yeah." Fatigue lines pulled at his eyes. "We're both shell-shocked."

She moved closer, placing one hand on his shoulder. "Come on downstairs. I'll make you dinner."

"That's a lot of trouble. Why don't I run the evidence sack into the station, stop by Vinnie's, and bring back a supreme deluxe?"

"I have an idea." She paused to kiss him. "Why don't I ride along with you? It's a gamble, but I'd like to try it."

"You sure? That's a big step."

"You've already seen me at my worst. I'm feeling confident. Or maybe I just don't want to be left alone. With my mood swings, it could go either way." She said it as a joke, but she prayed for courage.

He nodded. "What about Harold?"

"I'll check on him and make sure he's settled."

"You think he'll be upset that you're leaving with me?"

"He might not like that I'm leaving with you, but he'll be proud of me for trying this. He . . . he and I talked today. Really talked. About my attack, my therapy. About my mother, too."

"You can tell me about it on the way."

"You can call in the pizza order while I stop by Dad's room. Get a couple. Dad likes pizza, too."

"Any taboo toppings, or can I order whatever I want?"

"I'm not an anchovies bigot, if that's what you mean. But I do like the thin and crispy crust."

"Me, too." He nodded toward her sweatshirt pocket. "You'll have to leave the weapon here."

"I know. Jamie says it could take months to get my permit."

"How did she fingerprint you for the background check without taking you to the jail?"

"Wil brought home an old ink machine. He said the digital was a lot better, but the FBI still reads ink, too." She lifted her chin with determination. "I've inconvenienced a lot of people. That has to stop."

"Good for you." He followed her downstairs. "I'll call from my cell and meet you on the porch."

She followed him to the front door. "First, there's something I want to say."

He stopped, facing her, his gaze dropping to her lips. "Me, too."

Her pulse quickened. Did he intend to kiss her? *Dear God, help me say the right thing*. "I have feelings for you, Adam. Strong feelings. If you don't want to hear that, tough. But I think you feel something, too."

"I do." He met her gaze. "I've fought it like crazy, but you've taken the fight out of me."

She grinned. "Great."

He lowered his mouth to hers for a long yet gentle kiss. She closed her eyes, savoring the taste of him and the comfort of his embrace. Never had she yearned so for a happy-ever-after. Could he want the same? If only Adam learned to forgive her family. His bitterness stood between them and in the way of happiness.

Adam ended the kiss. When he opened his eyes, he couldn't stop staring at the horrible gash at Taylor's throat. A sudden knot of rage squeezed his chest. How dare that scumbag hurt such a beautiful person!

Sensing his gaze, she fingered the scar. "I know it's hideous, but the surgeon said it will fade eventually."

He trailed kisses over her throat, following the path of the scar. The path of the murdering bastard's knife. "Sweetheart, nothing about you is hideous."

"Except maybe my haircut."

He laughed at that. "I figured it was the latest style in California."

"Not hardly. You know, I'd never do plumbing or perform my own dentistry. Why did I think I could cut hair?" Her laughter, raspy and low because of her injured throat, was damned sexy, and it lightened his heart.

The dark clouds that had hung over him all day thinned. "I suppose some things should be left to the professionals." He swept the renegade tendrils from her eyes. "But you have a beautiful face. Somehow the hair suits you."

"And you have a beautiful smile, Adam. Try using it more."

"*You* make me smile."

"So what's holding you back?"

"You've been through a lot lately. I care about you, and I want you to be sure—"

"Don't start with the rubbish about how I've been through a life-threatening trauma and I see you as a hero and I'm feeling transference—"

"Whoa. Take a breath, woman. I'm trying to say you can trust me."

"I know that." Her swift reply did funny things to his gut.

"I still think—"

She placed her index finger across his lips. "Stop thinking. It gets in the way."

"In the way of what? It's not like we have a future."

She frowned at him. "I'm sorry you see it that way."

How else could he see the future? When Taylor was strong again, she'd leave. How often must he remind himself? She had a globetrotting career. He hoped to be Foster County's sheriff. He planned to stay put.

"We have a lot of cards stacked against us, starting with my mother and your father. Then there's the matter of what happens when you go back to work."

"Work? It's not as if I have a steady job waiting for my return. I'm freelance. I work whenever and wherever I want."

"Right. You won't win any Pulitzers photographing Sticky Swamp or the Christmas lights on the Suwannee. You'd have to go back to Iraq—"

"No, never." She shuddered. "Once was enough, thank you, and the Pulitzer was unexpected. I didn't go there looking for a prize-winning shot."

"It was amazing. Very evocative."

"You saw it?"

"Amy printed it on the front page of the *Democrat*. I guess I'd forgotten you took the photo in Iraq."

"I tend to focus on people rather than the landscape. That little boy's face . . . well, it spoke of so many emotions that summed up war."

"It did. I noticed in your photos of the Teamsters' strike how you captured faces and expressions. You're very talented."

"Thank you. I didn't realize I'd done much to impress you."

Was she kidding? She continued to dazzle him. "I was impressed you learned how to use a weapon and didn't hesitate to fire it when you needed to. Many folks buy guns, don't learn to use them properly, then wind up having them stolen or used against them in a crime."

"That's what Jamie says."

"You let me bully you into leaving the house and—"

"Bully is too strong a word. You challenged me."

"Okay, I challenged you. You showed spunk."

"And yesterday I showed you a serious anxiety attack."

"From which you recovered." He tapped the end of her nose. "But what impressed me the most? Your homemade pizza."

She laughed. "I can take a hint. Call in the order. I'll tell Dad."

His gaze followed her down the hall until she disappeared. Thoughts about his mother's illness intruded, but he'd deal with those emotions later. Right now his head spun from Taylor's kiss and dreams he shouldn't be having. Could he and Taylor have a future? Would she stick around after she recovered?

Could he love her enough to forgive the Drake family? He'd have to think long and hard about that. Could Amy be right? Was the hatred standing in his way of happiness?

Taylor breathed a sigh of relief and fastened her safety belt. She'd made it to Adam's cruiser without a single shiver. "So far, so good."

Adam started the engine. "You're doing great, champ."

"I guess you can't hold my hand since we're in a county vehicle."

He reached for her hand and gave it a squeeze. "Sure I can."

"That helps, but you need both hands to drive."

"Afraid so." He released her hand to shift into reverse. "How'd it go with Harold?"

"I told him you were helping me with a desensitization exercise."

"And what'd he say?"

She laughed. "Dad's no fool. He said 'if that's what you want to call it.'"

"So he suspects something's going on between us?"

She shrugged. "Probably. But as long as we bring him pizza, he'll be appeased."

Adam drove through the gate, slowing to turn left on County Road 471. "Since even *I'm* not sure what's going on between us, let's keep him in the dark for now."

"I'm not ashamed of my feelings. Are you?"

"Ashamed? No." *Frightened? Yes.* He drove past the Alibi Bar, where earlier he'd talked to Luke. "There's something I need to tell you. It's about your mother."

"I didn't think you had time yet to do any digging."

He crossed Ortega and slowed to turn left on Coronado. "I talked tonight with Luke Meiners. He owns the Alibi and has for many years."

"He knew my mother?"

"Not really. But he remembers the night of her accident." He pulled into the lot at the Foster County sheriff's office. "Just as the letter said, Connie met my mom. Earlier Mom had seemed ready to tear her apart limb by limb, according to Luke, and he expected a heated confrontation, but Connie apparently defused the situation. She left after a few minutes and didn't appear to be drunk or even tipsy."

"If she apologized to Phyllis, it wasn't enough to keep your family from hating us."

"Mom never mentions Connie. She blames Harold for driving Dad to drink and ruin." He parked and shut off the motor. "I'll be right back . . . unless you want to go inside with me."

"Not if you don't want us seen together." She couldn't ignore the pang of disappointment when he shook his head. "I'll stay here."

The quick but firm touch of his mouth against hers caught her off guard. "Don't read anything into it. I'm not ashamed to be seen with you."

"I understand."

He locked her inside the cruiser then disappeared around the corner of the building. She would be all right alone in the car. She would. Alone miles from her safe place—not that it truly was safe, as evidenced by the latest break-in—she could hardly find a spot any safer than right outside the county sheriff's office, sitting in a police car with the doors locked. She'd be fine.

Yet her body started to tremble from the inside out, and she shook as if she'd been soaked in an icy lake. A flutter deep in her abdomen burgeoned into an angry growl. She drew in quick, shallow breaths.

Dizziness swept over her.

No! She had to fight. Squeezing her eyes shut, she prayed for strength and courage. She inhaled a lungful of air then released it, repeating it three times.

Calmer now, she no longer shivered. Her breathing normalized. Dad believed in her, so she should believe in herself. She *was* strong and resilient. She had the choice to decide her destiny, and her faith to reinforce her for the battle. Maybe her world had been shattered after the killer's attack, but she could recover. If she cowered in fear the rest of her life, her assailant won. She might as well have died alongside Roz.

Taylor had escaped the killer because of her will to live and her strong faith. Now she sat straighter in the police car, her chin lifted and her resolve strong. No way she'd give Roz's killer power over her. She chose life.

How sad that Adam's mother couldn't choose to live. He'd want to make her last weeks as comfortable as possible, which meant she couldn't know about Taylor. She certainly wouldn't add to Adam's stress by going public with their relationship. They had to be sensitive to his mother's feelings because of a stupid feud.

Adam reappeared, jingling his keys and striding toward the car, his cell phone to his ear. When he caught her gaze, he smiled. This time the quiver seizing her body had nothing to do with anxiety. Her thoughts bounced from his mother to something he'd said earlier that tap-danced at the edges of her mind, something she needed to question. What was it?

He snapped the cell phone shut, slid behind the wheel, then closed the door. "You okay?"

"I'm good now." She swallowed. "I had a scary moment, but I got past it."

"I knew you could do it."

"I'm regaining my confidence. That's something."

"That's progress." He brushed a strand of her stringy hair away from her eyes. The tender smile he gave her warmed her.

She leaned her face into his hand. "You can be charming when you try."

"I can?" He removed his fingers from her cheek, and she immediately missed his touch. "I called Fred Fischer. He'll be armed when he comes out tomorrow."

"Did he see anything suspicious today?"

"He didn't see anyone but the two maids." He started the motor. "The pizzas should be ready by now."

She gazed out the window on the way to Vinnie's, taking in the small town in which she'd grown up, where Gram had built an arts college and Dad once served as a county commissioner. What was it she'd meant to ask Adam about her mother?

"You said something about the night our mothers had met at the Alibi Bar, about my mom not appearing intoxicated. Yet that contradicts what Dad said about the autopsy."

"I'm having Zelda pull the autopsy report, but it's buried under thirty years' worth of archived files."

"I'd be curious to know what it says." Would the report explain where else her mother went before wrapping her car around a tree in the middle of the national forest? How did she wind up with barbiturates and alcohol in her blood, on County Road 12, the opposite direction of the Alibi and Drake Oaks? "Thanks for helping me."

"A deal's a deal." His tone reminded her he wouldn't question his mother.

Yet without Phyllis, would she ever know the truth about that night?

Taylor held the two pizza boxes in her lap while he drove back to Drake Oaks. She looked almost serene, a promising sign of her progress against her agoraphobia. He fought the temptation to pull over to the side of the road and drag her into his arms. He longed to kiss her senseless.

"This aroma is driving me insane." She tapped the boxes in a show of impatience. "Can't you drive any faster?"

"Patience. We're almost there."

"May I ask you something personal? How'd you manage to still be a bachelor at forty?"

How did he answer? She'd run from the car screaming if he rushed to tell her the whole truth. "Guess I'm not that good with women."

"I know better than that. Seriously, why did you say you didn't date much?"

"I'm not very good at dating. Women find me too intense or too boring."

"Intense, maybe, but boring? I don't get it."

"Is this where you ask my dating history?" He slowed for a group of students crossing Main Street headed toward campus.

"Oh, no. I didn't mean it that way. It's just . . . I feel so fortunate that you want to be with me, even if you've been fighting it for days."

"That's funny. I'm thinking the same. What did I do to get so lucky?" He passed Ortega and the Alibi Bar, where Main turned into County Road 471. "As I said, I haven't much of a track record."

"You keep saying that. Whoever they were, these women were foolish not to latch on to a catch like you."

"Thanks." Taylor knew how to stroke his ego. Was that how Ben felt with Amy? Did he gaze at Taylor with the same lovesick fool look he'd seen on his brother-in-law's face?

"So explain."

"Okay. A couple years back, I took a lady out who was new in town. Cathleen Hodges and I attended the Suwannee River Jam for our first and only date. Turns out she didn't like country music or me. About a month later, she was murdered."

"Was she the vet? Wil told me about her."

"Yeah. In investigating, Wil found out she'd been in an abusive relationship before moving here. Maybe she just wasn't ready to date yet."

"That would do it for me. I'll never understand domestic violence."

"For all his faults, Dad treated Mom with respect. I never saw him abuse her, not even verbally."

"You can't let an abuse survivor who's reluctant to get involved convince you you're boring. It wasn't about you."

"Maybe you're right. But after Cathleen, I took out a friend of hers, Kris Knight. I honestly thought we could be good together. She was funny and smart. We had two dates, and then she told me she just didn't think we had chemistry. She'd been married once and admitted she was extremely selective about guys she dated."

"I'm very selective, and I don't think she could've done better than you." She reached for his hand and squeezed it. "But lack of chemistry doesn't mean *boring*."

"After Cathleen's murder, Kris seemed to have a change of heart. She called one night and invited me over to watch a movie with her, but I'd already promised Amy I'd be there for dinner. It was Ben's birthday. I tried to get Kris to go with me. Amy wouldn't have minded. She loves company. I've wished a thousand times Kris had gone."

"Oh, no. Is this the school teacher who was murdered?"

He nodded. "So after having two women I dated turn up dead . . . ."

"You didn't jinx them, Adam, if that's what you think. Wil told me all about that case. The killer went after Fia next."

"Yeah, I know, but after Kris died, other women shied away from me. I guess I scared them off."

She gave a low chuckle. "You don't scare me."

"Even though some probably suspected me of being a serial killer?"

"That's not funny."

"I'm not joking. Ask your brother. He had to question me about both homicides."

"I'm sure you weren't a suspect."

"Anyway, I never married." He was certainly finished with the topic of old girlfriends. Only one woman mattered, anyway: Taylor. "So how did you reach thirty-one without some guy marrying you?"

"Thirty-two. My story's fairly boring. I was married to my camera." She didn't elaborate. After a moment she sighed. "There's something about almost dying that forces you to reevaluate priorities."

"I can imagine." They reached the gate to Drake Oaks. The open, unlocked gate. "Did you follow up on having a coded gate opener installed?"

"Jamie helped me set up the automatic opener and the home security system with a company she vetted. They're scheduled to come tomorrow morning."

"That's the earliest appointment you could get?" Damn. Drake Oaks sat isolated at the edge of Osceola National Forest. "At the risk of scaring you, with Russo's killer at large, I'd like to stay out here tonight. Let's run it past Harold over pizza."

"You're going to eat with Dad?"

"I will if he will." Like it or not, Adam needed to get along with Taylor's father. He wasn't ready for forgiveness, but he had to try. As Zelda said, Taylor had been a toddler when the trouble between their two families began. She shouldn't have to suffer for the sins of her parents. "You told him all about Russo, right?"

"He knows what's going on. Just talk to him as if he's not in a wheelchair, okay?"

His stomach tightened at the thought of making nice with Harold Drake. How often, though, had he reminded the deputies *you can't let emotion cloud your judgment*? "I'm a professional. I know how to talk with people."

"Of course you do. I'm advising myself. Wil cautioned me that Dad needs to be independent. Seeing him in that wheelchair, though, just breaks my heart. He looks so . . . so broken. I catch myself babying him, and he hates that."

"Wouldn't you?"

She nodded. "The golden rule: Treat others as you would have them treat you. Such wise advice, and yet we forget."

He parked beside the porch stairway and cut the motor. "You and Amy have a lot in common."

"I'll take that as a compliment. Amy's a smart lady."

"Stay put. I'll come around and grab the pizzas from you." He hurried to the passenger door, but she already had it open. "So how do you feel after your outing? You made it back in one piece, champ."

Her smile beamed up at him as she handed him the boxes of pizza. "Yeah, I did. Thanks for letting me tag along."

Tag along? He treasured every moment he spent with her. Yeah, he had it bad. He was just too goofy happy. He forgot to be scared or worried, bad news for an acting sheriff who needed to focus on finding a killer. For all he knew, the guy could be lurking in the surrounding woods right now with a rifle scope trained on Taylor.

Sobering, he motioned her out of the car. "Let's get inside."

Thankfully she didn't argue. She joined him, skipping up the steps at his side. "What's wrong?"

"I just don't want to be an easy target out here."

She pushed him inside. "You think—"

"I'm being cautious."

She locked both deadbolts and then secured the chain. "So am I. Will you take the pizzas into the kitchen? I'll be right back."

"I thought you were hungry."

"I am. But I'm going upstairs to grab my gun."

Had he alarmed her unnecessarily? Unraveled her newfound confidence? No. Someone wanted Russo dead after he'd spied on Taylor. Adam couldn't ignore the danger to her. And he was already in too deep. She was no longer an assignment, merely the sister of his boss. Taylor was much, much more.

He couldn't bear it if he lost her now. How the hell had he let himself fall in love with her?

Chapter Eleven

Taylor sensed the tension in the kitchen the moment she ushered her dad through the door, but she trusted Adam to know what to say. She trusted Adam to safeguard her. She trusted Adam, period. The revelation should have unnerved her, yet she'd never felt more convinced about him. He was the one who registered at the top of her hero meter. Mr. Right. The man she could love.

Adam slid a slice of pizza onto his plate. He'd already put two slices on Harold's. "I wasn't sure which kind you'd like, so I gave you one of each. There's plenty more."

Dad positioned his chair at the end of the table and stared at the plate. "Either's fine."

She took her seat across from Adam. "Adam got us one with everything and one vegetarian with extra cheese. But first, Adam, will you ask the blessing?"

Maybe she put Adam on the spot, but she wanted to gauge his reaction. After her ordeal in Long Beach, she had found comfort in her faith. She needed to know if Adam shared her beliefs. He bowed his head and recited a brief prayer. If he was uncomfortable doing so, he hid it well.

Her dad managed to pick up a pizza slice one-handed and drag it to his mouth, leaving a trail of sauce and toppings, but she refused to get his bib. Hazel or Judy might find it practical, but she saw the embarrassment in her father's eyes whenever he wore it. She'd get him a clean pajama top when she returned him to his room. Her only concession to his disability was the flexible straw in his soda can.

By the time she and Adam had eaten their third slice of pizza, Dad had finished his first. He managed well on his own, considering. He stared at the second slice but didn't reach for it.

"Would you rather have the supreme, Harold?" Adam's sensitivity toward her father drove him further up on her hero meter—and he was already at the top. "I'm not too fond of the vegetarian, either."

"Yes." Dad's clipped response and his frown said he wasn't happy about having Adam at his table. But he needed to get used to it. If she had her way, Adam would be a frequent guest at Drake Oaks.

Adam slid a slice of supreme onto Dad's plate. "Here you go."

She couldn't help but smile. Her father, in true curmudgeon mode, couldn't resist Adam's cheery efforts. That he'd try so hard to be nice to Dad touched her. The two men had made no secret of their mutual hatred, but Adam was trying.

"Dad, until Jim's killer is caught, Adam thinks we might be in danger."

Her father chewed, swallowed, then scowled at Adam. "What do you plan to do about it?"

"With your consent, I'd like to spend the night out here. I can sleep on the sofa."

"With my consent?"

Adam shrugged. "It's your house, sir. If you'd rather not have me under your roof, I'll sleep out in the car."

Her father grunted. "I'm not an ass. You'll sleep on the sofa."

The three dined together without further conversation, like family. Almost. Dad shot an occasional glare her way, which she ignored. The melodious trill of the kitchen wall phone broke the silence, and she ran to answer it.

"Are you all right, darlin'?"

"Fine, Wil. Stop worrying."

"Adam told me what's going on. I don't like the idea of you and Dad out there by yourselves. Until they catch this killer, you could be in danger—"

"Relax. We aren't by ourselves. Adam's staying here."

A long silence. "Let me speak to him."

"Sure." She held out the phone to Adam. The ancient telephone had a long cord, but not long enough to stretch to the table. "He wants to talk to you."

Adam scooted from the table to take the phone, and Taylor rejoined her father. While Adam spoke in low tones, she turned to Dad to distract him from his blatant eavesdropping. "Wil's concerned about the killer, too."

"You like Gillespie, don't you?" The accusatory tone of his question startled her, although she should've expected it.

"Yes, I do. Very much."

"Watch yourself." Dad lowered his voice to a whisper. "I don't trust him."

"You should. He's a good man."

"Humph." He took another bite of pizza.

"The trip into town went well. I didn't panic. You may be right. I'm stronger than I thought."

His eyes softened then, and he nodded. Adam hung up the phone and returned to the table. Again they ate in silence until she pushed away her plate. She couldn't remember the last time she'd been able to eat so much. Another sign of progress? "That's enough pizza for me. I'm stuffed."

Adam met her gaze and winked. "Leaves more for me and Harold."

Her father didn't respond, but that was all right. At least Adam tried, and she loved him for it. *Loved* him? Better not to think in terms of love, or she'd run him off for sure. Hadn't she felt crowded and pressured by Jim Russo when he'd professed his love?

But nothing in her behavior had encouraged Jim's attentions. Adam said he had strong feelings toward her, that he wanted to be with her. He bent over backwards to be cordial to her father, a man he detested. She hadn't misread him. He *could* be falling in love with her, too. Or was it too soon to know?

Adam blew out a breath, a huge sigh of relief. Harold had refused his offer to help Taylor move him into bed, but at least he'd agreed to let Adam stay the night.

Taylor followed the dog to the back door. "I need to let Sophie out."

"Is Harold good for the night?"

"Yes. It took a long time, but he managed the bathroom by himself.

Plus we have a hydraulic lift that helps me move him." She stood by the back door, watching the dog.

"Get away from the door, Taylor."

"Oh, yeah. I guess that is risky."

"I don't want you near any windows, got it?"

She nodded. Soon the dog scratched at the door. Taylor wasted no time letting her back in then securing the locks. Sophie trotted off to Harold's room. Taylor paused to pull the door shut.

"Thanks for cleaning up the kitchen."

"No big deal. All I did was toss the pizza boxes and stick the plates in the dishwasher."

She turned off the hallway light. "Can't you just say 'you're welcome'?"

"You're welcome."

It would take time to figure out the next step for them. Despite his vow not to think about tomorrow, he let the future intrude in his mind. The sheriff's election loomed, less than three weeks from now. Regardless of the outcome, he'd give the campaign his best. He had his mother's illness to deal with, and Taylor needed to heal from her agoraphobia. He might never win over the Drake family, especially if he defeated Wil in the election, but he'd work on making peace. Taylor and Amy seemed willing to forget past offenses. Couldn't he?

With a flash of clarity, he got it. This was how Amy and Ben felt. With love in his life, he could treat others generously, just as they did. He bubbled over with happiness, enough to share. Amy wished for him to find someone. She should be glad he had.

Would she? When his twin sister hoped for him to find a woman to settle down with, she hadn't counted on the woman being a Drake. Hadn't she warned him against falling for Taylor?

Too late.

Now he needed to focus on security. Tomorrow the alarm company would install a system and automatic gate opener. Tonight Drake Oaks stood vulnerable and accessible. Why hadn't he stopped to lock the gate on the way in? If he ventured outside now, he'd frighten Taylor. If she didn't hear him leave the house, she'd hear the driveway alarm, and Harold would awaken. Adam would need to keep watch on the driveway.

His best vantage point was from the living room window. After about an hour, he struggled to hold his eyes open. He needed to stay alert. Suddenly a dark shape appeared beneath the security light at the entrance. At first he didn't trust his vision. Was that an SUV without its headlights turning in at the gate? He blinked, squinted, and confirmed a vehicle idling at the gate, at a point just shy of the motion detector that would trigger the driveway alarm. An SUV, perhaps, although he couldn't be sure without binoculars.

The hair at the back of his neck stiffened. Abruptly the driver reversed, backed out onto County Road 471, then sped away. Was the driver lost? Or had the presence of the FCSO vehicle scared him off? Most likely the latter, since a lost driver typically used headlights. Would the mystery driver return, possibly taking a different path to access the Drake house? If so, Adam would be lying in wait.

Taylor fought against waking from a deep sleep. Man, she hadn't slept so well without medication in months. Someone gave her a gentle shake, and she bolted upright in bed.

"Taylor, honey, it's Adam. I hate to wake you, but I need you to go downstairs and lock up behind me. I have to go home and change."

She yawned. "What time is it?"

"Five-thirty. Come on. We both have a busy day ahead."

"How long have you been awake?"

"All night. I told you I'd keep watch."

"But you need your sleep."

"I'll grab a nap later. Now get up and meet me downstairs."

He left, pulling the bedroom door closed behind him. Still struggling with grogginess, she padded to the dressing room, where her robe hung from a door hook. After wrapping the robe around her, she hurried downstairs.

At the door, he paused to kiss her goodbye. She curbed the impulse to ask when he'd be back. He had a busy schedule. He certainly didn't need a clingy, whiny woman to add to the pressures of his day.

He spared her from asking. "I'll be back when I can, babe. But we're having a family meeting today with Mom. Not sure when or how long."

"You take the time you need. I have my pistol, and Fred will be here with his. By this afternoon I should have a coded gate and a security alarm system. Plus Judy Wood will be here by eight or so to help with Dad. So don't worry about me, okay?"

"Can't help but worry. Promise you'll be careful." He unlocked the door but didn't open it. "I'll let you know as soon as I find out about your capsules, but the lab has a backlog."

She shuddered. "I don't plan to take any meds today, anyway. I've made a lot of progress in twenty-four hours."

"You're tough, champ." He gave her a brief kiss. "Remember that."

He stepped outside and waited while she locked and chained the door. Then she heard him step off the porch. Like a giddy schoolgirl, she raced to the dining room window to watch him. He strolled to his car, looking about as if monitoring his surroundings. Cop behavior, as she'd seen with Wil.

Good thing she couldn't vote in the upcoming election, because she'd struggle to choose between the two men she loved. Her brother, a skilled and competent law enforcement officer, was no less dedicated than Adam, who looked exhausted this morning from keeping vigil all night, denying himself much needed rest.

She watched until his car disappeared from view. The driveway alarm buzzed when he passed through the gate, but this time the noise didn't startle her. Although someone wanted her dead, she couldn't contain her newfound happiness. She was healing, and she was in love. With a lighter step, she bounded upstairs for a shower. She had plenty of time to primp and dress before her father needed her help getting up. Maybe by that time, Judy would arrive.

Adam poured his second cup of coffee, although it was barely eight o'clock. He needed the caffeine to stay awake. Earlier he'd had to force Devon to go home for some shuteye. The guy had been at the computer most of the night, researching Russo and all his known associates. Both he and Adam suspected a tie to something in California, but what? Jamie could pick up where Devon left off when she arrived.

"Got a sec, Adam?" Brady Newcomb entered the break room and followed him to his office. "This may be unrelated, but I think you need to hear about it."

"Grab a chair." He indicated the seat across from his desk. "What's going on?"

"Suwannee County has a homicide. They found a woman's body yesterday hidden under some brush behind a vacant house off Highway 90. Blunt force trauma to the head, although that's not official. The ME still has to do the post mortem."

"What's that have to do with our investigation?"

"Early this morning at the same lot, hidden behind debris, they found the stolen Yamaha, along with the purple helmet."

Adam nearly choked on his coffee. "Have they ID'd the victim?"

"Not yet. But they're checking missing person reports in both North Florida and South Georgia. I'll let you know soon as I hear back."

"This could be a break in the case. We need one."

Brady nodded. "I'm betting she had a vehicle. Probably car-jacked, unless she's Russo's killer."

"Why would she be a suspect?"

"Well . . . in a way, she fits the description. Silver hair, sturdy shoes like nurses wear, and she was dressed in medical scrubs." Brady shrugged.

"Geraldo said the impostor was short, stocky, and had a hairy mole on her chin. Any of that fit?"

"I'll find out. But if she killed Russo, who killed *her*? This is sounding like a game of musical chair murders."

"Let's stick to the facts and not theorize. We can't do much with this until we know who the victim is. Keep on it. Get Geraldo involved, since he's our best eye witness."

Brady left, then Zelda poked her head in the door. "Amy wants you to call her cell. And Geraldo Blanco needs to speak with you."

"Thanks. Tell Geraldo to give me five minutes." He picked up the telephone and dialed Amy's number.

She answered immediately. "Adam, we're meeting with the doctor at eleven. Then I'll head home. Mom had an easy night, probably because they pumped her full of drugs. I told them to keep her pain-free."

"Yeah, it's not like we have to worry she'll get addicted."

"Amen to that. I want her to be comfortable for as long as she lives. If you can get away from work, we're meeting at her house around six. Ben's picking up a rotisserie chicken dinner from Miller's. Mama Sawyer is keeping the boys."

"I'll be there."

"Thanks. But if something comes up on your murder case, Mom will understand. You know how committed she is to your campaign."

"Get real, Amy. You think this matters more than family?"

"I hear ya, little brother, but you know Mom."

After ending the call, Adam stared into space, his thoughts scattered. He certainly didn't have the election in the bag. Four years ago it had been a tight race, and Wil Drake hadn't been the incumbent then. If Adam lost, his mother would be devastated. He needed to win, if for no other reason, as a last gift to her.

If for no other reason? Winning the election wasn't a priority for Adam. When had that happened? Or had it ever been as important to him as it was to Mom? Sure, his pride had been injured when he lost his police chief position. He'd resented taking second in command to Wilson Drake. But many of the officers had had to adjust to consolidation. Now the department had begun to recover their team culture. Frankly, he enjoyed working as the chief deputy. Was he after the golden ring only to please his mother . . . his *dying* mother?

Geraldo peeked in the door, interrupting Adam's reverie. "Come on in, Geraldo."

"I need a favor. I caught Buzz at Cari Mercer's window last night, luckily before her mama called it in. I'm at my wit's end with the kid, so I sort of . . . arrested him."

"Sort of?"

"Call it a mock arrest, though my dumbass kid brother doesn't know the difference. I threw him in a cell overnight. Mama knows about it, and frankly, agrees with me."

"About what?"

"Well . . . ." Geraldo sighed, his gaze darting around the room. "I sentenced him to community service, to be served after school each day for the next five school days."

"So what's the favor? Want me to talk to him?"

"No, I want you to give him something to do. I figure if he serves out this so-called sentence here at the sheriff's office, I can keep tabs on him."

Adam couldn't help but smile. "Actually, I have just the thing for him. Let's assign him to Zelda. She has plenty of filing, copying, and errands. I'll discuss it with her now."

Geraldo smiled. "That's a great idea."

"So is your mock arrest. Buzz needs to know, though, next time it goes on his record."

"Oh, I already warned him of that."

After Geraldo left, Adam made a list of everything related to the Connie Drake auto accident, starting with her autopsy. He intended to keep his promise to Taylor and get all the information he could about her mother's death. Pulling old records at the musty archives building would keep Buzz Blanco out of trouble and Zelda at her desk handling current business.

Taylor stood in the kitchen with nothing to do. After cleaning up the breakfast dishes, she'd started the dishwasher. The camera she'd ordered online wouldn't arrive before Friday. The personnel from Cameron Security, having wired all the windows with some kind of sensors, had left for a lunch break. Judy helped Dad with his shower. Fred Fischer hammered in the barn, putting the finishing touches on the horse stalls. Adam would be tied up all day, possibly all night. Who knew when she'd see him again?

On impulse she located Hazel Porter's number and called her. After identifying herself, she said, "I need your advice."

"Sure, Taylor. Is it about your daddy?"

"No, it's about cooking. I found a pork tenderloin roast in the freezer. I haven't a clue how to cook it, but I thought it might be nice to make dinner tonight for Dad. We could eat leftovers tomorrow."

"Got any garlic cloves?"

"Sure do."

"You can roast it in the oven or the large slow cooker. The secret is to cook it low and slow." Hazel gave her detailed instructions, which Taylor jotted on a notepad. "How's Miss Judy working out?"

"Fine. Never offers to cook, though. I'll be glad when you return."

"Soon as that murderer's caught, honey, I'll be there. Tell Judy hi for me."

Taylor ended the call. Just as she replaced the receiver, the telephone rang. "Hello."

"It's Adam. Just checking to see if Fred got there." The sound of his voice brought happy flutters to her chest.

"He's here. So are Judy Wood and the techs from Cameron Security, although they just left for lunch."

"Will they be able to finish today?"

"Yes. They said everything's done except for finishing up the control panels by the doors and then the gate opener."

"Amy called. We're having dinner tonight at my mother's house, so I don't know when I can stop by. But I'll be there later."

"You sound tired."

"I am, but I'll grab a nap before dinner. Do you have your weapon with you?"

"In my apron pocket."

"Keep it close. There's been another homicide, next county over, but

154

we think it could be related. I'll fill you in tonight."

"I'll be vigilant."

"I'll call when I leave Mom's so you can give me the gate code."

"It's one-two-three-four. They said I have to reset it."

"Be sure you do. It's important."

Could she leave the house and walk two blocks or so to the gate? The one time she'd tried to walk to the mailbox, she'd made it no farther than the porch steps. But that was last week. She'd made a lot of progress since then. "I'll try."

"You need to. Get Fred to go with you. I don't want you out there alone."

"I can do that. I'm going to beat this silly agoraphobia."

"Sure you are, champ. Don't underestimate your inner strength." Someone's muffled voice in the background interrupted him. "I need to go. Check back with you later."

Dial tone. She would have preferred a *love you, babe* or at least a *goodbye*. Of course he hadn't said he loved her, either in person or over the phone, much as she wished he would. Adam was the consummate professional, though. He couldn't sweet talk her and say he loved her from the office. But would he say it at all?

By late afternoon, Adam's battle with drowsiness worsened. Excessive ingestion of caffeine failed to keep him awake.

"Go home, Adam. I can call you if anything comes up." Zelda stood at the corner of his desk. He hadn't heard her approach, which spoke volumes about his alertness.

"It's only three-thirty."

"I can tell time. I can also see that you pulled an all-nighter."

He gave her a wry grin. "Yeah. I'm too old for this crap."

"You need a couple of hours' rest before going to see your mama tonight."

He didn't ask how she knew. Zelda shamelessly eavesdropped and seemed to have her finger on the pulse of the entire station. "Did that kid

Buzz Blanco show up after school?"

"Sure did. I just sent him to the archives."

"All right. We're at a standstill until Jamie or Brady learn more about Suwannee County's latest victim. Promise you'll have either of them call my cell if they find out anything new."

"Promise." Zelda stood, hands on hips, and glared until he got up to leave.

"Okay, okay. I'm out of here." He opened his middle desk drawer to put away his deputy scheduling sheet. There lay the report Jamie had prepared on Judy Wood. He scanned it, then tossed it on his desk. "I guess I don't need this anymore."

"I'll file it. Now, get out of here." She added foot tapping to her stern routine. "Go home and straight to bed."

He locked his desk. "Yes, ma'am."

Jamie rushed into his office almost barreling into Zelda. "Devon compiled this list of the various missing persons. I think we have a serious problem."

"What's wrong?"

Her gaze dropped to the report on Judy Wood. She tapped it with her index finger. "It's Judy Wood. She's on the list. Last seen yesterday morning."

"What?" His heart jack hammered his chest. "Then who the hell is the woman out at Drake Oaks claiming to be her?"

Zelda withdrew to her desk, and Jamie picked up the report on Judy Wood. "My gut tells me this is Suwannee County's homicide victim. Matches the description. We have a *be-on-the-lookout* issued on her vehicle."

"Let's go. You drive. I'll call Taylor." They raced out to her Ford sedan. When he got in, he dialed Taylor's cell phone. After seven or eight rings, it transferred to a voice mailbox. She'd plugged it in its charger last night. Had she left it there? "She doesn't answer her cell."

"Call the house."

"What if the line is tapped?"

"It's not anymore. Phone company security is monitoring it for us."
He scrolled to the number and punched the send button. And waited.

Taylor worked up her courage to program the new gate code. She could do it. First, she needed to walk out back to the barn and get Fred Fischer. Judy had Dad settled in his chair to watch television, and the Cameron Security technicians had walked Taylor through arming, disarming, and re-coding the control panel. So what was keeping her from venturing outside?

She could do this. Both Dad and Adam had confidence in her. She patted the pistol in her apron pocket, then moved through the laundry room to the back door. Taking a deep breath, she unlocked the deadbolts. Just then the telephone rang.

"Saved by the bell." She returned to the kitchen and answered it.

"Taylor, listen carefully and don't argue." Adam's calm tone didn't hide the urgency in his voice. "Go get Fred. Now. Judy Wood is dead. The woman there is an impostor. Get out of the house. We're on our way."

Dead? Another murder? She tried to breathe. To move. "I—I can't leave Dad," she whispered.

"Hurry. Get Fred now. Leave the phone off the hook—"

The line went dead. Taylor spun around and came face to face with the impostor, who had broken the connection. *Stupid, stupid Taylor*. Of course the woman wasn't Judy Wood. If she'd paid attention, she would've seen the signs. Beneath the caked makeup hid a much younger face, with an ugly mole on her chin that all the concealer in the world couldn't hide. She lifted weights, judging by the thickness of her arms.

Adam said he was on his way, but where was he now? She had to keep her wits, to play along with the disguise. She reached for the phone, but the woman knocked her aside. Who knew she could pack such a strong punch? Stunned, Taylor managed to recover her balance and eased back toward the door. She'd left it unbolted, hadn't she? She didn't have a second to waste.

The impostor yanked the receiver from the phone, then unplugged its spring-coiled cord. "You won't need this."

She forced herself to focus. "Judy, what are you doing?"

"I think we both know I'm not Judy." The woman took the phone cord and stretched it between her hands, stepping toward Taylor as if she planned to—

No! The impostor intended to wrap the cord around her neck. *Move, Taylor. Run!* She rushed toward the door, but the impostor was too quick and too strong. She grabbed Taylor's arm and dragged her stumbling into the kitchen.

"Why are you doing this?"

But the impostor wasn't explaining. Much as Taylor struggled, the woman overpowered her. She shoved Taylor to the floor, knocking the breath from her lungs. Face mashed against the tile floor, she tried to fight back, but the woman's weight bore down, robbing her of precious oxygen. Spots danced in her eyes, and she gasped for air.

The attacker then did what Taylor dreaded most—snaked the phone cord around her neck and tightened it against her throat. Still tender from the knife injury, the healing scar throbbed. Worse yet, Taylor couldn't breathe. If only she could stay conscious long enough to reach her pistol. She wriggled her hand beneath her, slipping it into the pocket holding her Cobra .380. She thumbed off the safety, for all the good it did. In her current position, she'd be able to shoot herself in the thigh. No way could she hit her assailant.

She tried to inhale. She couldn't. Worse than any anxiety attack, she couldn't even swallow. Hot pain sliced through her neck. Her head swam. Darkness edged her vision and closed in. *Dear God, please help me!*

Chapter Twelve

Siren blaring, Jamie sped down County Road 471. The narrow highway, which primarily carried tourists and hunters to the national forest, wasn't designed for high speeds. The meandering blacktop tested Jamie's driving skills . . . and Adam's patience. Better that he let Jamie drive, though. His body vibrated tension, and his knees threatened to collapse. Fear held him in its grip. Surely Taylor hadn't hung up on him. His instincts said someone—the killer?—had broken the connection.

"Oh, God." If anything happened to Taylor— "Hurry."

"We're no good to her if we panic." Jamie gripped the steering wheel and whipped around a curve. "Stay focused on saving her, okay?"

"Damn it, I am."

"I care about her, too, you know. We've gotten to be friends." Jamie slowed for another curve, but not enough to keep from locking up their seatbelts. "I'm thinking the killer learned of Taylor's plan to hire Judy Wood from the wiretap. Then she—or he—made the substitution."

Adam swore. "The impostor was in the house all day yesterday. That's probably when she tampered with Taylor's medicine."

"Did you hear back yet from the lab?"

"No, but my money's on cyanide. It's hard to mistake that odor. Thank God Taylor didn't take any."

"Lucky that cleaning service was there all day, too." She stomped the accelerator. "Almost there. Hold on."

He strained to see into the distance, watching for the turnoff to Drake Oaks. He barely made out the weathered sign beneath the security lamp towering over the gate. "There!"

Jamie braked, fishtailed, then ground to a stop at the closed gate. She lowered her window to access the keypad. "I sure as hell hope you know the gate code."

"Try one-two-three-four." He hoped Taylor hadn't reprogrammed it yet, even though he'd urged her to.

Jamie punched in the numbers and waited. After a three second delay that seemed like three minutes, the motor hummed and the gate crept open. "Too bad there isn't a speed adjustment on these things."

The gate finally opened enough to let them through. A red Honda Pilot backed in at the house could have been the suspicious vehicle he'd seen at the gate last night. Jamie pointed. "That's the BOLO, Judy Wood's vehicle." As soon as Jamie parked, they jumped from the cruiser, then raced up the porch steps to the door. The *locked* door. "Ring the doorbell?"

But Adam wasn't wasting another second. He had to get to Taylor. "Hell, no. Let's test this new security alarm."

He hoisted a heavy wooden rocking chair from the porch and crashed it through the living room window. The report of a gunshot echoed from the back of the house.

Was he too late?

Taylor fought to stay conscious, her cheek pressed into the cold tile. The attacker relentlessly twisted the cord against her tender throat. Suddenly aware of a faraway rumble, she felt the floor vibrate. At the same time, the cord at her neck slackened. She tried to gulp air, but managed only a tiny breath. The rumble morphed into a whine, like a motor—

Like a motorized wheelchair. Dad! She tried to twist her head to see. Suddenly the attacker shifted, freeing Taylor from her deadly hold. A tangle of bodies and wheelchair toppled over her, pinching and mashing her legs. But then she could move. Dizzy and gasping for breath, she rolled to her side. She needed to take advantage of the distraction. Her finger slipped over the trigger of her pistol. She had to make every second count. Aiming for the impostor, she held her breath, squeezed the trigger, then collapsed against the floor.

She had no idea if she hit the woman. At least the noise would be enough to summon Fred Fischer from the barn. Sophie cowered in the corner barking nonstop. Like a distant siren, the cacophony rang in

Taylor's ears. Then she thought she heard the sound of breaking glass. The odor of burned fiber from the hole in her apron compounded her efforts to catch her breath. Although no longer choked, she still couldn't seem to pull enough oxygen into her lungs.

Her gaze found her father, lying opposite her attacker. He winked at her. Thank God, he wasn't hurt. It took enormous effort to move her hand to reach the cord still looped around her neck. She rose to her elbows and stared at the blood oozing from the attacker's shoulder. She couldn't make her voice work to speak. If her vocal cords were injured again, she'd sound worse than ever.

"Strawberry?" Her father lay on his side facing her. "I think you got *Mrs. Doubtfire*."

Mrs. Doubtfire? Dad had taken her to see that movie for her fourteenth birthday. Although at the time she'd thought it funny, he hadn't liked the idea of a man disguising himself as a woman. A man disguising himself . . . .

Meeting her father's gaze, she tried to question him with her eyes.

"Beneath all that makeup is a man."

The attacker groaned, so she—no, *he* had survived Taylor's shot. Fred banged at the door, then stepped inside, gun first. Suddenly Adam and Jamie Peterson rushed in from the hallway. How had they gotten in? Everyone yelled at once, pounced on *Mrs. Doubtfire* to subdue her, and fired questions at Taylor. But her vocal cords produced only a rasping sound.

"Get her some water," Dad said.

Jamie handed her a cup of water. At first she couldn't swallow. But after a few sips, she drank normally. "Thanks," she whispered. She could talk again, even if she did sound like a bad case of laryngitis.

Meanwhile, Fred helped upright her father and his wheelchair. She rushed to Dad and buried her face in his neck. "Oh, Dad, you saved my life." All the stress of the attack caught up with her, and she sobbed.

More police arrived on the scene in response to her alarm system. Adam explained he'd shattered the windowpane, which explained the sound of breaking glass.

Fred edged toward the back door. "I have a sheet of plywood on the truck I can nail up for tonight. I'll pick up a new window tomorrow."

Dad was the hero of the day. In giving his statement, he explained how he'd set his wheelchair to its highest speed and plowed into the attacker, the momentum knocking pseudo-Judy off balance and freeing Taylor.

"Good job, Mr. D." Fred gave Dad a thumbs up.

The same two paramedics who had treated Taylor on Tuesday arrived and checked out her injuries, while two deputies arrested her attacker. One of the deputies, a heavyset woman named Tracy Sinclair, handed Jamie the impostor's large vinyl purse. "Before we bag this, you may want to check out the cell phones."

Jamie snapped on latex gloves then delved inside the cavernous handbag. "Lots of medical paraphernalia, too." She pulled out two cell phones. One was an older model white iPhone with a chipped corner.

Taylor gasped. "That looks like Roz's. Hers was damaged at the corner from when it got caught in the recliner."

Adam peered over Jamie's shoulder. "Is it?"

"I'll see." Jamie beeped through several screens. "This is the phone that e-mailed the photo of you two." She held it out to show them the picture. "This links our offender with Taylor's attack in Long Beach."

Adam's jaw tensed. "I'll be curious to see how he explains this."

Tracy snorted. "Good luck. He ain't talking to either me or Kurt."

The night Jim lay on the stretcher, he'd seemed confused when Taylor confronted him about the picture. *I don't know what you're talking about.* "So Jim really didn't know anything about the e-mailed photo."

"Maybe not," Jamie said. "But don't forget he set up the Bluetooth on your barn."

Adam nodded. "I know you thought him a friend, but he stalked you."

Yet Taylor couldn't forget her last words to him. *You sick bastard.* Now he was dead. Even if guilty of stalking her, he hadn't deserved to be murdered.

Karen saw Dad to his room before the EMTs left. Fred went outside to board up the window. Cameron Security reset the system and temporarily bypassed the living room window sensor. The two deputies left with their prisoner, and Jamie stepped outside to place a phone call.

Finally Taylor had a moment alone with Adam.

Seated at the table in the breakfast room, she tried to smile. "I guess you're tired of having to respond to all my crises."

He leaned against the kitchen doorjamb. "That was some shooting, champ."

"Lucky shot." She showed him the hole in her apron pocket. "You know each time Dad retells this story, it'll be the *Mrs. Doubtfire* tale."

"What Harold did took guts." Was that a tiny bit of respect in his voice? "He's earned the right to brag about it. I shudder to think how it could've gone wrong."

"Yeah, but you know what? I didn't panic. I mean, no more than a normal person would. And now I realize how wrong I've been in thinking of this as my safe place. Both times some bastard's tried to kill me, it's happened inside my home. So how is it sane to be afraid to leave?"

He shrugged. "I'm no psychiatrist."

She huffed an exasperated sigh. "At least you could say something affirming, like 'It's not sane, and you are, so you must be recovering'."

He tried for a chuckle, but fatigue clouded his eyes. "Don't forget to clean your weapon now that it's been fired."

"I remember."

His gaze softened. "I need to kiss you."

"I need that, too." She bolted from the chair and into his arms. "But don't be surprised if I start boo-hooing again."

He covered her lips with a firm, almost desperate kiss. She leaned into him, savoring the taste of him and the warmth of his embrace. She didn't care if Dad rolled in and saw them. No way she'd be embarrassed or ashamed of loving Adam.

"I don't want to feel that kind of fear again. I thought I'd lost you, babe."

She laid her cheek against his shoulder. "I'm not that easy to get rid of."

He kissed her again. And again. Then with great reluctance, she stepped away. "We'll continue this discussion later. I know you need to get back to town."

Adam hesitated, scrubbing his face in a gesture of weariness. "Honey, who is that guy? Did you know him?"

"Never saw him before yesterday, although with all that makeup, it's hard to say."

"He wasn't your attacker in Long Beach?"

"I never saw him. He wore latex gloves and held me in such a way I couldn't look at his face."

"If you don't know him, we need to find out his motive. He may have killed Russo, too. Think. Did you and Jim work together on any assignments where you could've made enemies?"

"Not that I can remember, but I'll think about it."

"I wish I could tell you this is over, that we have the bad guy in custody."

"We don't?"

"It's possible someone hired him. Who and why is a big question mark, and so far, *Mrs. Doubtfire*'s not talking. So stay alert, watch your back, and take another look at that last photo shoot of yours."

She nodded. "Maybe if Jamie can get the photos enlarged for me, I can see something I missed."

"I'll have her bring the enlargements out later. Tell her what you need."

"All right."

"We're working with Detective Raizor out in L.A. to see if Russo's death could be related to your original attack." He glanced at his watch.

"It's after five." She walked him to the kitchen door. "You better get to your mother's house."

"I need to. But whatever you have in the oven has me drooling."

"Yikes! I forgot about my pork roast. Hazel told me 'low and slow,' but I'm sure it's done by now."

"You'll have to make it again sometime." He winked. "For me."

"It's a date." She planted a quick kiss on his lips. "But be glad I'm practicing first."

She'd love to cook his dinner every night. Would that idea send him running? Although she didn't want to scare him with talk of the future, she couldn't shake the overwhelming sense that they were running out of time.

During dinner, Amy and his mother tossed about words like *Hospice* and *advanced cancer* as if they were discussing a stranger's case. Adam wanted to scream. *This is* Mom*'s life we're talking about!*

He hardly tasted the rotisserie chicken or the roasted vegetables. The green beans with new potatoes, usually a favorite of his, disappeared from his plate without any memory of his having eaten them. The dull ache in his temples burgeoned into a full-blown headache.

"No more treatments. I want to feel well enough to enjoy my grandsons."

"I plan to tell the boys the truth," Amy said. "Travis is at such a tender age, though."

Finally, Adam asked, "Isn't there anything we can do?"

"Just keep me comfortable. I refuse to be a burden to my children—"

"We'd never think of you as a burden, Granny Gee," Ben said.

Amy asked Ben to pick up their sons, even though Ben's mother offered to keep them another night. "I've missed them. I want to be with all three of my guys tonight."

"Go on with Ben. I'll help Mom clean up."

"I'll take you up on that offer, little brother."

Amy seemed so sad, but so was he. Exhausted from no sleep, he'd fought his emotions all through the meal.

After they left, his mom closed the door and faced him. "Leave the dishes. I'll get them later."

"Go sit. It'll just take a minute to rinse and load the dishwasher." He welcomed the moment alone to get a grip.

"I need to talk to you, son. It's complicated, and it's important." Never had she seemed so defeated. The fleece warm-up suit she wore drooped from her thin body. She'd given up.

"I'll be right in."

She wasn't about to let him clean up in solitude. Still the control freak he knew and loved, she stayed in the kitchen until the dishes were loaded to suit her. Then he followed her into the den, where she collapsed in her worn recliner.

He sat in the nearest chair. "Are you sure you don't want to try more chemotherapy, Mom?"

She shook her head. "I've been all through that with Amy. It won't save me. It will buy me a little more time, is all, and I refuse to spend my last weeks, especially the holidays, sick and unable to enjoy being with my family."

"I'd feel the same way, I guess. But I'm selfish. I don't want to lose you."

She smiled. "It's funny, isn't it? A mother tries to spare her children from hurt, yet how can she when she's the source of their pain?"

He swallowed the lump in his throat and fought for composure. "It's not as if you can help it."

"No. But I can't say I'm surprised to learn I have cancer. I don't want you wasting your life in bitterness the way I have. Amy's been warning me for years about holding onto hate and resentment—"

"Stop it!" What hogwash had his sister been feeding her? "Your feelings didn't give you cancer."

She shook her head. "Guilt is a destructive emotion, son."

"Guilt? Why are we talking about guilt?"

"Because something has been eating away at me a lot longer than cancer. I need to tell you, and what you do with the information is up to you."

Anxiety squeezed his gut. "What?"

"I did something wrong, very wrong. Illegal."

"Mom, wait. You know as an officer of the law—"

"That's why I have to tell you. If I'm to be arrested, I'd prefer my son do it."

He bristled. "Nobody's arresting you—"

"Please, Adam, stop interrupting. Let me get this out, all right?"

He nodded, forcing his fists to unfurl. Tension seized his spine and his shoulders throbbed. Pounding in his ears matched the pulsing inside his chest.

She picked up a book and thumbed through it. "Zelda Brooks brought over this Malachy McCourt book. I guess I needed it, but I wish I'd read it thirty years ago." She found the passage she sought and read "'Resentment is like taking poison and waiting for the other person to die.'"

"That sounds like some of Amy's karma crap."

"It's not crap; it's true. Please don't waste another minute of your life hating the people I've taught you to hate. I'm not saying be their best friends, but stop nursing my old grudges."

"What's this have to do with guilt?"

Laying the book aside, she sighed. "I haven't been honest with you about your father. But then I haven't been completely honest with myself. All those Sundays I sat in church and prayed for forgiveness—"

"Forgiveness for what?" The unease in his gut tightened. "You had every right to hate the Drakes after—"

"I've been a world class hypocrite. Your father took risks he shouldn't have. He went into debt and spent every dime we had on a scheme, without adequate research. The county commission acted responsibly in turning down his zoning request."

Lack of sleep, along with his mother's revelations, culminated in a killer headache. "Why did you blame Harold Drake?"

She flipped a hand like swatting at an annoying insect. "Harold Drake was a sanctimonious asshole. I blamed him for everything because I couldn't blame Jed. I loved Jed, too much. Much more than he loved me."

Adam wouldn't argue. Had there ever been a time when his parents showed genuine affection for each other? He'd seen nothing between them like he saw now with Amy and Ben. "The commissioners could have compromised with Dad."

"How? He'd bet the farm, quite literally, on building that water park and hotel. Stuck with the land, all we could do was sell what little we owned and move out there in a trailer."

Amy would be offended to hear Mom call a manufactured house a trailer, but he let it slide. "We kids didn't mind. It was a fun place to grow up."

"It was no fun for your father and me. We struggled, and he drank, and then he became obsessed with revenge. He told me his plan, you know, to seduce Connie Drake, and I was a gullible fool."

"You didn't object?"

"Wouldn't have mattered. The sordid truth was Jed loved her. The revenge story was a cover for their affair."

Adam's head reeled. Sweat dampened his spine. "When did you know?"

"A woman knows, son."

Sweat turned to icy prickles. Dread filled his chest. The bottom dropped from his stomach. He had to ask the question he'd vowed he'd never ask. "What happened the night Connie died?"

She laughed, more of a humorless terrible snort. "That's what I'm getting at. It's the real reason I've hated Harold Drake all these years."

"Which is?"

"He wouldn't take Connie back or forgive her. If he had, Jed would've gotten over her, and eventually we could have patched things up. But Connie had nowhere to go, and Jed said he was leaving me . . . for her. Can't you see? I couldn't let that happen."

His blood roared in his ears. "What. Did. You. Do?"

"Your father had already bankrupted us, honey. Then he was going to leave me to raise three kids with nothing? I could've killed him. But instead . . . ." She shrugged.

He closed his eyes, but he couldn't shut his ears. He couldn't block the awful thing he suspected she wanted to confess. "Instead?"

"I killed Connie."

Chapter Thirteen

Soon after the police and paramedics left, Sam called, and she invited him to dinner.

"Only if you'll let me bring a dish."

Taylor laughed in spite of her sore throat. Something definitely had changed in her brother's life. "Stop by the deli at Miller's and get whatever vegetable dish they have that goes well with a pork tenderloin roast."

"Sounds delicious."

"Curb your high expectations, bro. It's my first attempt. I make no promises." She hesitated. "Uh, we had some excitement out here this afternoon."

"So I heard. No one was injured?"

"We're fine, although I'm going to have some bruises and sore muscles. I shot the bad guy, but just in his shoulder."

"You shot somebody?"

"He was trying to kill me. But Dad saved my life. He'll tell you all about it at dinner."

"That's twice you've shot that pistol of yours. I'll remember not to sneak up on you."

"Which reminds me, we have an electric gate opener now. You need the code to open it. It's one-two-three-four."

"How enigmatic."

"I'm supposed to reprogram it, but I'll do it tomorrow."

At seven, she served her family not-too-bad pork tenderloin, cranberry muffins she'd baked from a mix, and the bowl of green beans cooked with new potatoes that Sam brought from the Deli.

"My sister has become domesticated. I am utterly impressed."

"Thank Hazel. She talked me through it. In all the excitement, I forgot the pork and left it in the oven too long, which is why it's not sliced. It just fell apart." A bonus, as it turned out, because her father had no trouble eating the tender meat. Just as Hazel promised, low and slow made a roast foolproof and juicy, too. "Thanks for being my test subjects."

"You can try out recipes on me anytime," Sam said. "Now I want to hear about my father, the hero."

"Taylor fired her gun," Dad said around a mouthful of pork. "Hit *Mrs. Doubtfire* in one shot."

"Adam says you showed a lot of courage, Dad."

Sam's gaze ricocheted from Dad to her. "So does Gillespie know why the guy wanted to kill you?"

"He's working on it. Actually, local detectives think it could be tied to the original attack in Long Beach." She shrugged. "My photography equipment, along with my picture files, was stolen. I'm reviewing my last photo shoot to see if maybe the answers are in the pictures."

"Mind if I take a look?" Sam asked.

"Please do. A fresh set of eyes couldn't hurt."

Adam stared at his mother, trying to make sense of her confession. She had killed Connie Drake? How? Luke Meiners told him Connie seemed fine when she left her at the Alibi Bar. "You'd better explain."

Mom folded her hands in her lap. "Connie wanted to meet for a drink. To talk, she said. I had nothing to say to that woman, but I agreed to get together. And then I doctored her drink."

"You poisoned her?"

She shook her head. "I sedated her. I had a prescription for pills to treat insomnia. It was pretty strong stuff, but I've forgotten the name. Whatever it was, it wasn't refillable. I remember that. I emptied the bottle and crushed all the tablets into powder."

"So you mixed a sedative with alcohol. No wonder she crashed into a tree. Oh, Mom, how could you?" How the hell could he tell Taylor? "Connie wanted to apologize to you. She was trying to reconcile with Harold."

"Who told you that?"

"Taylor found Connie's letters. So did she apologize?"

Weariness dragged at her features. "I guess, but by that time, she'd drunk most of her wine."

"Damn. Do you realize how much damage you've—"

"There's more, son. I should've come clean a long time ago, but who would've raised my children if I was in prison?"

"More than murder?" The roaring in his ears competed with the pounding of his pulse. "You have any aspirin? I suddenly have a killer headache."

"In my medicine cabinet, son."

"Be right back." In the bathroom, he located the aspirin bottle and shook out three tablets. Three hundred wouldn't cure the pain in his head. Could his day get any worse? After downing the pills with a cup of water, he returned to the den to face the rest of his mother's confession. "All right. What else?"

"I'm fairly sure Megan knew. She walked into the bathroom as I was crushing the pills."

Adam gasped. "No."

"She overheard my telephone conversation with Connie, so she probably put it together. But she was barely fourteen. I didn't count on her being so perceptive. From the time she heard about Connie's death, she gave me a rough time. It was as if she was blackmailing me. She deliberately misbehaved and tormented me, though she never came right out and accused me."

That could explain his sister's rebellion. "Then she died in a car wreck, too."

"Don't think I missed the irony of that. I thought God was punishing me by taking my firstborn and my unborn grandchild, too. But that's not how God works. God didn't have to punish me. I've done a splendid job of raking myself across the coals."

Heat flushed his skin from trying to contain his rage. What good did her confession do? He wanted to hate her for what she'd done, especially the grief she'd caused Megan. But she had little time to live. How could he waste it being angry with her?

She held his gaze. "Tell me what you're thinking."

"I don't know what I'm thinking!" He stood and paced the room, beating his fist into his palm.

"Please don't hate me, Adam."

"I don't hate you." But he was damned angry with her. "First, you tell me you're dying, and then before I can get my head wrapped around the idea of losing you, you tell me you're a criminal. And your twisted scheme destroyed my sister, too."

She'd destroyed more than their family; she'd destroyed his future. How in the world could he tell the woman he loved, the one he now knew he wanted permanently in his life, that *his* mother had killed *her* mother?

Taylor met him at the door at eleven-thirty with a shy smile. Harold must have been asleep since she whispered her greeting. She'd done something different with her hair. Everything about her looked damned good. He stepped inside the foyer and waited for her to lock up.

Then he swept her into his arms and kissed her as if it would be their last embrace. After he told her what he'd learned about her mother's death, he doubted she'd want to kiss him. She'd probably kick him out of her life. He was so screwed, and just when he thought they might have stood a chance.

"You got my message about the photo?" In reviewing the enlargements, she'd recognized the man in the suit as a businessman who'd been indicted, but she couldn't remember his name or the nature of his trouble.

"Yeah. E-mailed the file to LAPD. Now we wait."

"You must be exhausted." Taking his hand, she led him toward the kitchen. "I have some decaf."

He stopped. "Honey, I don't think I can stay awake to drink any."

"Then sleep. I have the sofa made up for you."

He stifled a yawn. "First I need to talk to you. It's important."

"It'll wait until morning. Get some sleep.

He had to tell her about her mother. "First we talk."

She pushed him toward the sofa. "We'll talk in the morning. I'll make you breakfast."

She gave him a quick kiss then disappeared. He removed his shoes and stretched out, sinking his head in the soft pillow. But he needed to tell her something. What was it? Closing his eyes, he savored the taste of her kiss on his lips and the lingering scent of her hair. The tension in his spine dissolved. He needed to tell her . . . *what*? Drowsiness swept over him, dragging him down like a mind-numbing elixir.

Whatever he needed to say could wait until morning. Surrendering to fatigue, he sank into oblivion.

The digital clock read 5:05. Taylor eased out of bed and dressed in the dark. She crept downstairs, feeling her way along the wall for the light switch. The glare from the sudden brightness blinded her for a few seconds until her eyes adjusted. Typically she slept later, but Adam would need to go by his house to shower and change.

What she wouldn't give to wake up every morning with Adam, to make his breakfast and kiss him goodbye. Where had that fantasy of domesticity come from? She'd never been the homemaker type. But she'd never been in love, either. Funny how loving Adam put a different spin on everyday living. Now she got it. All the sappy lyrics of those romantic ballads made sense.

She started the coffee. What did Adam like to eat for breakfast? She had so much to learn about him, and she looked forward to every minute spent getting to know him. She preheated the stainless steel griddle, buttered sandwich bread to grill, and then she grabbed the carton of eggs from the fridge. While arranging the toast on two plates, she glanced up to find Adam standing in the doorway. With eyes at half-mast, he sported an adorable stubble on his face, and his hair needed combing.

He squinted. "You're up early."

"I promised you breakfast." She grabbed the spatula to turn each egg. "Sleep well?"

"Unbelievably, considering." He walked behind her and planted a kiss

173

at her ear.

She turned her face to kiss his lips. "I hoped you'd rest."

"I still need to talk to you."

"Okay." She poured coffee in a mug and handed it to him.

He took a sip. "You brew good coffee."

"Thanks." She slid two fried eggs onto one of the plates. "Is over medium all right?"

"Perfect." He took the plate and gave her another quick kiss before he sat down at the table.

She turned off the burner, added eggs to her own plate, then sat across from him. "Eat. Then tell me what's so important."

They ate their eggs and toast in silence, yet it was a comfortable silence. She could get used to mornings with Adam. Or would her thoughts run him off? He hadn't seemed commitment-phobic, yet their romance was still new and fragile. *Be patient, Taylor*. She took away their plates, then rejoined him at the table.

"Thanks for breakfast. I usually grab a muffin or sticky bun." He grimaced. "Usually from the vending machine."

She smiled. "Glad you liked it."

He drank the rest of his coffee. "You need to program your gate today. Get Fred to go with you when he comes out to replace the window."

"Bummer. I'm expecting a FedEx delivery. I ordered a Sony Alpha DSLR like Amy's."

"I know the gate is a pain. Have you considered closed circuit TVs?"

She sighed. "I'm trying not to think of this place as my prison, yet I'm making it more like one."

"Well, think about it." He got up and grabbed the coffee carafe, then refilled both their mugs. "I'm glad you're getting back into your photography."

"I miss my cameras. We have so much wildlife out here, and I see opportunities for a lot of good shots." When he sat down again, she asked, "So how did it go last night at your mother's? Was it difficult?"

174

"More difficult than I imagined." He set his coffee mug in the center of the placemat. "I need to talk about it with you."

"About your mom?"

"Yeah. She's not willing to go through any more treatment, although I can't say I blame her. Chemo at best would buy her a few months, and at worst would make her miserably ill during the time she has left."

"I know it's rough on you and Amy."

He stared into his coffee but didn't take a drink. "It's going to be rough on you, too."

Because he had to hide his relationship with her from his mother? She'd expected as much. "How do you mean?"

"After Amy and Ben left, she made a sort of deathbed confession. A *horrible* deathbed confession." He closed his eyes and grimaced. "It concerns your mother."

"*My* mother? Is this more about this feud between our families—"

"Yes, and there's no easy way to tell you, so I'll just say it. The night Connie died, Mom admitted they met for a drink, and she . . . put something in Connie's wine. A sedative."

Taylor's hand trembled, threatening to topple her mug of hot coffee. She used both hands to steady the drink and set it down. "Phyllis . . . *drugged* my mother?" He nodded. "You're saying she made sure my mother was too impaired to drive? She caused her to wreck?"

He finally met her gaze. "I'm sorry, but . . . yes."

A slow burn in her chest stole her ability to speak. What could she say? She had her answer now about her mother's death. She'd pushed him into finding out, and now this? The unfairness of it all overwhelmed her. Rage filled her. Fisting her hands, she struggled to breathe. Phyllis Gillespie had robbed her and her brothers of a mother.

Finally she found her voice. "Did she say why?"

"She claims my father was in love with Connie and planned to run away with her. She didn't know Connie regretted the affair and wanted to reconcile with Harold. You discovered that from Connie's letters."

"She cold-bloodedly murdered out of jealousy?" Her voice rose. "To eliminate her rival?"

"I was just as horrified as you are when she told me."

"For thirty years your family hated mine, blaming us for all your troubles. Now I understand how you could hate that much because right now I—"

"We both need time to readjust our thinking."

"Readjust our thinking? What a perfect political response. Suddenly you're eager to make peace between our families." Her throat ached from fighting back sobs of fury but she couldn't calm her anger. "Funny how you weren't so charitable when you blamed the Drakes for everything. Phyllis taught you to hate us, playing the injured party—"

Adam stood. "I'm leaving before I say something I'll regret."

"Like what?" She stood, too. "What can you possibly say in your mother's defense?"

"Nothing." A muscle tic twitched beneath his ear as he clenched his teeth. "What can you say about your brother getting Megan pregnant and abandoning her? He didn't even have the decency to attend her funeral."

"You are such a jerk. Megan never told Wil she was pregnant. He never knew—"

"According to your brother."

"No." She glared at him. "According to your sister."

His face lost some of its tautness. "Amy said that?"

"Ask her. She intended to set you straight on that score, but getting your mother to the Mayo took priority—"

"As it should."

"Of course it should. Don't imply I meant otherwise. I'm not the enemy here."

"And I am?" Even upset, Adam seemed sad and vulnerable. She hadn't meant to lash out at him. He sighed. "I told you we had too many obstacles."

She got the message. He thought their romance doomed. She searched for something to say to ease the anguish and gloom that stretched between them, but she came up empty. "What are you going to do about Phyllis's confession?"

"I took an oath to uphold the law. I'll do the right thing."

"Wait." While she hated what Phyllis had done, Taylor wasn't without sympathy, at least for her family. "Your mother is gravely ill. You can't mean to—"

"I mean to turn this over to the sheriff when he gets back. Then you Drakes won't need to have anything more to do with us Gillespies."

She reeled from the bitterness in his tone and the sheer despair in his eyes. Was he declaring their relationship over? Wait a minute. She didn't want to lose Adam. He couldn't mean to walk away from her forever. But how did they cope with the years of collected poison between their two families? What could she say?

He spun on his heel and left, quietly clicking the front door closed. She half expected him to slam it. His news about her mother's death had shocked and enraged her, but had she been fair to him? Or had she shot the messenger?

The bottom dropped from her stomach, and her breakfast rebelled. She should run after him. But then her father called for her. Six o'clock was too early for him to be getting up, though why wouldn't he be awake? She had yelled at Adam, ranting and screaming until her throat was raw. Of course she'd disturbed Dad. He would ask what was wrong.

Dear God, how do I tell him?

She hurried to his room. "Just a second, Dad. I'll get the lift."

"I don't need to get up yet. Just tell me. Is it true?"

"You heard?"

Her father shook his head. "I'm pretty certain Gabe Reesor heard, clear down at his place."

She winced. "Sorry. I guess I was loud."

"Uh huh. So did Gillespie find out his mother drugged Connie the night of her wreck?"

She strained to understand him. Had she heard him correctly? "Sorry?"

"Did Phyllis drug your mother? Is that why she wrecked?"

Yeah, he'd overheard. "Yes. After I found those letters, I asked Adam to look into what happened to my mother. I couldn't make sense of how she ended up out on County Road 12 when that's the opposite direction of the Alibi Bar. But drugged, she would've been disoriented and . . . ." She choked on the words. What chance did her mother have of driving safely to Drake Oaks?

"Aw, Little Strawberry, don't cry. If I hadn't thrown Connie out in the first place, she wouldn't have been out driving that night. I sure can't forgive Phyllis, but—"

"What are you saying? You hate her, as well you should."

"She hates me. But you were right about her son. Took a lot of character for him to tell you the truth. And to turn her in to Wilson, that's a tough call." He peered up at her from his pillow, his eyes sad yet wise.

"You heard all that?"

"These walls aren't soundproof, you know." He hesitated. "Did he say Wilson got his sister in trouble?"

"Wil never knew, and I don't think we need to tell him. Megan died a long time ago."

"You don't think he'd want to know?"

"Megan didn't want him to know. I think we should honor her wish."

"What about Adam? You going after him?"

"Go after him?" She shook her head. "He thinks we have no future, that we can't get past this . . . this history hanging over us."

"So you love him, yet you threw him out? Sounds to me like you're repeating my mistakes."

"Wait a minute. You're saying—I thought you didn't like Adam. You said you don't trust him."

"I didn't, but I was wrong. Like I said, it took a lot of guts to do the right thing."

"Phyllis hasn't long to live, you know. Her cancer is inoperable."

"I reckon that makes it doubly hard for Gillespie to turn her in. Not sure what good it'll do now. Won't bring your mother back."

"But now that I know the truth, I'm so angry, Dad. Phyllis robbed me of a mother. I was just a toddler. I missed so much. Why did she do it? Why did she hate her enough to kill her?"

"I heard what he said. Jed wanted Connie."

"But she wanted you. We know that now from the letters." She fought back more tears. "It's all so sad."

"Yes." Dad closed his eyes. "I wish I could go back and do things differently. I drove Connie away."

"You had help. Gram interfered, or you would've known about the letters." But Phyllis had interfered, too, with her permanent solution to a temporary problem. "What Phyllis did is unforgiveable, though."

He opened his eyes again. "Don't say that. Look where being unforgiving got me."

"I guess we all have regrets, including Phyllis. She felt the need to confess, even if it was a long time coming." She snorted. "Hope it made her feel better."

Dad didn't respond to that. "I guess I may as well get up. Maybe you'll fry me an egg, too."

"Sure I will. But you'll have to talk me through this hydraulic lift thingie. One thing about our impostor—he had no trouble lifting you."

"Has Gillespie found out anything about why he wanted to kill you?"

"He didn't say, and I thought it too soon to ask."

Adam undoubtedly would have Jamie or one of the other deputies get back to her. She'd never see Adam again, and it was his mother's fault. Just one more reason to hate the woman. How could Dad feel so charitable all of a sudden? It would snow in Miami before she forgot the damage Phyllis Gillespie had inflicted.

Chapter Fourteen

Friday morning at nine, Adam rushed into the conference room, where Devon and Brady stood crowded around Jamie and her laptop. "Good morning, people. Have we ID'd the guy locked up in our jail?"

"Yep." Brady pulled out a chair and sat. "Mike Lobo. He has a long list of priors. Lately he's hired himself out as a contract killer . . . a budget hit man. Before he got arrested for dealing drugs, he worked as a male nurse in a convalescent home."

"Hence his familiarity with hospitals and hypodermics." Devon snapped his fingers. "Which reminds me, I got a call from the lab about those capsules in Taylor's prescription bottle. They were cyanide, just as you suspected. FDLE's going to try to get prints, but Lobo probably used gloves."

"What about that big purse Tracy found? Lab may find traces of the cyanide inside," Brady said.

Jamie nodded. "It'd be great to tie Lobo to tampering with Taylor's medication, but I really want to pin Russo's murder on him."

Adam frowned. "I hear you, but what's Lobo's motive for killing Russo, Jamie?"

"I need to back up. Detective Raizor, LAPD, recognized both guys in Taylor's photo, and he wants to extradite. Well, the FBI is involved, so maybe they're pushing to extradite so they can make a deal."

"Both guys? Who are they?" Adam asked.

Jamie tapped her laptop screen. "Kenny Robb Johnson, now deceased, is the guy with all the tattoos. The suit he's talking to is Dan Dilliard."

"That name sounds familiar."

"It should." Devon moved aside so Adam could look at Jamie's laptop. "He served time for insider trading, then made a comeback building a successful retail business, mostly on the west coast."

"What else do we know?"

Devon pulled out a chair at the conference table. "He's been on the feds' radar for a while, and now this photo puts him in contact with an assassin right before he killed state representative Sheila Woosley—"

"—who just happened to be actively sponsoring a state bill that Dillard opposed. Long story short, it would have put him out of the retail business. He's already suspected of substituting parts that don't meet safety requirements." Jamie pointed to the photo of Johnson. "Troy Raizor thinks Johnson killed Rosalind Williams, although it was wrong-place-wrong-time. He targeted Taylor because she took pictures."

"Didn't you say they had a piece of biological evidence?"

Jamie nodded. "A strand of hair. Troy's still waiting for the DNA profile to see if it's a match for Johnson."

"But Taylor had the photos backed up. Why kill her?" Brady asked.

"They didn't know she had copies online," Jamie said. "The killer took every bit of camera and computer equipment from her apartment. If it's Johnson, I'm sure he thought he'd covered his and Dillard's tracks."

"I don't get it," Brady said. "There is nothing in those photos worth killing for. A jury wouldn't convict Dillard solely on a picture showing him standing with Johnson."

"He never saw the photos," Jamie said. "There's no telling what her camera missed that he may have thought she saw."

"Shows what a ruthless son-of-a-bitch Dillard is." Devon shook his head. "If Taylor wasn't famous, he might not have been able to find her."

"Oh, he would've found her." Adam grabbed a chair and sat. "Even if he'd had her followed."

"So the local cops kill Johnson after he assassinates Woosley. How convenient." Brady turned to Jamie. "How does Lobo tie in?"

"It's supposition, but Troy thinks Lobo, working for Dillard, used James Russo to case out the place. Played on his obsession with Taylor."

"That would be easy enough. Russo stalked Taylor," Brady said. "I doubt he knew his surveillance fed intel to a killer."

"Lots of unanswered questions, but right now the biggest one is, is Taylor safe?" He hoped so. He still broke out in a sweat just thinking about her narrow escape with Lobo.

Devon nodded. "If LAPD and the FBI have copies of her photos now, what good could come of eliminating her? Besides, they've issued a warrant for Dillard's arrest. That's one reason they're pushing extradition on Lobo. They need him."

Adam met Jamie's gaze. Although he'd feel better once Dillard was behind bars, Devon made sense. "Call Taylor and let her know. Meanwhile, I'll talk to the district attorney, but I think we can turn over Lobo to the Feds or the state of California without waiving our own extradition rights. Meanwhile, we can build a case against him for the Russo homicide."

Brady shrugged. "Why waste tax payers' money? Let them put him away."

"Because something could go wrong with their case," Devon said. "Or he could make a deal. At least we'd have another shot at putting him in prison."

"Devon's right." Adam stood. "Good work, everybody."

What would Brady or any of the deputies say about spending tax money to prosecute a senior citizen dying of cancer? What would Wil say? Adam would find out soon enough.

Friday turned out to be sunny and mild, and Taylor had to turn the air conditioning back on. Trying to keep her mind occupied—and off Adam, she placed phone calls to the insurance company, Hazel, and Miller's IGA Market. She even managed to hook up the leash to Sophie and take her for her morning walk.

After running out of busy work, she invited Dad to sit with her on the porch. "It's too beautiful to stay indoors. I have dinner cooking in the Crock Pot, so I don't need to be inside to mess with that."

"You're becoming a regular chef," Dad said.

"It's just beef stew. I'm a beginner cook."

"I'm glad you feel like getting out again."

"Me, too." She'd kept them both isolated too long. "I'm so much better than I was a week ago."

Soon Fred Fischer's familiar pickup truck bounced up the drive. Sophie raised her head to check out the arrival. "It's okay, girl," Dad said, and the dog relaxed.

Fred jumped from the cab and handed her a large FedEx box. "Good morning, folks. Found this by the gate."

"My camera. Thanks." She broke a nail tearing into the package, but what was a messed up manicure compared to getting her hands on a camera again? "I saw deer out back this morning and wished I could've shot them."

Fred grinned. "You shoot deer?"

She held up the new camera. "Only with this." She read through the brief manual and tested the camera with a shot of her dad.

Fred secured the new window, then stepped back to survey his work. "This one's double-paned, so it won't be so easy to break next time."

"Jeez Louise, let's hope there isn't a next time."

"Yeah. Now Cameron Security needs to come back and reattach the sensors. Otherwise, you're all set."

"Thanks. I need to call them anyway. I'm thinking about installing an intercom or TV camera for the gate. Do you think it's all right if I leave the gate code as is for awhile?"

"It should be. The bad guy's in custody." Fred gathered his tools and the crate that had held the window. "When is Hazel Porter coming back to work?"

"Not till Tuesday. Monday is Judy Wood's funeral, and she wants to attend." Just another victim she'd led a killer to. "If only I hadn't called her—"

"Don't go there, young lady." Fred shook his finger at her. "You aren't to blame for anyone getting killed. Understand?"

"I hear ya." But she'd be a long time getting over the deaths of two people—three counting Roz—brought about because of something she inadvertently photographed.

Sunday, Adam followed Ben and the boys from church to his mother's house, where the family gathered for lunch. He and Amy had agreed to have regular family dinners as long as Mom felt up to it. Of course, Amy didn't know her mother's dark and terrible secret. So far, only Adam bore the burden of that confession.

Amy stayed behind to cook and met them at the door. "Hope you're hungry for lasagna."

Adam patted his stomach. "I'm always hungry for lasagna."

They gathered in the dining room. After Ben asked the blessing, Amy served lasagna. "Adam, did you see the paper?" she asked. "I made you look very capable as the acting sheriff. Should swing some votes your way."

"I saw it. You gave me all the credit for making an arrest in the Russo homicide, but it was a team effort."

"Yeah, but the team isn't running for sheriff. You are."

His mother met his gaze. "It's good press, son. Early voting starts next week."

He steered conversation away from the campaign. Who knew how voters would react when he turned in his own mother for a thirty-year-old crime? "He's being extradited to California, so it's not much of a coup."

"Bringing in Mike Lobo for the murder at Foster County Medical is the big news. The locals aren't interested so much in California crimes." Amy took a sip of iced tea. "Anyway, that was my angle for the front page and that's what's up on the Drake Springs website."

He may get the credit for the arrest, but it was Taylor who shot the offender, and Harold who helped bring him down. Adam doubted he'd ever forget the terror of hearing the gunshot and struggling to reach her in time. If he dwelled on that memory, though, he'd be unable to digest his lasagna. He might never have all the answers to the motive behind the attacks, but he could live with that as long as she was safe.

"So what's for dessert?" he asked.

"Yes, Mom, what's for dessert?" Travis echoed.

"Just brownies."

"Hooray for brownies." Adam picked up his and his mother's plates. "I'll make coffee."

Amy gathered the rest of the dishes. "And I'll clean up."

"No, honey." Ben reached for the stack of plates in her hands. "Adam and I will clean up. You cooked."

"You serve the brownies," Adam said.

"Granny Gee, can we watch TV?" Ray asked.

"Sure you can, boys. We grownups will have our coffee in the living room." His mother smiled. Any other time she would've scolded them for staying indoors on such a beautiful day.

Although her sluggish movements suggested she was ill, her face shone. She had serenity and peace in her eyes. He'd heard confession was good for the soul. But her confession had been pure hell on his. When he followed Ben into the kitchen to load the dishwasher, his mother didn't come in to supervise, a further testament of her newfound tranquility.

"Your sister has me trained in after-dinner cleanup. Watch and learn."

He couldn't stop the sigh of wistfulness that escaped. "Aw, Ben, you two are so well suited."

The plate Ben rinsed froze in midair. "Is that envy I hear? What's going on with you?"

He hadn't intended to broach the subject, but pure longing filled him. Pipe dreams, yes, but he couldn't suppress them. He'd love to clean up after Taylor's cooking every night. "I guess I want what you and Amy have."

"You mean two car loans, a mortgage on land we can't even access, sky high utility bills, and two boys growing so fast we can't keep 'em in clothes?"

He nodded. "Yeah. I guess I do want all that. It doesn't sound so bad when weighed against the fun and affection I see every time I'm with you guys."

"Whoa." Ben took the rest of the plates from Adam's hands. "You do have it bad. Welcome to the club."

He shook his head. "I didn't get the girl, so it's not gonna happen for me."

Taylor Drake?" Ben laughed. "Don't look so dumbfounded. Amy figured it out."

He gave Ben a rueful grin. "She *is* a newspaper lady."

Amy entered the kitchen. "That's right, I'm a reporter, and I'm here to investigate what's taking the coffee so long."

"Oops," Adam whispered. "I forgot."

"Never mind, I'll do it." She pushed him aside with her elbow and reached for the coffee brewer. "You can pour a couple glasses of milk and take them to Ray and Travis."

"Adam was too busy envying us, honey. He seems to think we're perfectly happy."

She moved to the sink to fill the reservoir. "Uh-uh, little brother. We're just happy. If you strive for *perfectly*, you'll never get to *happy*."

"You're right." He poured the milk for his nephews. "Thanks."

"For what?" she asked.

"Oh, I guess that's just something I needed to hear." Amy made sense: Perfection didn't equate to happiness. "Once in a while you come up with a pearl of wisdom."

By the time they had the coffee and brownies ready to serve, Mom had settled in the living room. She peered through the window. "Who's this parking in front of the house?"

His gaze followed hers. He'd seen that Ford Escape with California license plates, parked at Drake Oaks. His pulse quickened, and his breath caught. The driver climbed out—Taylor! Her short red hair caught in the breeze, and she took off her sunshades to squint at the house as if verifying the address. Had she come to see him?

But wait. This was his mother's house. What the hell? Why was Taylor here? He wasn't about to let her tear into his mother, no matter what. He raced to the door, but Amy got there first.

The half of a turkey sandwich in Taylor's stomach wouldn't digest because of the bee hive she'd swallowed. Well, at least it felt like a hive of bees swarming inside her. She couldn't declare herself cured of her anxiety disorder yet, not when her hands shook like a cement mixer and her knees threatened to buckle with every step.

"What's the worst that can happen?" Suddenly, all sorts of unfortunate ideas flooded her mind. She could vomit all over Phyllis Gillespie's front porch. She could hyperventilate and pass out. Or she could trip, fall, and break a bone. Oh, God, was she a mess!

None of those dire consequences materialized, though, and she found herself pressing the doorbell. Amy answered the door.

"Taylor, this is a surprise. Come in and meet my family."

"I hope I'm not intruding—"

"Nonsense." Amy closed the door and turned to Adam, who looked about as uncomfortable as a guy who had wandered into the ladies room by mistake. Another man she suspected was Amy's husband stood in the archway "Adam, you know. This is Ben Sawyer, the most wonderful husband in the world."

"My pleasure, Taylor." Ben, an attractive guy with a pronounced receding hairline, shook her hand. "She only says that because it's true."

"And modest, too." Amy chortled. "Have you met Mom?"

Adam flinched when Taylor stepped forward and offered Phyllis her hand to shake. Uncertainty filled the woman's eyes, but she shook Taylor's hand. "Mrs. Gillespie, it's nice to finally meet you."

"Call me Phyllis."

"Phyllis. I'll only be a minute, but I'd like to talk to you."

Adam moved to Phyllis's side and placed his hand protectively on her shoulder. "Why are you here, Taylor?"

"Where are your manners, little brother?" Amy turned to Taylor. "May I get you a cup of coffee?"

"Oh, no, thank you." She spotted a small three-legged stool and set it down at Phyllis's feet. Sitting on the stool, she met Phyllis's questioning gaze. "Adam told me." She didn't want to say more in case the rest of the family was in the dark about her confession. Phyllis would know what she meant.

"I don't suppose it does any good to say 'I'm sorry,' but I truly am."

"Actually, it does." The tremors in her stomach calmed. She could do this. "I came here to talk about forgiveness. I guess you know I was almost killed last summer." She pointed to her scarred throat. "I suffered an anxiety disorder and had some counseling, and my therapist advised me to forgive my attacker."

"Forgive?" Phyllis whispered the word. "But how can you forgive—"

"The person you forgive doesn't have to ask you for forgiveness. He doesn't have to earn it or deserve it. He doesn't even need to know you've forgiven him. My attacker will never know. As my therapist explained, forgiveness is about the injured party's mental health."

Phyllis nodded. "You mean letting go of resentment and anger so it doesn't poison you?"

"Exactly. So whether you want my forgiveness or deserve my forgiveness, Phyllis, I give it to you."

Phyllis's eyes watered, and tears leaked down her cheeks. "How can you? After what I did . . . all that I've done . . . ."

Her tears softened Taylor's heart. "Thirty years is too long for our families to be at odds. What kind of legacy is this feud to your grandchildren? I refuse to pass it on to another generation. It stops now."

"Amen to that." Amy moved behind Taylor. "I stand with Taylor on this. I don't want Travis and Ray to hate anyone."

"For what it's worth"—Phyllis reached for Taylor's hand—"I'd do anything to undo the past. Anything. I'm so sorry."

Taylor enveloped Phyllis's hand with both of hers. This woman who had played a role in killing Taylor's mother was a pitiful shell. She'd punished herself already. "Well, that's all I came to say. I won't impose further."

She rose from the stool, and Amy walked her to the door. Adam hadn't moved from his mother's side. At least she had her answer. He wouldn't acknowledge his feelings for her to his mother no matter what. She glanced at him, but his face was inscrutable.

Amy stepped outside and pulled the door closed, giving them a moment of privacy. "I'm not sure what just happened in there, but thank you. I understand why you did it, you know."

"You do?"

"You're in love with my brother, and don't deny it."

How could she? "I have to get home. Wil and Fia are coming in soon." She had to get out of there. Now. "Goodbye."

Amy gave her a finger wave. "See you again, I hope."

Taylor fled, as fast as her legs would carry her, and jumped in the car. She wouldn't cry. She wouldn't. If she could forgive the woman responsible for her mother's death, couldn't Adam budge? What more did he want? She replayed the visit, each time puzzled that he hadn't run after her. If only he had, she would have told him how much she loved him.

Perhaps he didn't want to hear that. On the drive back to Drake Oaks, she pulled over once, because she couldn't see through her tears. Checking to be sure the road was clear, she pulled onto the narrow country road heading toward home. Suddenly a car appeared in her rearview mirrors, approaching at too fast a speed for the road. What on earth?

Suddenly the car bumped her, jolting her and locking up her seatbelt. Her heart raced. A quick glance in the mirror confirmed the driver intended to collide with her. He closed the short distance between vehicles and rammed her again. He pulled into the center of the road as if to pass. Instead he collided with the left rear bumper and sent her into a spin. Fighting for control, she skidded off the pavement toward the trees.

Chapter Fifteen

Amy leaned against the door and glared at Adam. "Well? Are you just going to let her leave?"

Ben gripped his shoulder. "She loves you, man. Anybody can see it."

"I'm sorry, Mom." Adam searched his mother's eyes for understanding. "I never planned to get involved with her."

Instead of censure, she gave him a smile filled with understanding. "She's a good person, son. Don't let my old grudges ruin your life."

"You aren't upset that I—"

"That you're in love with a Drake? Maybe this is what the two families need to bring peace between us. God forgive me, I caused enough damage."

When he rushed to open the door, he saw no sign of Taylor's SUV. "I have to go."

He hoped her destination was Drake Oaks, because that's where he headed. The road narrowed at the city limits sign, and his thoughts returned to the sheer terror of racing to save her from Mike Lobo. At least now he could drive at a safe speed. He urgently needed to see Taylor, but this time her life wasn't at stake.

Taylor squeezed the steering wheel. Shaking and dizzy, she tried to catch her breath. The beating of her heart pounded in her ears. Why had the driver deliberately run into her? With great effort, she focused on her surroundings. She had sideswiped an oak tree and landed in the wetlands. She looked to her left, where the white Chevrolet idled, pointed in the opposite direction. The driver scowled at her through his open window, a large gun pointed at her.

No!

She'd had enough of living in fear. She grabbed the gearshift, engaged her four-wheel drive, and eased the SUV free of the mud. She cut the steering wheel as hard as she could toward the gunman. *God help me do this right.* Flooring the accelerator, she held her breath and rammed the other car.

The impact jolted her. The airbag filled her vision, crowding her against the seat. Her hand throbbed from the implosion. She struggled to breathe. Had she managed to dislodge the man's weapon? Injure him? *What next, Lord?*

She strained to listen. Not a sound came from the gunman. Then a siren whooped a sudden, shrill burst. Her heart raced. Pushing against the airbag, she peered through her cracked windshield. A police cruiser screeched to a stop, blocking the road. *Thank you, God!*

The officer emerged, his dress jacket pulled back and his right hand hovering over the firearm at this hip. Adam! But wasn't he at his mother's? Had he followed her, after all? A mixture of joy and relief swept over her. He'd keep her safe. She let out a long breath and slumped back against the headrest.

"Turn off your motor." His commanding, even tone reassured her. Whether he addressed her or her attacker, she couldn't say, but she switched off the ignition. He stood with his back to her. "Taylor, are you hurt?"

"No. What about him?"

"I think he's unconscious. What happened?"

"He had a gun pointed at me." Her throat ached, and she had to force the words. "After he ran me off the road."

Adam drew his gun and trained it on the man. "I called for assistance. Go sit in the cruiser."

She shoved open the driver's door, got out, and then forced her wobbly legs to move just as the EMS van and another FCSO cruiser sped toward them. The familiar face of EMT Karen Fox greeted her.

"I think you're in shock. You better sit." Karen led her to the van, where Taylor collapsed on the doorstep.

Shock maybe, but she hadn't panicked. With God's help, she'd kept the other driver from—

From killing her? Why had he wanted her dead? Who was he?

Twice in one week Adam had tasted fear unlike anything he'd known. Twice he'd almost lost Taylor. Thank God she wasn't hurt. He used both hands to hold his firearm on the offender for fear he'd start shaking. When Brady Newcomb and Tracy Sinclair arrived, he resisted the urge to sag with relief.

"He's injured, but keep an eye on him. He tried to kill Taylor."

"You bet." After the EMTs revived the suspect, Brady recited him his rights.

"Ride with him to the hospital and don't let him out of your sight," Adam said.

Tracy called the wrecker service to tow in both vehicles, and Adam had a brief moment of privacy. His emotions a jumble, he followed Brady and the suspect to the EMS van, Tracy following.

Taylor gazed up from the step where she sat. Her eyes were puffy and red. "I didn't have my gun, so I turned my Ford into a weapon."

"Are you sure you're all right? You've been crying."

"I'm not injured," was all she said, but he understood. He had hurt her by ignoring her earlier at his mother's house. If only they were alone, he'd find a way to explain.

"I didn't have an anxiety attack, either."

"Told you so, champ."

"Who is that man?" she asked. "He looks familiar."

"I think he's the guy in your photo, the one wearing the suit, a guy named Dan Dillard. We'll know soon."

"I didn't focus on his face. I was too busy trying to keep him from killing me."

"I'm glad you did."

Then she grinned. "Good thing I have four-wheel drive, huh?"

"Good thing you kept your head and rammed his car."

Her smile faded. "I may need you to explain that to my insurance company, though."

Adam didn't have a chance to say more. He longed to hold her close and hug her, to talk about the tangled up emotions that had him questioning himself and yet hoping for their future. Now wasn't the time or place. Instead he summoned Tracy. "Will you drive Miss Drake home? I need to follow the ambulance."

It's not what he wanted to do, but he couldn't risk a repeat of the Russo murder. He couldn't afford to lose another suspect in his custody.

Monday morning, Adam hurried to work, eager to arrive before Wil. He needed to talk to him in private. Wil must have entered via his private entrance, though, because he was already at his desk. Although Wil looked enough like his arrogant brother to be his twin, he was a lot more down to earth. Could Adam have misjudged him?

"You're here mighty early."

"I need to talk to you alone. A lot happened in your absence."

Wil's smile disappeared when he picked up a tattered, slim file folder. Connie Drake's autopsy report. "Let's start with why Zelda had that kid Buzz Blanco dig up this file."

"Taylor asked me to look into Connie's accident." Adam gripped the arms of his chair. *Might as well get this over with.* From Taylor's finding the hidden letters written by her mother to his mother's awful confession, he told Wil about his investigation into Connie's death.

Wil clenched his jaw but didn't say anything. Finally, he blew out a deep breath. "I need coffee."

Adam volunteered to brew a fresh pot. He followed Wil into the break room and started the brew. "You're too quiet about this."

"Just absorbing it," Wil answered. "I accepted the accident ruling on Mom's death. Never questioned it. Wonder why Taylor did?"

"The letters. I gather your grandmother hid them from Harold."

"Yeah, I can see how that would happen. Gram made no secret of what she thought of my mother." Wil leaned against the counter. "We weren't allowed to mention Mom in her presence."

"Your grandmother sounds a lot like my mother. Very controlling."

"Except Gram didn't kill anyone," Wil said.

He winced. "True."

Wil plucked a Styrofoam cup from the cabinet. "Still, I can't deny she compounded the trouble between my parents."

Adam poured Wil's coffee, then filled his own cup. "A number of people had a hand in Connie's death, but only my mother's actions showed premeditated intent." He followed Wil back to his office. Neither spoke until they sat.

Finally, Wil asked, "How long does your mother have?"

"Two or three months. She hopes to make it through the holidays before she needs Hospice." He stared into his coffee. "Did you know Taylor went to see her yesterday?"

"That's where she'd been? I thought it remarkable she could drive again."

"Not as remarkable as what she did for Mom. She . . . she forgave her. Mom cried. It really touched her. Said it was unexpected and undeserved."

"None of us deserves forgiveness."

"I've had a hard time accepting that. Doesn't speak well of me as a church-going Christian."

"Church is a hospital for sinners, not a sanctuary for saints." Wil sipped his coffee. "Taylor would be the first to forgive, though. She looks for the best in people. You can see it in her photography. That's why it hurt so to see her brutally attacked."

"Did you know she forgave her assailant, too? Not that he knew it, but—"

"She told me. Said her doctor suggested, but I think she would have, anyway. Taylor reads her Bible."

"She said 'forgiveness is good mental health'."

Wil nodded. "For what it's worth, I agree with Taylor about forgiving Phyllis."

"How can you?" Adam scrubbed his face. "After Taylor's visit yesterday, I did little else but think about what she said. I asked myself, if the situation was reversed, could I forgive Harold? The ugly truth is no."

"It's high time we made peace between our families."

"I agree, but is it possible? You're a bigger man than I."

Wil leaned back and patted his stomach. "After all I ate on last week's cruise, I'm bigger than lots of folks."

Adam smiled. "I wish I had your gift for humor. You have a way of using it to relieve tension."

"Not everyone thinks it's a gift." Wil sobered. "What do you plan to do now?"

"It's inconceivable to me that you and Taylor can so easily forgive my mother. The fact remains, the state of Florida doesn't. She has to be held accountable, same as anyone breaking the law. I won't cover this up."

"What do you suggest we do?"

"That's up to you. I'm officially turning this over to the sheriff of Foster County. She asked that I be the one who arrests her, though."

Wil leaned back in his chair and sighed. "Nobody's arresting your mother."

"I can't accept favoritism—"

"It's just common sense. How many people know about this confession?"

"You, Taylor, and probably Harold."

"Let's keep it that way. Sometimes a secret should stay a secret, especially if revealing it will cause nothing but hurt. Think about Amy and her boys—"

"It's more than a secret, Wil. It's a capital offense."

"I'm not going to spend valuable law enforcement hours building a case for a thirty year old crime based on nothing more than a verbal confession. Especially considering the defendant won't be alive to stand trial."

"Can you do that—legally, I mean?"

"If we take what we have to the DA, he'll throw us out of his office. We have nothing but the confession of a woman who just got out of the hospital. A good defense attorney could argue she's hallucinating from her pain meds."

"She'll plead guilty. Mom expects to be punished for her crime."

"It won't be by the county court system." Wil leaned forward and narrowed his eyes. "What's this really about?"

"I don't know what you mean."

"Reading between the lines, I think you want your mother punished. My question is, why?"

"I don't." Or did he? He'd been furious about his mother's hypocrisy. It had cost the family dearly. He wanted somebody to pay for his sister's death. "How well do you remember Megan?"

Wil's eyebrows lifted. "That came out of left field."

"Humor me."

"I'll never forget her. So lively and full of fun. To an eighteen year old boy, she was awesome . . . and a little scary."

"Reckless, yeah. But Amy and I idolized her."

"I was shocked to hear she'd died. So tragic."

"She'd been drinking, you know, the night of the accident."

"No, I didn't. I was at the academy when it happened."

"So you never heard from her after that one prom date?"

"No. I got the impression she just went to the prom with me to piss off Phyllis, not that I objected. She was older, a pretty college girl, experienced"—Wil grimaced —"Sorry."

"I know you two had sex the night of the prom."

"You do?" Wil had the decency to look embarrassed. "Did she tell you?"

"No." Adam squeezed the arms of the chair until his hands ached. He wanted to hate Wil for what he'd done to his sister. Or at least throttle him. "She told Amy."

Wil stared into his coffee, as if lost in a memory. "Did you know Megan was my first?"

Adam shook his head. "I figured Amy was. You two dated a long time."

"No, she saved herself for Ben Sawyer." Wil grinned. "Why'd you bring up Megan?"

Here was the opening to tell Wil about the baby, but he couldn't say the words. Megan didn't want Wil to know she was pregnant. Maybe it wasn't Adam's place to tell him.

Sometimes a secret should stay a secret, especially if revealing it will cause nothing but hurt.

"Megan caught Mom crushing the pills she used to doctor your mother's wine. She *knew*, Wil. Don't you see? All that reckless, self-destructive behavior makes sense now."

Wil frowned. "So you blame Phyllis for Megan's death?"

"Indirectly. Imagine being thirteen or fourteen and discovering your mother's guilty secret. She couldn't handle it."

"A child can't handle that kind of guilty secret at any age, Adam. Look what it's doing to you now. Your mother caused a lot of harm, but if you aren't able to let this go, it will destroy you."

"I wish I could."

"Fia's eighty-five year old grandma would quote you scripture about forgiveness and then tell you to get over it." Wil leaned back in his chair. "Take today off, okay? You've earned some down time, and you really need to forgive your mother. She hasn't long to live."

If Wil and Taylor could forgive her, couldn't Adam? "But—"

"No *buts*. Devon can bring me up to speed. Any questions I have for you can wait until tomorrow."

"Thanks, Boss." He stood and offered Wil his hand.

"Boss?" Wil shook hands with him. "I think that's the first time you called me that."

"I guess I'm getting used to the idea of working for you."

He had the day off and a lot to think about. For the first time since his mother's revelations had rocked his foundations, he saw a ray of sunshine break through his dreary world. With hopefulness and optimism, he jumped in his car and drove to his mother's house, the first of many stops he needed to make. With God's help, he could free his heart and find his future.

Taylor left her father sitting on the front veranda enjoying the mild weather, Sophie sprawled at his feet, while she ran upstairs to grab her new camera. She hoped to capture the magnificent cardinal perched in the magnolia tree.

She skipped down the stairs from her suite like a lighthearted schoolgirl. Why dwell on Adam? If he couldn't move beyond the past, it was his loss. Nothing she could do about it. She recalled something Fia said. *Misery loves company, but the feeling isn't mutual*. No more pity parties. She needed to count her blessings and focus outside herself.

Photography was an easier passion to indulge. And she did love the feel of a camera in her hand. Just as she reached the front door, the driveway alarm buzzed. Her heart raced a bit, but she didn't freeze in terror at the sound as she would have a week ago. Adam's FCSO cruiser emerged into view. Hard as she tried, she couldn't stop the burst of pleasure at the sight of him. No way she could control the flutter of her heart.

She stepped onto the porch and headed toward the swing. "Hello, Adam."

"I need to talk to you."

"Have a seat." She indicated the rocking chair next to the swing.

What in the world? Adam squeezed in beside her on the swing, forcing her to make room for him. "I want to talk about your talk with Mom."

Dad reached for the toggle on his motorized wheelchair. "I'll leave you two alone."

"Don't leave. I want to talk to both of you."

"What's this about?" she asked.

"First, I want to thank you for what you did. I know you said forgiveness benefits the forgiver, but your words to my mother went a long way in helping her, too."

"I'm glad." And she meant it. "I hate what she did, but I don't hate Phyllis."

"Amy said you did more to bring peace between our families in two minutes than what the rest of us could do in thirty years."

"Does Amy know . . . everything?"

"No, and Wil wants to keep it that way. I'll let him explain it to you." He took her hand. "Taylor, what you said to Mom about forgiveness. You inspired me to rethink my . . . well, my whole life."

Her heart pounded, and her pulse echoed in her ears. Dare she hope? "And what did you decide?"

"I'm withdrawing from the sheriff's race."

"What?" Had she heard him correctly? Of all the things he could've said, she least expected that. "Why?"

"A couple of reasons. Your brother and I talked about a lot of things."

"What about Megan?" she asked. "Did you confront Wil—"

"No, and if he finds out, he won't hear it from me." He held her gaze. "I've always been honest to a fault, or so I've been told. But Wil said sometimes a secret should stay a secret, especially if revealing it will cause nothing but hurt."

"As Amy says, Amen to that." What good would knowing the sordid truth about Phyllis do Amy and her family?

"I had to reevaluate my motives in running for sheriff. I guess pride got in my way. I'm okay working as the chief deputy. I enjoy it."

"Are you sure?"

"Fred Fischer said he never ran for the position because as chief deputy he had almost as much clout as sheriff but without the headaches, and he's right. Besides, Foster County has a good sheriff."

Talk about a change of heart. "Have you told Wil?"

"No, but he'll know soon enough. I told Amy, and she's the town crier." He smiled then, and his gaze met hers. Gone were the tight lines of tension. Had Adam found peace at last?

"Wow, this is quite a turn of events."

"So I have a question for Harold and one for you."

Dad lifted one eyebrow. "A question for me?"

"Yes, sir. Do you think a chief deputy in the sheriff's office is good enough for your daughter?"

What? Adam wouldn't resort to asking her father's blessing if he didn't love her. Excitement flushed her skin, and her breath caught.

"Depends on what you plan to do with my daughter."

"Well . . . that depends on how she answers the question I have for her."

"The answer is yes."

"I haven't asked you my question yet—"

"Yes, I love you. What else do you need to know?"

He fished a gold and diamond solitaire from his shirt pocket. Holding it out to her, he said, "I love you, Taylor Drake. Do you think you could marry a chief deputy in the—"

"Yes, I'll marry you." He'd said he loved her! Pure joy filled her to bursting.

Beaming, he slid the ring on her finger. A perfect fit. "One more thing. I told my mother about us."

She lifted her gaze from the beautiful engagement ring. "You did?"

"She didn't seem all that surprised." He pressed his lips to the back of her hand. "Would you consider getting married before . . . while Mom can still attend the wedding?"

"Yes." Her vision blurred. "Yes, yes, yes." She threw her arms around his neck, and then gave him a very long kiss.

Her dad cleared his throat. "Gee, Little Strawberry, at least play hard to get."

Oops. She'd forgotten about Dad.

Adam ended the kiss and gave her a sheepish grin. "Please don't."

She shook her head. "Not a chance."

With a harrumph, her father turned his wheelchair toward the door. "Then get the door for me and Sophie, and we'll leave you two alone." A smile in his voice softened his words.

After they were alone, Taylor wrapped her arms around his neck and kissed him. Really kissed him. "We have lots of planning to do for our future. From now on, we'll have peace between the Drake and Gillespie families."

Adam glowed. "As Amy says, 'Amen to that!'"

Recipe for Taylor-made Chili

Ingredients:

- 1 ½ pounds lean ground turkey
- 1 12-oz. can beer, any kind
- 2 onions, minced
- 2 cloves garlic, minced
- 1 bay leaf
- 1 Tablespoon chili seasoning mix
- 1 10-oz. can Rotel® diced tomatoes and green chilies
- 1 8-oz. can tomato sauce
- 1 large can chili beans
- (Optional) hot sauce to taste

Directions:

Place a 4-qt. saucepan over medium heat. Add beer and bring to a boil. Cook the ground turkey breast in the beer, using a spatula to break apart the meat When cooked, add all other ingredients, return to a boil, then cover and reduce the heat to low. Simmer for thirty minutes or transfer chili to a slow cooker. Slow-cook on low for at least four hours. Remove bay leaf before serving. Recipe can be tripled in a six-quart pot.

VEILED THREAT

A Drake Springs Short Story

by Cheryl Norman

Taleah Wright once loved weddings. Bridal wear had been her favorite part of the business she co-owned with her mother, Gowns and Roses. Her mother handled the floral arrangements and bouquets for most occasions in Foster County. Taleah designed the gowns. Between proms and weddings, the two women made a living. Now weddings were a chore.

Early one December morning, she opened the door to her latest client.

"Hope I'm not too early." Taylor Ann Drake stepped inside the shop and shivered. "I promised Adam I'd meet him for lunch."

"Early is better for me, too." She closed the door against the chilly air. "Want hot tea or coffee?"

Taylor shook her head. "No, thank you. I'm eager to see my gown."

"Come on back to the fitting room."

Taleah led the petite, red haired woman past the Christmas tree, the poinsettias, and the potted plants. Often a rush job on a wedding gown suggested a pregnant bride, but in this case, Taleah knew better. Adam's mother, an ovarian cancer patient, had only weeks to live. The whole town had pulled together to make the wedding happen so Mrs. Gillespie could attend.

In the fitting room, the dress form holding Taylor's wedding gown took center stage. Unlike the flowing, lavish gowns one might expect a member of the prominent Drake family to wear, Taylor's dress had no train. The father of the bride, a stroke victim, would be walking the bride down the aisle riding in his motorized wheel chair, and Taylor wanted no excess fabric to get in his way.

Taleah pulled the floor-to-ceiling curtains to give them privacy.

"Oh, it's beautiful." Taylor clutched her throat, where an ugly scar marred her slender neck. Was she thinking about the gown's high neck design? Or perhaps reliving the brutal attack last year that nearly took her life?

Taleah didn't know the details, but she knew Chief Deputy Adam Gillespie had solved the case—and fallen head-over-heels in love with Taylor Drake in the process. At the time, Taleah had been too distraught over Keith Montgomery to pay attention. Now she needed to focus on her client's happiness.

"I'm glad you like it. You'll be beautiful walking down the aisle Saturday."

"It's what I wanted, simple yet elegant. I can't wait to try it on." Taylor slipped out of her clothes, stripping down to her strapless bra and briefs.

Taleah helped Taylor lift the gown over her head. Starting at the waist, she fastened the thirty buttons that ran all the way up the back and to the neck. Taleah had sewn each tiny pearl button by hand. "You'll need help Saturday fastening the dress."

"I'll give Amy that job." Taylor turned toward the mirrored wall. "It's a perfect fit. Thank you so much for the quick turnaround. I know it wasn't easy."

"All worthwhile, seeing how lovely you look in it." Not to mention the premium she'd collected for the rush job. But money was hardly an issue with the Drake family, and Taylor had agreed to Gowns and Roses' fees without debate.

Taleah unbuttoned the gown and helped Taylor remove it. While

Taylor dressed, Taleah carefully packed the gown for transport.

"Whose dress is *that*?"

She followed Taylor's gaze, where her own bridal gown hung in protective plastic. She couldn't bring herself to put it in storage. The gown had been her masterpiece. Grief punched her in the stomach, and tears burned her eyes. Forcing a smile, she said, "Mine."

Taylor nodded. "I'm sorry. I'd heard something about your cancelled wedding, but it must have happened before I moved back to town."

"Yeah."

"It's beautiful. The color makes it look like a treasured heirloom."

"Thank you. Fair-complexioned blondes look ghastly in white, so I chose ivory fabric. " She'd planned to weave ivory roses into combs that pulled her blond curls back from her face. Keith loved her long curly hair, or so he'd claimed. Who knew what he loved? After cancelling the wedding, she'd had her hair cut to a chin-length bob.

"I'll be sure to recommend you to anyone needing a gown."

"I appreciate that." Taleah swallowed a sob and composed herself. She shook off her own sorrow to concentrate on her client's happy event. "Let me show you the bridesmaids' dresses."

There were only two bridesmaids: Adam's twin sister Amy, and Taylor's sister-in-law Sofia, two women practically the same size, coloring, and build. Making the simple green gowns had been a cinch. Both Taleah and her mom were involved in the Drake-Gillespie wedding. Not only did they handle the flowers and gowns, but they were invited guests. Such was life in a small town like Drake Springs.

Taylor waited while Taleah brought out one of the green gowns. "Oh, my. That is so perfect."

"Glad you approve. I took your suggestion about the one-shoulder drape."

"It's better than I could imagine."

Taleah returned the gown to the closet. "All either gown needs is a final fitting. Both women are stopping by this afternoon. Everything is on schedule."

Taylor left the fitting room and walked through the shop to the door. "Taleah, you will be attending the wedding, won't you?"

"Wouldn't miss it."

"I know the invitation was to you and Mrs. Wright, but feel free to bring a date if you like."

"I hadn't thought about bringing a date." Since Keith's defection, she refused to think about romance or dating. And the last place she wanted to go on a date was a wedding.

"It's just that we ran into Jerry Zales at the courthouse. He said you two were going out. Bring him if you'd like."

He said what? "We'll see. Thanks for including him."

Long after Taylor left the shop, her words lingered. So Jerry told people they were dating. That was a stretch. Taleah considered Jerry a friend. He'd been pressuring her for more. Didn't he know the agony she'd suffered? Keith and Jerry were once friends. Keith had run out on him, too.

She didn't want to date Jerry Zales or anyone, yet she was so lonely. How long was she supposed to mourn? It wasn't as if Emily Post had a rule for jilted brides. As long as she shut herself off from socializing, she'd never get on with her life.

The time had come to emerge from her pity party. Who knew what fun and games Keith had been up to while she pined for him?

Enough!

If Jerry asked her out on a real, honest-to-God date, she'd go.

Keith Montgomery rubbed his eyes. He'd been staring at the computer screen so many hours he no longer focused. He never thought he'd admit it, but he missed dressing in suits and reporting to work in an office. To think he'd complained about the drive from Drake Springs to Jacksonville. Now he'd welcome the commute. Working in isolation sucked.

He stood and stretched, his joints popping like a senior citizen's. Good grief! He was only thirty-one.

"Taking a break?" Claudia lowered her iPad. "I can walk you to the workout room."

"Yeah, that'd be great. Let me change clothes."

She nodded. "Sure." She stood and holstered the handgun she kept within easy reach. Claudia and Tom handled security at the safe house, which should have been called a safe *condo*. At least he'd been safe so far. Until the suspect was arrested, tried, and imprisoned, this townhouse would be Keith's home, and the U.S. Marshals his roommates.

He shouldn't complain. At least with the workout room downstairs he could stay physically active. He pulled on his gym shorts and grabbed his Nikes. The feds were doing everything they could to keep him entertained. Everything except allowing him to contact anyone. The one letter to Taleah had been a concession, and a third party had to deliver it.

Taleah.

What she must think of him. The lies he'd written were to protect her as much as him, but she didn't know that. By the time his ordeal ended, she'd probably be married. Hadn't he told her to get on with her life? He'd had to make it sound credible so she wouldn't try to find him.

His gut twisted at the thought of another man holding her. His pulse rate jumped. Yeah, he needed that workout bad. He stretched on his sweatband and grabbed a hand towel before joining Claudia in the living room. She had changed into a warm-up suit, something too warm for vigorous exercise but perfect for concealed weapons.

Claudia frowned. "You look ready to kill somebody."

"Sorry. I know this is no picnic for you, either."

"My job." She waved him ahead of her. "Let off steam with some exercise and you'll feel better."

Keith had learned to time his workouts for early afternoon when few people used the facility. The exclusive high-rise condominium offered its residents 24-hour access. His security card, which unlocked the elevators and outside door, admitted him to the workout room, although he never actually held the card. That was Claudia's job. Or Tom's.

He draped his towel over the bar of the treadmill and stepped on.

Claudia claimed a cycle facing the glass doors and began pedaling. He started jogging fast then increased his pace, pushing his heart rate to the upper limit of his target range. His running shoes blurred when he looked down. He ran harder, as if trying to outrun his frustration. His heartbreak. He'd chosen to do the right thing, and now he was the one in prison. How fair was that?

If he had it to do over, would he have made the same choices? But life didn't offer do overs. He had to live with his decision, knowing at least he'd kept Taleah safe. He'd had no choice. Not really. He loved her too much to put her in danger.

The ringtone of Claudia's cellphone interrupted his thoughts and her cycling. "Yes?" She glanced at him. "I'll tell him."

He slowed the treadmill speed to cool down. He sensed the phone call delivered important news, judging from Claudia's expression as she approached the treadmill.

Fortunately, she didn't keep him in suspense. "That was Special Agent Cory. They have enough evidence to corroborate the files you copied to arrest your boss."

Keith slowed to a walk. Elation filled him, along with a feeling he'd all but forgotten.

Hope.

"That's great, right? I can go back—"

"Slow down, Montgomery. We need your testimony. Then we need a conviction. We'll see after the trial if you can return to Drake Springs or if you'll enter WitSec permanently and be relocated."

Keith's mood plummeted. What was left of his patience vanished. What good was his life if he lost Taleah? She had no way of knowing his real situation, and he couldn't tell her. How many times had Tom or Claudia reminded him that any contact put him at risk? No witness under the U.S. Marshals' protection who'd followed the rules had been killed. He understood the importance of the restrictions, but he'd underestimated the sacrifice.

"You really think I'm in danger from one man?"

"It's not one man. He's connected. You're going to help us bring down organized crime in Jacksonville."

He snorted. "I find that hard to believe."

"One organization, anyway. We have to try."

Would sacrificing the life he'd had make a difference? "Claudia, you aren't married, are you?"

"Not yet. This job kind of gets in the way of relationships." She narrowed her gaze. "Why?"

"I'm hoping you'll understand what I'm about to ask. Even if it gets me killed, I need to go home." He couldn't leave Taleah thinking he didn't love her, that their life together had been a lie. "I have to see Taleah. Please?"

The frown on the marshal's face was her only answer.

Taleah sat across from Jerry at the best dining spot in Drake Springs, the Hurricane Lantern. True to its namesake, a hurricane lantern topped each table and gave the dining room a soft, rustic glow. She'd once found the ambiance romantic, but she struggled to fit romance into her mood tonight. God knows she wanted to. Now that she'd accepted a date with Jerry, she had to give romance a shot. Yet every time she thought of love and passion, she saw Keith's face, not Jerry's. Why couldn't she forget Keith as he so easily forgot her? He'd seemed sincere about being in love with her. How had she misread him?

"You ever hear from Keith?" Jerry's baritone pulled her from her reverie.

Guilt flooded her. How had she betrayed herself? Were her anguished thoughts of Keith imprinted on her forehead? "Never. Nothing since that one letter."

"He's never called?" Jerry's tone hardened, as if he doubted her word. Or maybe she just looked for reasons to be annoyed with him. Jerry frequently asked if she'd heard from Keith.

"No. I'd tell you if he contacted me."

Jerry frowned. "Strange. I don't understand him."

"Obviously, I don't, either. But may we please talk about something else?"

"Of course." He smiled. "I didn't mean to be insensitive."

"Here's a new topic. The Drake-Gillespie wedding is Saturday. Taylor tried on her gown this morning and it was a perfect fit. I'm so proud of it."

"As you should be. You put in a lot of hours to finish on time."

Another wave of guilt washed over her. Although she'd done much of the hand stitching at home, she'd used Taylor's gown as an excuse several evenings to avoid seeing Jerry. "I was well paid."

He smiled. "Good. I'd hate to see you taken advantage of again."

Again? She bristled at his words. "What do you mean?"

"Well . . . Keith, of course. But that was out of line. I apologize." He picked up the menu. "I can't decide if I want steak or the fried catfish."

She opened her own menu to study the evening's specials, but the print blurred. She blinked back tears and swallowed. Keith had loved the filet mignon with a side of sautéed mushrooms. He once teased her about ordering a salad then having mud pie for dessert. So many memories. How could she dine in this restaurant with another man? So much for getting on with her life.

Jerry cleared his throat. "Taleah, you're obviously upset. I'm sorry. I get so nervous around you, afraid of saying the wrong thing, and then I do."

"I make you nervous?" Remorse filled her, pushing aside her heartache. Here she sat on a date with a nice man, feeling sorry for herself. How lame and selfish.

"I really like you." Jerry still wore his suit and tie, having driven into Drake Springs after work. He reached across the table and squeezed her hand. "I wish you'd give me a chance."

She forced a smile. "We're here, aren't we? This is a big step for me."

"I'm honored to be a part of it." Something about the way he spoke sounded slick, as if he'd rehearsed the line. Or was she nitpicking again? *I wish you'd give me a chance.*

The server arrived with their wine, a pricey merlot. She whipped out two stemmed glasses. "Are you ready to order, or do you need more time?"

Jerry waited for the woman to pour the wine before answering. "We're ready. We'll share the chateaubriand-for-two."

Taleah closed her menu. Why had she bothered looking it over if Jerry ordered for them both? Maybe it was acceptable etiquette, but she bristled at not being included in the decision. He may claim to like her, but Jerry was no candidate for the man to replace Keith.

Unfortunately, no one could replace Keith. A sudden rush of tears filled her eyes. "Excuse me." She fled to the ladies' room.

At least Tom was willing to discuss Keith's request with him. Claudia had regarded him as a toddler making an impossible demand. "You understand the risks, not only to you but to me or Claudia, whichever of us is lucky enough to accompany you."

Keith snorted. "You mean *unlucky* enough."

"Yes. That *is* what I mean."

"I'm willing to wear a disguise." He had grown a full beard during his months in exile, and added muscle definition from his regular workouts. "If I dyed my hair, I doubt my own mother would know me now."

Tom nodded. "I'll talk it over with Cory. We'll see what we can do."

"Really?" Dare he hope he'd get to talk to Taleah? Could he work it so she wouldn't be in danger?

"What exactly do you hope to accomplish by talking with your girlfriend?"

He shrugged. "I guess I just want her to know I didn't mean what I wrote in the letter. She's the one person on earth I need to tell the truth."

"Then answer me this: Why didn't you marry her so she could go into hiding with you?"

"No, I couldn't ask that of her. She's part owner of a business, and she loves designing gowns and dresses. I won't ask her to give up her dream just because of my misfortune."

"Don't you think you should ask what she wants? If she's in love with you, she'd be willing to do whatever it takes to be with you. At least that's how I feel about my wife."

"I won't do that to her."

"Okay. Just remember you're robbing her of the choice. You're making the decision for her."

Was he? He'd seen Taleah as his partner—his soul mate. He never intended to control her life or make her decisions. "I suppose I didn't consider it that way."

"Take it from me, pal, women don't like that. At least no woman I know."

"I wish I'd thought of it sooner, before I told her to get on with her life." He grimaced, and his stomach tightened into a painful knot. The lies in the letter he'd written had been too convincing.

Taleah,

I'm sorry. I can't marry you knowing I don't love you. I thought I did, and I feel like a heel running out on you like this. It's better this way, though. You can move on and forget me. You'll find a man who truly loves and appreciates you the way you deserve. I wish I could've been that man, but I'm not.

I hope you someday forgive me. I wish you only the best.
Keith

Tom walked to the window and looked out, although the view was mostly bare trees covering the North Carolina mountainside. "Maybe she believed the letter, maybe she didn't. But if you're going to do this, make a plan and be quick about it. In and out, while we have the creep in custody. He could post bail and be out of jail if the judge sees no flight risk."

"I'm not writing another letter. It could fall in the wrong hands. I need to talk to her face to face." Keith joined him at the window.

"If we could zip you into town on Saturday, would you know where

214

to find her?"

"At her shop, I guess."

"A public place is better. They may be watching her shop and home. I'll have Claudia do some recon and set it up, but only if the boss approves. Understand?"

"Tell Special Agent Cory I'll do whatever he says if he'll just let me make this trip back to Florida. I'll even shave and dress up like a woman."

Tom chuckled. "Let's hope it doesn't come to that."

Taleah struggled to open her eyes. Her eyelids seemed weighted down, much like the rest of her body. She tried to lift her arm. What on earth—?

From a distance, Jerry's voice spoke in hushed tones. She strained to listen. "She's empty, I tell you. Doesn't know a thing."

She managed to open her eyes and studied her surroundings without moving her head. One light shone in a corner of the dark room. Judging from the odor, she was in an old cabin or shack, lying on a broken down sofa. Her cheek stuck to the vinyl upholstery when she tried to lift her head. Nothing made sense. Where was she? And how long had she been asleep? No. Not asleep. Unconscious.

More questions arose. Why had Jerry brought her here? And who was he talking about being empty . . . her? Her last memory was drinking a glass of wine after she'd returned from the ladies' room. She'd been having dinner with Jerry, and he'd insisted on her trying the merlot. To be so costly, it had tasted bitter and cheap. She'd had to down her entire glass of water to dilute the taste. Surely one glass of wine hadn't gotten her drunk.

The hairs at the back of her neck stood to attention. She remembered nothing else. Had Jerry drugged her? Did he give her one of those date-rape pills? So many questions. Why had he brought her here? And where was *here*?

From across the room somewhere behind her he spoke again. "I'll make it look like an accident."

Say what? Was he talking to someone about *her*? She started to get up then reconsidered. If—for whatever reason—Jerry meant her harm, her best defense was surprise. She'd fake unconsciousness, learn what she could, then escape at the first opportunity. Even if she didn't know her whereabouts, she knew she needed to distance herself from him. Too bad she didn't have her purse or she could call for help. Her gaze swept the area around her, though, and found nothing. No purse, no keys, no phone. Worst of all, no exit. Not even a window. The only way in or out must be a door beyond where Jerry stood.

Once again she'd misread a man. She was a lousy judge of character. First Keith, now Jerry. If she got out of this mess, she'd go on her next date after she was old enough to draw social security and not before.

For what felt like an hour, Jerry paced the floor, ignoring Taleah. She continued her ruse of unconsciousness, although her body buzzed with tension. Didn't the man ever take a bathroom break? Not that she'd seen a bathroom in the rundown cabin, but he'd need to step outside soon, wouldn't he? If he did, she'd make her move.

His cell phone rang. "Yeah." A pause. "Arrest me?" He cursed. "Call Eddie Morgan."

Eddie Morgan was a well-known Jacksonville attorney. So Jerry faced arrest. Wonder why? And what did it have to do with her? Or was this about Keith? They had worked together at the same accounting firm. With a sudden flash of insight, she knew. Whatever the charge against Jerry Zales, it was related to Keith's disappearance. But how?

A chill seized her. Keith may have written that farewell letter, but had he done so willingly? Was he still alive? If so, was he in danger? Her drugged mind spun with questions. She had to focus. Escape. And somehow find Keith.

Jerry spoke again. "I have her car, so I need you to pick me up."

Taleah froze. Her car was here? Did Jerry plan to do away with her in her own vehicle? Calm spread over her. She had no intention of making it easy for Jerry, whatever his plans for her. She would run now, while he was preoccupied with his phone call, and lock herself in her car. The plan had flaws, such as what if he had the keys, but so be it. She had to try.

Testing her limbs, she surreptitiously stretched. Then as quickly as she could, she bolted from the couch, ran past Jerry, then out the flimsy wooden door. He'd made a grab, scraping the flesh on her arm, but she broke free. He rushed after her and was too fast, but luck was with her. He stumbled and tripped, cursing as he hit the ground. As she raced toward her beloved Camaro, three things struck her at once: it was dawn, the middle of the swamp, and—praise God!—she knew where she was. The cabin was within view of the County Road sign. If she drove east on CR 471, she'd be on Main Street in ten minutes.

She grabbed the door handle and her luck held. The Camaro wasn't locked. She leapt inside, slammed the door, and hit the electric door locks just as Jerry regained his footing and pursued her at a dead run.

He grabbed for the door handle just as the locks engaged. Cursing, he banged on the window. "Taleah, wait. Let me explain."

I don't think so. What was to explain? He'd asked her out on a date then drugged and kidnapped her, taking her to the edge of the national forest. Her hands shaking and her heart pounding in her chest, she reached for the horn to summon help. Then she smiled. There in the ignition dangled her set of keys. And there in the floorboard lay her purse.

Jerry beat against the window with a hard metal object, and her heart jumped into her throat. Dear Lord, it was a gun! Trembling, she started the engine. Would his next move be to shoot her? She had to get to town. Now! Slamming the gearshift into drive, she gassed the car and spun the tires in the loose leaves. Jerry's image in her side view mirror pursued her, but he was no match for the Camaro.

Then he stopped and took aim. She slid deeper into the seat and floorboarded the accelerator. But could she outrun a bullet?

The ride from Jacksonville International Airport seemed shorter than usual, perhaps because Tom ignored the speed limit. He took the Highway 12 exit off the interstate and drove north into Drake Springs on Main Street.

They'd left North Carolina in the wee hours, shortly after Tom had gotten the call.

"What do you mean she's missing?" Keith had yelled. Had he sacrificed everything to keep Taleah safe only to have her in danger anyway?

"We're on it. The good news is we're taking you to Drake Springs. Claudia and I both will accompany you."

Hardly placated, he waited for the catch. "Okay, great. What are you not telling me?"

Tom hesitated. "Well. How do you feel about blond hair?"

Keith didn't care about his hair. "I'll shave it off and go bald as long as it means I get to see Taleah." *And please, dear God, keep her safe.*

He repeated the prayer now that they'd reached the city limits sign.

"Cory said go directly to the Foster County sheriff's office. Where is that?"

Keith leaned over from the back seat and pointed. "Turn right up here on Main then right again on Court Street." The station was just three blocks from Gowns and Roses, the shop where Taleah should have been at work. Where was she?

As they pulled into the parking lot, Tom parked next to a familiar white Camaro. Dread settled in Keith's gut. "That's Taleah's car. What does that mean?"

Claudia looked over her shoulder. "Don't jump to conclusions. We'll find out soon enough."

The three hurried inside the sheriff's office. Tom stepped up to the counter that separated dispatch from the small lobby. "I'm here to see Sheriff Wilson Drake."

Chief deputy Adam Gillespie came out to greet them. Keith didn't know Adam well, but they had attended the same church.

Adam shook hands with the two marshals. "Wil's interrogating a witness but he'll be with you shortly." Adam turned to Keith and squinted.

"Don't you recognize me?"

"Not until you spoke." He lowered his voice. "Well done."

"I have Claudia to thank for the hair."

Adam glanced around the lobby, as if making sure no one else was around, then whispered, "Taleah's in with Wil. She's okay."

Keith nearly collapsed with relief. "Can you tell me what happened?"

"I'll let Wil fill you in."

A few minutes later, Sheriff Drake ushered them back to his office, but Taleah was nowhere in sight. He closed the door and turned to Keith. "I had Deputy Peterson take Taleah to the hospital to be checked. I'm sure she's fine, but Zales drugged her."

Keith fisted his hands and ground his teeth, suppressing a string of expletives. Claudia touched his arm. "Easy."

"Based on Taleah's testimony, you can add kidnapping to whatever charges you have against Jerry Zales."

"I assume Special Agent Cory told you?" Tom asked.

The sheriff smiled and nodded. "Cory and I worked another case together, a couple years ago. He said the feds were charging Zales with twelve counts of investment fraud."

"So when can I see Taleah?"

Claudia gave him a sympathetic smile. "We need to wait till Zales is in custody. We think he's trying to run."

Keith sighed. "Okay. I've waited six months. What's another day?" He prayed another day was all it took to get his former boss arrested.

The bride began her walk toward the altar, her father's wheelchair buzzing along beside her. Taleah choked back a sob. So pretty, and so touching. Everyone stood to watch father and daughter make their way down the aisle.

A blond-haired man slipped in the pew beside Taleah, forcing her to scoot over. She never took her eyes off Taylor, although she'd lost her vantage point. Not that she blamed the latecomer for taking a seat in the last pew, but she'd hoped to slip out quickly after the ceremony. She had so much to do to get her affairs in order. She'd already confided in her mother that she planned to go into hiding, and her mother agreed. Not that she liked it. But Taleah's safety was Mrs. Wright's number one priority.

Jerry had been captured this morning, and she intended to testify about the kidnapping. As she'd suspected, he had a lot more charges against him, but kidnapping was enough to send him to prison. If only she could find out what had happened to Keith. In her heart, she knew he hadn't left her voluntarily.

The bride reached the altar, and the congregation sat. Suddenly the blond-haired man reached for her hand. What the—?

She tried to tug her hand free, Then she saw his face. The hair threw her for a second, and a heavy beard covered his face, but she knew him. Stifling a gasp, she whispered, "how?"

His answering smile allayed any doubt that he loved her. "I didn't mean what I wrote."

"I know."

"Don't look at me or act like you know me, okay?" He released her hand, and she nearly wept.

She turned her attention toward the bride and groom at the altar, but she barely saw them. "Okay."

"I love you. I should've told you the truth."

She considered all the hurt, the anguish she'd suffered after he'd left. But hadn't he done so to protect them both? So filled with joy at seeing him alive and at her side, she dismissed any reprimands. Whatever it took, she planned to spend the rest of her life with him.

Barely moving her lips, she muttered, "Don't let it happen again."

Eight Months Later
French Quarter Casino–Las Vegas, Nevada
Leah Preston adjusted the wedding dress on the twenty-something woman. "I just need to shorten the hem a bit. It'll be ready for this afternoon."

"Thanks. I can't wait to get married."

Leah stooped to pin the hem in place. "I know how you feel. My wedding was in this very chapel the day we moved to Vegas."

"Really? How romantic." The young woman sighed. "So how did you go from quickie bride to casino wedding coordinator?"

Leah smiled. "It's what I wanted to do. I was determined to make my ceremony as special as any that had taken months to plan. I wanted to do that for other couples, too. It's what sets the French Quarter's apart from the other Vegas wedding chapels."

"And what about your hubby? What's he do?"

"Jack works for the French Quarter, too." He was an auditor, but she thought it wise to keep his profession to herself.

"Cool!"

"Okay, we're finished here."

The bride-to-be stepped out of the gown, exposing two different tattoos along her shoulder. "This casino is so cute."

Leah thought so, too. The casino was a scaled down New Orleans French Quarter on the Las Vegas strip. Its buffets and cafés offered Creole and other southern cuisine reminiscent of the Prestons' previous lives in the South, where they once lived as Taleah Wright and Keith Montgomery.

The Witness Security Program changed their original plans for a life together, but the Prestons had found happiness within the parameters of their new identities. And their new hair colors. Contact lenses turned Leah's blue eyes brown to go with her chestnut color hair, and Jack still sported the beard and freakishly white-blond hair. Even Taleah's mother had joined them in hiding, working for a florist under her new identity as Heather Bishop.

Whether temporary or permanent, their names and addresses—or hair color—had little bearing on their happily ever after love story. As for missing the big wedding day of her dreams, Leah had the *man* of her dreams, and that's what really mattered.

Besides, every day was a wedding day at the French Quarter Wedding Chapel.

ABOUT THE AUTHOR

Cheryl Norman grew up in Louisville, Kentucky, where she wrote her first mystery at the age of 13. She earned a BA in English at Georgia State University in Atlanta.

After a career in the telecommunications industry, she returned to fiction writing and won the 2003 EPPIE award for her contemporary romance, Last Resort. Her debut with Medallion Press, Restore My Heart, earned her a mention in Publisher's Weekly *as one of ten new romance authors to watch.*

Running Scared, a romantic suspense set in Jacksonville, Florida, and Washington D.C., earned a Perfect 10 from Romance Reviews Today. *Reviewer Harriet Klausner called her writing "Mindful of Linda Howard."* Rebuild My World *is the third book in the "Mustang Sally" trilogy.*

Cheryl helps writers with grammar via her Grammar Cop *blog, newsletter articles, and workshops. Visit Cheryl at her website:* **http://cherylnorman.com**.